W9-CBZ-243

THOMAS CRANE PUBLIC LIBRARY
QUINCY MA

CITY APPROPRIATION

BY THE SAME AUTHOR

Other People's Rules

Forbidden Fruits

Julia Hamilton

St. Martin's Press ♏ New York

FORBIDDEN FRUITS. Copyright © 2002 by Julia Hamilton. All rights reserved. Printed in the United States of America. No part of this book may be used or reproduced in any manner whatsoever without written permission except in the case of brief quotations embodied in critical articles or reviews. For information, address St. Martin's Press, 175 Fifth Avenue, New York, N.Y. 10010.

www.stmartins.com

ISBN 0-312-30504-4

First published in Great Britain by HarperCollins*Publishers*

First U.S. Edition: November 2002

10 9 8 7 6 5 4 3 2 1

For Trevor

PROLOGUE

Summer 1999

Sir Jack Macarthur (affectionately known to all and sundry, including his children, as the Old Man) came out of his house at number twelve Ainslie Place in Edinburgh's New Town, shutting the imposing front door gently behind him, having first made sure that Bella, the rather dim spaniel of whom he was exceptionally fond and who accompanied him on his journey from home to his office in Moray Place, had her tail out of the way. She was sometimes careless about such matters. It was exactly nine o'clock in the morning and Jack had just lit his first cigar of the day. Needless to say, they had tried to get him to stop smoking but he wasn't having any of that.

As usual, Jack's mind was fixed on several different subjects at once – he swore that the cigar helped this scattershot kind of focusing. He thought of his wife of many years, Jean, whom he would encounter again later that morning at the consulting rooms of his doctor, Professor Lamont, and he also thought of his mistress, Justine Mackenzie, an editor in his own publishing house, the Eglinton Press, who was going through one of her periodical bouts of putting pressure on him to prove that he loved her, which he did, but he also loved his wife and would never leave her, a fact Justine was perfectly well aware of although she pretended not to be when it suited her. He was also thinking about the problem of his younger son, Ben, whose life was in a mess after his divorce.

He had taken care of Justine, however, and she had nothing, in Jack's view, to complain of and much to be grateful for: their child, Eleanor, Elly as she was known, was now sixteen, was a boarder at St Leonard's School in St Andrews, Justine and Elly had a beautiful apartment in Howe Street and would be taken care of in the future. Gerry Lamont of Lamont & Lamont WS had seen to that on the Old Man's instructions. Nevertheless, it perturbed him that she still felt the need to make waves and it perturbed him even more that he was susceptible to her whims. The Old Man had reached a time of life where he no longer wished to be susceptible to any whims but his own, for he was aware that his time was limited.

The first heart attack had shocked him. At seventy plus he had still, remarkably, thought of himself as invincible; good health had followed him all his days (apart from a small problem with his prostate in his fifties) and he knew no other condition.

He had been with Jean, down at Ardgay, their estate

in Kirkcudbrightshire, when it had happened, up a ladder in the walled garden pruning the espaliered fruit trees that grew against the south wall, an occupation he enjoyed hugely; luckily, Jean had been with him and the ambulance had come quickly from Kirkcudbright and taken him on Jean's instructions straight to Dumfries Infirmary where he had been looked after as if he were royalty. Years before, not long after he married Jean, he had been the principal fundraiser for a new children's ward, which had been named after him and although it had been forty years ago they had not forgotten. He loved Scottish nurses with their mixture of jocularity and motherliness underpinned by a deep compassion for the sick and surmised that he would not have recovered so well as he did elsewhere.

His hair, until then still dark and thick, had gone white overnight and he had lost well over two stones in weight, so that when he came out of hospital he looked like a negative image of his former self; the leonine quality had gone, the massiveness (he had played rugger for Scotland as a young man) and he had resembled a husk, a burnt-out thing, a wraith. He had regained some of the weight but his unshakeable faith in his health had gone for good. He knew that very little now separated him from his Maker, an encounter the Old Man did not entirely relish.

As Jack entered the handsome building that housed his publishing company, the Eglinton Press, Doug, the janitor, came out of the glass box he occupied to one side of the imposing entrance hall.

'Morning, Sir Jack, morning, Bella,' he said, bobbing slightly, playing his rôle of pantomime half-wit, a part he had perfected over the last twenty years.

'Morning, Doug,' replied Jack, handing him Bella's lead, before going on up the staircase to his office on the first floor, with Bella at his heel. Justine, who was in the outer office going through the post as he came in, looked up and then down again at what she was doing, without greeting him; a bad sign.

'Good morning, my dear,' he said, passing her by and, as he did so, gently tapping her behind.

'Don't do that,' she said, giving him a look. 'It sets a bad example.'

'Come, come,' Jack persisted, 'it's just a wee show of affection. I've got Archie Maclean coming in towards lunchtime to discuss the portrait of Elly. Maybe you'll join us?'

'It's the book committee meeting this morning,' came the reply, 'in case you've forgotten.'

'Anything interesting?' enquired Jack, peering over her shoulder, who, although the figurehead of the firm, paid little attention to its daily workings, preferring to use his office as headquarters for his numerous other interests, charitable and otherwise.

'The agenda is on your desk, Jack.'

'Well, come for lunch then. I know Archie Maclean would enjoy your company. He likes attractive women.'

'So I hear,' she said drily, without looking at him, taking up a sheaf of post and going into her own office, which was across the passage from the Old Man's.

Justine sat down behind her desk and switched on her computer. She knew she ought to be turning her attention to the book committee meeting that lay ahead – they were being offered several interesting new books: a novel that promised to be a bestseller (that she was determined to get Duncan to sanction), the biography of some pioneering eighteenth-century Scottish feminist, hitherto only a name in footnotes, the ghosted autobiography of a Scottish footballer and so on, but all she could think of was the appointment she had seen in Jack's diary at ten thirty that morning to see Professor Lamont. She knew what that meant – his heart was playing up again but he hadn't told her – although marking the appointment 'Patrick Lamont' instead of just putting down a time, was his oblique way of doing so.

She had started life at the Eglinton Press as an editor nearly twenty years before at the age of twenty-seven, when there had been three editors, not including the Old Man who was doing then very much what he was doing now, playing publisher, financier, patron of the arts, restorer of the New Town, whilst leaving the actual business of the firm to his staff.

They had become lovers after eighteen months. Justine had lived with a gang of girls in a tenement block in Marchmont in those days and had gone on doing so for a further year or so, meeting Jack in the flat in Howe Street that he kept for visitors. During the summer in those days, Jean had gone to Ardgay for the ten weeks of the school holidays with Duncan and Ben, and Justine and the Old Man had been free to see as much of each other as they wanted.

She had loved him – there had never been any doubt in her mind about that – and he had loved her back – no doubt there either, but she had been young and incredibly naïve. To start with it had been enough that he loved her. He was nearly thirty years her senior and he knew how to make a woman feel wanted. He was also powerful and she liked power. She was not his first mistress – she knew that too – but still she had not understood that she would never be first in his life. Jean would always occupy that place. In 1982, she discovered she was pregnant, but when she had mentioned an abortion Jack was horrified. He had the double standards of the cradle Catholic: allow the woman to use contraception but if it went wrong then the consequences would have to be accepted. The child was sacred. Elly was born at the end of that year and Justine had taken her home to the apartment in Howe Street that Jack had bought her in the same building as the company flat.

After Elly's birth, Justine had tried to make him promise that he would leave Jean but he would never agree. Her friends urged her to make a move, but she had the baby and she was comfortable. She never wanted for anything. Jack was very generous like that. If it was a trap it was a very comfortable one. What Jean thought about the arrangement or whether she even knew of its existence, Justine had no idea. Duncan, who clearly did know, never mentioned the subject and neither did Ben. But it was hard to be on the edges of the family, of it and yet not of it, and, as she was beginning to realise, hard for Elly too, although the two boys were always exceedingly kind to her. Charles, Duncan's partner, employed Elly in his shop during the school holidays, and Ben sometimes took her on site visits, if he was working somewhere interesting. Ben had also promised to teach her to drive.

In 1986, Jack had been knighted and that had been the end of Justine's dreams of playing happy families with him. But why had she stayed? There had been so many reasons that had seemed so compelling at the time, but now she wondered whether they really had been as compelling as they appeared. There was Elly of course but Jack would always have kept up with one of his precious children (one of the great regrets of his life was that he had never had enough children) and she could have gone to London or Glasgow, but the truth was she had liked her life and was contented enough to stay. But when Jack died, what then?

As she was thinking this, Ben put his head round her door. He had his dog with him, a collie he'd found at a farm somewhere in Galloway and bought off the farmer who'd been about to shoot her. Apparently, the dog oscillated between wild exuberance (herding sheep a valley too far) and creeping paranoia of such an advanced kind that she wouldn't go near the flock for days on end.

'Morning, Justine,' he said, smiling at her. 'You look as if you're in a dream.'

'I am a bit,' she said, smiling back. She liked Ben;

everyone did. He was as cosy as the smell of toast, but also a worry to his father. An architect with a particular interest in the conservation of old buildings, he was not successful.

He would start a job for a private client and then dither about (sometimes losing the commission in the process) or tender for something and miss the deadline; it wasn't that the lad lacked talent, he just had a problem with following through, according to his father.

He was also recently divorced from his glamorous and rather wild wife, Diana, and was living in squalid bachelorhood at number twenty Ainslie Place, a house his father had given him years before as a twenty-first birthday present, and where he had lived during his short marriage.

Jack was nothing if not indulgent as a father – it was his Italian blood coming to the fore – but Justine had wondered quite how kind an act it really was to give your child such a large present so early on. The houses in Ainslie Place were even by a conservative estimate now worth several hundred thousand pounds each. Ben, rather like Justine herself, had never wanted for anything under the Old Man's aegis, but the flip side of not wanting could also mean that growth was stunted.

'I'm just going to see the Old Man,' Ben said, 'Doug told me he was in.'

'He's just arrived,' said Justine, thinking that Ben had made being scruffy into an art form. His shirt was unironed, his cords threadbare. On his feet he wore builder's boots with exaggerated soles like running boards. 'Non-spill,' Duncan, his elder brother, called them, the kind of boots you couldn't fall over in even if you tried.

'Have you got a minute?' Ben put his head round his father's door.

'Of course,' said the Old Man, putting down his newspaper. 'What brings you here so early in the day? Oi!' he added commandingly, 'that's enough!' turning in the direction of the dog basket where Bella was bristling at the sight of Lolly.

'Well, son, what can I do for you?'

'I've been thinking,' said Ben, sitting down in the chair opposite the desk, with Lolly on red alert sinking beside him, 'that I want to go into our Parliament. There's no one taking enough interest in the preservation of the city's building stock.'

'I'm not certain you've got a platform,' said the Old Man, consideringly. 'Manny Jamieson's hot on the New Town; has been since the seventies when we got together. You'd be in competition with me, for God's sake. I sit on enough committees to sink the New Town. Maybe you should concentrate more on your basic skills,' he added. 'Build from the business you already have. Where are you working at the moment?'

It was a wearying business, he thought, to continually have to crush the unreasonable enthusiasms of one's children, particularly when they were in their thirties, but this enthusiasm was like so many evinced by his younger son before, something possible but improbable; tomorrow, he would have thought of something else.

'Andrew Murray's taken me on at Barhill. Now that old Mrs Murray's dead they're doing a complete revamp. He's certainly got enough money to do what he likes with the place.'

'That's a pretty place,' said the Old Man approvingly – Barhill was a house in Galloway of considerable architectural distinction – on the other side of Kirkcudbright to Ardgay. 'You could make a name for yourself over that if you played your cards right. Murray strikes me as a man who likes to show off – you could really go places with him.'

'So you think the idea of my going into Parliament is ridiculous?'

'No, "ridiculous" is the wrong word, but it would take time and application. There's stiff competition, you know. It's the gravy train everyone wants in on these days, but I'll have a word with Manny if you want me to.'

'Don't bother,' said Ben, pushing back his chair, 'thanks anyway, Dad. I'll do it my way. Come, Lolly.'

He couldn't even believe he'd been stupid enough to ask, and then to hear himself saying 'I'll do it my way' was enough to make him despair of himself. My way. Jesus! But why hadn't he argued the toss more with the Old Man? Why did he always let him have the last word? Why had he gone to see him in the first place? Maybe that was the question he ought to ask himself.

As he went down the stairs he met his elder brother Duncan on the way up. Duncan was the financial director of the Eglinton Press, a financial whizz kid, and the apple of their father's eye: the positive to Ben's negative, or so Ben saw it. The only blot on the escutcheon was that Duncan was gay, not that that had ever stopped him from doing anything he wanted, Duncan being Duncan.

'Hello, my dear,' said Duncan. 'What brings you here so early?'

'Having a word with the Old Man,' said Ben.

'About?'

'Oh, just an idea I had.'

'Want to share it with me?' asked Duncan, trying to sound neutral. Charles, his partner, told him that he was often patronising towards his younger brother.

'It was just an idea,' repeated Ben, 'which the Old Man managed to squash flat, as usual.'

'Well, don't allow him to,' said Duncan. 'You give way too easily.' In spite of himself, it was like talking to a child. The guy was thirty-five, hardly a child and yet he seemed as helpless as a baby. 'How's the business?' he added, trying not to sound as if he were giving Ben a pat on the head.

'Not bad. Andrew Murray's retained me to do Barhill for him.'

'But that's fantastic,' said Duncan, 'a bit of a coup for you. Murray's an important guy.'

Andrew Murray was a financier who had made a killing out of asset management in London and had come north to re-establish himself and his young family at the old family home in Kirkcudbrightshire, a phenomenon of the eighties and nineties in Scotland, when the City had provided cash in sufficient quantities for such endeavours. Houses that would have been written off and sold two generations before were now enjoying a new heyday. Murray even wanted to add on a new wing at Barhill.

'Thanks,' said Ben, 'I'm just on my way to see him now.'

'What!' exclaimed Duncan, who was a dandy, aghast, 'Dressed like that?'

'What's wrong with it?' asked Ben, looking down at himself.

'You look like you've just walked off a building site,' said Duncan despairingly. 'Murray's a smarmy bugger. At least put on a suit if you're going to see him in town. He'll never respect you if you turn up looking like that.'

'It's not the way I dress that counts,' said Ben. 'He's already seen me like this in any case.'

'It's up to you,' said Duncan, frowning and glancing at his watch. 'Look, I have to go. See you later.'

He went on up the stairs two at a time.

Ben hesitated outside the building and then turned on his heel and walked Lolly back to his house. In his heart, he knew Duncan was right. He knew he had to do something about himself. It was as if he were determined to fail in whatever task he set himself, but why should that be? The therapist he had seen had told him it was the family dynamic: having a brilliantly successful father and elder brother meant that he didn't want to compete: too many bull males in the tribe or some such theory which was probably true, for it was not only his side of the family but his uncle Sandy too – the famous playwright – not to mention his cousin Luke who was a professor at the university; all men, all successful. Even the one girl, Sukey, Luke's sister, was a respected journalist; all bulls to his cow.

The only time he could remember earning his family's respect for a brief moment was when he married Diana Forbes. He had known Diana from when they were children in Galloway together, but had held her in awe. A shy, awkward boy, he had watched her at parties snogging the boys and smoking; she always seemed to be surrounded by a posse of admirers. Later on, when they were grown up, people had still surrounded her, mostly men, and he could see why. She had rather coarse auburn hair, a willowy figure and a pale skin; Burne Jones would have loved her, but it wasn't just her looks, which were good but not outstanding; it was the way she talked and made people laugh. Diana was the kind of person whom people gravitated towards, the epicentre of the gang, the mainspring. Her end of the room, her end of the table was always laughing. She also knew how to dress and had the kind of classical understated style his mother admired that she said hardly existed any more.

'Diana always looks just right,' Jean had said. 'She has an eye. She shouldn't waste her talent. She could design clothes or do people's rooms for them.'

And for a while she had played at those things; the Scots designer Macgillivray had used her as his 'muse' – there had been a point some years before where you couldn't open a glossy magazine without seeing a picture of Diana Forbes in one of Macgillivray's absurd creations, and she had worked for Charles Murray too, Duncan's partner, helping him undertake various large commissions for Scotland's new rich – 'returners' like Murray, whose family had been broke a generation before – but she had never stuck at anything. And, as Charles had said, it was no good having talent if you couldn't apply it, genius being an infinite capacity for taking pains, etcetera etcetera.

Quite how he had summoned up the courage to ask her out, Ben would never know, but when she had accepted he was astonished, then frightened. He was afraid he would bore her, but to his surprise they'd got on as if they were meant for one another. She made him laugh; he bolstered her confidence with his intense devotion. For such an attractive woman, she was surprisingly lacking in self-confidence: it was as if there was something broken in her that could not be mended; but in the beginning she was a goddess whom he had worshipped. Only afterwards had he realised that she needed to be understood, not admired, but by then it was too late. By then he had withdrawn from her because he couldn't cope with what he saw as her tyrannical demands on him, and the tables had turned: she had adored him; he was ambivalent towards her.

The combination had seemed to work for a while and they had married to a chorus of approval on all sides: Ben's family hoped Diana would galvanise him, Diana's family that Ben would anchor down their wild daughter.

For a while the approval of others had fuelled them, as if the image of themselves as a happy couple was enough to live off, but after a year or so this false energy evaporated like the Solway tide, leaving them beached but also bound to one another.

Diana loved to party and was witty (but always, he realised when it was too late, at other people's expense) and lovely to behold, but the subsequent hangovers made her a ferocious companion. Her sharp tongue wounded him where it hurt most. She tore and tore at him until he was in tatters. His shaky confidence had wilted and then vanished. At the end of it all he had thought of her as a siren combing her hair atop a pile of his bones. He knew he had failed her too, that he couldn't meet the need that forced her into her role as performer, the hollowness at her centre that somehow echoed his own. Since they had parted she was turning being a drunk into an art form. Several times lately he had been told by other people of her drunken behaviour in bars and restaurants as well as at private parties. Was he to blame for this? He didn't know.

At his house, Ben changed into a suit, one of Duncan's cast-offs that he could no longer fit into, a heavy but extremely smart dark blue cotton with an embarrassingly flashy lining of violet silk. Duncan was right about the clothes, as he was right about most things.

In the bathroom, however, where he went to comb his hair, he saw that Marianne had left her make-up bag behind when she had departed so abruptly in the middle of the night. He picked it up and looked at it and then put it down again. The mere sight of an object so intimately associated with her made him feel bleak and depressed.

Marianne Maclean, the daughter of the painter Archie Maclean, worked at the Eglinton Press which was where Ben had met her six months before, all part of the incestuous loop in which he seemed to have spent his whole life. She had had a kind of cherry-dark ripeness about her that had attracted his attention at once. They had started an affair almost immediately; too quickly, he now thought. She was a wonderful girl, warm, tender and loving as well as funny and witty, but as vulnerable in her own way as Diana had been, and he didn't feel able to cope with the needs of another person, as he was barely able to cope with himself. Her mother had recently died and sometimes he would find Marianne in tears, but unable to explain why; secretly, the tears made him recoil. He had had enough of women in tears – Diana had always used them as a weapon – maybe, he sometimes thought, he had had enough of women full stop and was destined to spend the rest of his days in an increasingly austere bachelorhood, in the company of a long line of Lollys.

The reason for the débâcle was that in the night,

after they had made love, she had told him she loved him. To his horror, he had not known how to respond.

'I don't know what to say,' he had said, already regretting his honesty as he said it. He knew it would mean the end of their affair.

'You don't have to say anything,' she replied, reaching for the light switch.

'What are you doing?' he asked.

'I'm going,' she said. 'What do you think I'm doing?'

'Please don't.'

'Of course I'm going. I can't stay after this.'

'Why not?'

'Work it out for yourself.'

She was pulling on her clothes as she spoke. What he had said hurt her so much that the place where she registered emotional pain had gone numb.

'Look, I'm very fond of you, you know I am.'

He sat up in bed watching her dress, wanting to stop her leaving but not (as usual) knowing how to.

'There's a big difference between being "fond" of someone and loving them. I don't want to hang around in an unequal relationship. I'm not that kind of person.'

'I didn't really mean it like that.'

'Well, how did you mean it then?'

'It's just that I don't think I'm quite ready to commit.'

'You won't ever be ready,' she said in a calm voice, pausing to meet his eye. He'd have preferred it if she'd

19

been angry; then it would have been easier to discount what she said.

'You're a classic ditherer. In another age, you wouldn't have had a choice; you'd have been married off to somebody and you'd have had to get on with it, but it doesn't work like that anymore. You'll never settle at anything, Ben. Your family, much as I love them, have disabled you so that you're unable to function. I'm sorry but it's true.'

And so she had gone, slamming the front door behind her. Another bloody balls-up. Somewhere in his being, he already knew he had made a terrible mistake. He wanted to love her, he did love her, but he didn't want to have it dragged out of him like pulling teeth. To love someone, and to admit it, meant that you were completely and utterly vulnerable to them and he already felt exposed enough as it was.

'Come, Lolly,' he said, patting the part of the bed recently vacated by Marianne, and the dog had leapt up eagerly, nestling in his arms as tenderly as any lover.

He slept and dreamed that he was tenderly carrying a little baby in his arms but when he looked at the child carefully he realised it was Marianne.

Marianne was late into work on account of her broken night. She had reckoned on staying at Ben's and strolling over in a leisurely manner, in plenty of time for the book committee meeting. Instead, she had overslept, couldn't find her make-up and had scrambled into work by cab, arriving at the meeting just as the preliminaries were over and the real discussion was beginning.

The meeting consisted of Justine, the publisher; Duncan, the money man; Marianne; her fellow assistant editor, Consuelo; and Hester Black, who had been with the firm since the sixties when publishing was a very different business to what it was now.

Justine was just beginning on her sales pitch for the novel she passionately wanted the Press to bid for. Marianne had read the book and had written the resumé that had already been circulated the day before via e-mail. The novel was a twenty-five-year-old female writer's début, a summer rite of passage novel (why did so many rites of passage novels take place in the summer, she wondered?), written with considerable brio, insight and humour. With the right backing the book would go places, that was certain. What was not so certain was how much Duncan would be prepared to pay. As Justine said, his sporran snapped shut very easily and it was very difficult to get him to open it again.

As Justine talked, Marianne's mind wandered. What had happened the night before with Ben had made her feel emotionally hung over. When they had started going out six months before, she had felt she had found the man she had been looking for and he had seemed to feel the same way. She liked his life and liked what she saw of his family. The Old Man, in particular, was very warm towards her and she felt he approved of her role in his son's life. It was no secret that the Old Man wanted to see Ben make a go of things and it had not been lost on Marianne that he regarded his younger son as a small child in need of parental guidance, the implication of his approval being that she would be the one to supply it. When she had said to Ben that she felt his family had disabled him she had meant it: it was as if he was preserved in aspic as the eternal child and never allowed to develop any further. The only way for him to change would be for him to leave the incapacitating, claustrophobic circle of family and strike out on his own somewhere different, as his grandfather must have done all those years ago.

But neither was Ben so simple a project for a woman as his family fondly imagined. He was warm and loving towards her but he was also capable of retreating emotionally; days would go by when he didn't phone, for instance, but if she protested he appeared not to know what she was talking about and if she persisted he would grow angry, a state he almost appeared to enjoy. When he was angry he felt powerful and Marianne would feel that he was more honest in that condition than when he was trying to please her. If only that emotional energy could be transferred to his everyday life then their relationship (which had enjoyed many good moments) might have had a chance.

His particular brand of bachelor squalor suggested he hungered for a woman – he adored it, for instance, if she tidied up or cooked for him – but his behaviour last night shouted ambivalence. Maybe she had been too hasty in leaving? If she'd played it differently, there might have been a happier outcome but, in common with most of humanity, she couldn't stand rejection, and Ben's had been a particularly wounding response, which when she had thought about it afterwards had made her angry, very angry indeed.

'I don't know what to say.' She shook her head, hearing his words echoing in her mind.

'Marianne disagrees,' says Duncan, noting her response. 'At least we have someone present with a sense of prudence.'

Marianne glanced at Duncan, at Justine and then wished she were somewhere else. The meeting was being held in Duncan's office, a high-ceilinged, important kind of room lined with bookcases containing the books the firm had published over the years since the Old Man had bought it for a song in the late fifties. Disconcertingly, her eye came to rest on a painting by her father that the Old Man had purchased years ago, long before he had ever met Archie, of a rumpled bed recently vacated by a pair of lovers; Archie was particularly good at painting hangings and inanimate objects; his paint surface had a kind of creamy depth to it that one knew was the touch of the master and ordinary objects took on what Marianne had occasionally thought of as 'inscape'.

'Well,' she stumbled, 'I think we should be cautious. If everyone goes crazy for it then we'll find ourselves in a dot com kind of situation with a lot of properties that aren't worth very much. I think it's a great book but we should be careful.'

'What do you say to that, Justine?' Duncan enquired, tapping his pencil on his pad.

'Well,' said Justine, giving Marianne a hard, cold, 'see me afterwards' kind of a look – they had already agreed to back each other on this one, 'if we miss this opportunity, we shouldn't be in publishing at all.'

'Consuelo?' asked Duncan, 'tell us what you think, then we'll take a vote on it.'

Andrew Murray had an office in a building in Charlotte Square, recently acquired when he had moved his operation north. When Ben arrived, he found Murray in this office wearing chinos and a flamingo-pink polo shirt with his Gucci-shod feet up on a vast inlaid desk of blonde wood, the kind of object Gatsby would have understood; not a partner's desk so much as a plutocrat's desk.

'I had it made for me,' said Murray proudly, mentioning a certain minor royal who went in for cabinet making. 'What do you think?'

'It's incredible,' said Ben, which was not a lie. It was, indeed, incredible. He tried to imagine his father commissioning the same kind of thing and failed utterly. The whole hierarchy was so strange these days: you had the Old Man with more new money than he knew what to do with masquerading as a gentleman and Murray who came from an old, respected county family playing at being a Texan millionaire with knobs on.

'Let me show you the rest of this place,' said Murray, springing up from his chair. He looked like a plump monkey with his bronze hair and his simian features. The backs of his hands were thickly covered in the same bronze hair as his head and Ben found himself wondering if they were dyed to match. Murray gave Ben a tour of the middle office, the outer office, the kitchen, opening and closing drawers proudly, even flushing the lavatory as if he had invented it himself. The power of his gigantic ego seemed to roll off him in waves.

'And the best thing of all,' he said, steering Ben back in to his own office, 'is I don't have to be here if I don't want to. And that's where you come in. I want Barhill to look perfect: I want the works, the whole caboodle restored to its original magnificence and yet to be as high-tech as the Pentagon. Get it?' 'Get it' was a Murray phrase, Ben had learned.

Ben nodded. 'I've brought the plans,' he said. 'Shall we go over them now?'

'Can't right now I'm afraid, old boy; I'm waiting for my wife. We're going to a prayer weekend in Texas. The helicopter's waiting.'

'You're what?'

'Don't look so surprised,' said Murray, gratified at Ben's astonishment. 'We're Alpha Christians and we're off to Texas. They really know how to pray there. Have you done an Alpha Course?'

'No, I haven't. I'm a Roman Catholic.'

'Oh, there's a version for Holy Rollers too,' said Murray, laughing heartily, 'you can't get off that easily. Here's my wife now. Have you met Suzie?'

'I don't think so,' said Ben, shaking hands with a

long, thin, tubular woman with short, dark hair and wire spectacles who could, without much effort, have been taken for a man.

'Hi,' said Suzie, flashing American teeth. 'I hear you've brought the plans for Barhill.'

'He has, darling, but I'm going to get Ben to come down to Barhill with us next week. We can go over them then.'

'I'll need some warning for next week,' said Ben, letting his irritation show, 'I'm pretty busy. What day did you have in mind?'

He realised that Murray had summoned him to show off, and that he had never had any intention of going over the plans that Ben had rushed to finalise. That was how this kind of rich behaved. The Old Man would never have dreamt of such behaviour. He was on the point of leaving but then he thought better of it. If Marianne was right, then using the Old Man as a yardstick was fatal. He was on his own now and he'd bloody well show them all. He realised he desperately wanted to make a go of this project.

'Hang on a minute,' said Murray, pressing a button on an intercom, no doubt to summon a post-modern version of Miss Moneypenny.

'Next week,' he said, when an efficient-looking Edinburgh lady in a suit appeared, with an old-fashioned diary in her hand, 'what's happening? Give me an afternoon and evening when we can take Mr Macarthur to Barhill.'

'Thursday?' said Miss Moneypenny.

'Thursday?' Murray enquired of Ben.

'I think that's the one day I can manage,' Ben replied. It was a lie of course, but one he was rather proud of. His diary for the whole of the coming week was alarmingly empty.

'Thursday it is,' said Murray. 'I trust Mrs Dewar with my life, as you can see. I'll see you then, old fruit. We'll pray for you.'

'Thanks,' said Ben, recalling with sudden pain the débâcle with Marianne. He could do with all the help he could get.

Summer 2000

A tall, elegant, terraced house constructed out of the famous Edinburgh stone quarried from Craigleith sometime in the 1790s, number twelve Ainslie Place had two windows to the right of the front door on the ground floor, and three windows on the two floors above, ending in a pediment with a porthole in it.

The house belonged to Sir Jack Macarthur, the local luminary, publisher, property tycoon and one of the forces behind the restoration of the New Town in the 1970s. Sir Jack had lived at number twelve Ainslie Place since 1965. Indeed, one of his children had been born in the bedroom and indeed the bed in which the elderly patriarch now lay dying on this day in the cold, wet summer of the year 2000.

As befits a patriarch, particularly a dying one in this city of patriarchs and elders, his family attended Sir Jack in much the same way as they might have done in another age.

Jean, in a forest-green cashmere cardigan and Speight plaid skirt, thin bird-legs in fine stockings, long, narrow feet in the Ferragamo shoes she ordered by the dozen, was just going back up the stairs when the door knocker sounded again, echoing in the hall, and making poor, wretched Bella bark and have to be firmly shushed again. She was Jack's dog and like dogs do she knew something was up. Jean would have had her sent down the road to her son Benjamin's house, but for the fact that Jack adored the beast (the last in a long line of Bellas dating from the time of their marriage) and liked to put down his mottled, transparent old hand from under the cover and feel the dog's silken, soft ears under his hand.

'Hush, Bella,' said Lady Macarthur without conviction. The dog had a streak of anarchy inbred in her and made a virtue of ignoring commands. She was a hopeless gun dog too, dithering about in the heather as if she didn't know what on earth she was there for, and if she did inadvertently stumble on a bird, she'd rather eat it rather than retrieve it. Nevertheless, Jack loved her and if Jack loved something it had to be endured.

Jean opened the heavy front door with its handsome fanlight above – a pattern of urns linked by swags of laurel (patterns laid down by Adam himself and not to be deviated from) – and stood face to face with Duncan, an imposing figure in one of those dark suits he favoured, and his lover, Charles.

Charles was dressed in jeans and an open-necked striped shirt in contrast to Duncan's sober hues.

Duncan reminded her very much of his father at the same age. He had the same massive, slightly leonine aspect to him; not a man you would trifle with, just like his father.

'I've mislaid my key,' he said. 'Sorry to drag you down here.'

'Never mind that,' said Jean, offering her son her cheek to kiss. 'Hello, Charles, how lovely of you to come as well.'

She had long ago accepted her son's homosexuality – after all what else could one do? – and had welcomed the faithful Charles into the fold as part of that acceptance. She often thought what a wonderful daughter-in-law Charles would have made – he was an interior designer with a successful business and a gorgeous treasure trove of a shop in Rose Street – with his ability to cook brilliantly, arrange furniture and flowers like no one else – and to be unfailingly civil, warm-hearted and tactful. Today, he had brought her flowers; marvellous colours wrapped in shell-pink tissue paper and tied with wired ribbon in a perfect bow.

'Darling Charles,' she said gratefully, kissing him. 'How lovely.'

'Just a little *bonne bouche*,' said Charles, steering her indoors by putting his hand on her elbow, something men rarely did any more. When she had been a girl, men had always steered women like that as if they were delicate beings made of porcelain. Now, they held the door open if one was lucky and certainly didn't get up on buses to offer one a seat unless one gave one's best, most governessy glare.

'How is he?' asked Duncan, putting his briefcase on the hall chair and taking a swift glance at his reflection. He had the same immovable, thick, glossy dark hair as his father, with a slight wave in it that looked as if it had been sculpted. 'Stone hair', he had called it when he was a child.

'Not good,' said Jean quietly, placing Charles's flowers on the hall table next to Bella's lead, and a copy of that day's *Scotsman* that she had judged her husband too exhausted to have read to him. At death's door he was still liable to be made apoplectic by the news and his old heart would gallop like a dog chasing rabbits in its sleep.

'Has the doctor been?'

Duncan turned to face her, looking so like his father: large, dark and foursquare, the same beetle brows and black eyes, that she felt quite pierced by tenderness. Why was it that love had to lacerate one instead of soothing or stroking? All the imagery of love was of piercing and tearing or destroying. That poem of Blake's: 'And his dark secret love/ Does thy life destroy.' Why that now? Lines of poetry lying about in one like unexploded bombs.

'He came this morning and he'll be back before supper, he said. Come on up. Your Uncle Sandy's sitting with him now.'

Sandy Macarthur, Jack's brother, was a playwright whose huge hit, *Atlas Revived*, a satirical examination of Scottish nationalism, had earned him the nickname

34

of the 'Pinter of the North' years before. Like his brother Jack, he was an Edinburgh bigwig and retired grandee who lived round the corner in Moray Place with his wife, Hannah, a teacher at the university. Luke, Sandy's son, and his wife Alice, both academics, lived just across the water in Stockbridge in one of those beautiful houses (although some thought them twee) in Ann Street, designed by Sir Henry Raeburn. All the Macarthurs lived in this part of Edinburgh – it was sometimes jestingly referred to as Macarthurtown, but Jack had liked a family atmosphere; it was his Italian blood coming out, she supposed. He had even given Luke the house in Ann Street as a wedding present when he married Alice: 'Have it now rather than later,' he had said, 'when you really need it.'

The house had been in a terrible state and the brothel down the road meant prices were not then what they were now, but it was still a very generous gesture: that was Jack for you, generous to a fault where his family were concerned. Not every uncle, however rich, would give his nephew such a very munificent gift.

Sandy was a big, burly man like his nephew Duncan and his brother Jack, though illness and impending death had shrunk Jack down, making him look bonier and baggier. Parts of his body were coming into view – scrawny ridges and hollows – that Jean had never seen before, as if the seabed of her husband's body was being revealed as the life force drained out of him, poor old darling.

Sandy was sitting on a chair by his brother's bed like some sort of saggy Colossus. He had his hands in his lap clasped over his stomach as if he was praying and his eyes were closed. He had taken his pipe out of his pocket and laid it carefully on the table by Jack's bed where all the medicines were kept. A little ash had spilled out onto the white linen cloth. Sandy was messy like that; he always had been. Hannah, his wife, said she could follow his movements around the house by the trail of receipts, bus tickets and small change that Sandy left in his wake like the wash of detritus from some great liner.

'Uncle Sandy.' Duncan put his hand on his uncle's shoulder and Sandy came to, rising to his feet to embrace his nephew and then Charles, who was family and merited the treatment of a clan member.

'How is he?'

The same question, thought Jean, making a sort of mental shrug, to which there is no answer. The timetable of the sickroom was like that of a war; long periods of watchful inactivity punctuated by crises during which death occurs without warning.

'I don't think he knows I'm here,' said Sandy, 'but I thought I'd stay awhile in any case. Maybe I'll yield my place to you now you're here, laddie. How's the business?'

Duncan was the financial director of the Eglinton Press, in which his father had a majority shareholding.

'Not bad, thanks; surviving.' The business was in fact flourishing – a novel bought the previous

year had been in the bestseller lists for several con-
secutive weeks and the biography of a well-known
footballer had been selling out as fast as it could
print – but Duncan was a Scotsman and preferred
the cautious version of his balance sheet. 'We're
reprinting a special edition of *Atlas Revived* in time
for the Festival performance. Did you know that?'

Sandy nodded. 'Aye,' he said, 'good lad.'

The dying man, waxen-faced, took a sudden breath
that failed. What had been a cough turned into a par-
oxysm. His hands clutched the covers convulsively,
reminding Duncan of Levin's brother's death in *Anna
Karenina*. The curse of being literary, he thought, was
that one could always think of a fictional parallel for
everything. It meant that one did not always live in
the moment, as one should. When he remembered
his father's dying, he would also remember Levin's
brother. In the end, he might only remember Levin's
brother, Tolstoy's choreography of death being what
it was.

Duncan watched his mother take charge, smoothing
the brow of the dying pharaoh, holding his hand,
bending over him like some graceful, angular bird.
Nursing his father had worn her down; always slender
and elegant, she was now verging on gaunt. They
needed a nurse for the day as well as the night;
he must say something to his brother about it, he
thought, going to the window and looking out across
the gardens whilst his mother soothed and tended to
the effigy in the bed, wiping away the string of dribble,
stroking the flaking skin of his poor old hand. There

really was a lot to be said for choosing when to make one's exit, Duncan thought, in terms of dignity. He did not want to think of poor Charles on bedpan duty.

A commotion in the doorway of the bedroom made him turn from his scrutiny of the tree tops. Benjamin had arrived and was going through the family ritual of greeting. Macarthur men embraced, Italian warmth breaking the frost of Calvinism that otherwise might have paralysed them. Their paternal grandfather, Massaccio, had been an Italian immigrant in the Gorbals after the First World War. He had married Aileen Mitchell, a Galloway lass in service in Bearsden, and they had had the two gifted boys.

Grandfather had wanted the children brought up as Catholics and Aileen had acquiesced in this after a certain amount of struggle. For those reared on Knox and his rantings, the whore of Rome was a hard one to swallow, but swallow she had. Grandfather Giuseppe had changed his name to Macarthur. Jack had said that Giuseppe had spoken broad Scots with an Italian accent; quite an achievement, and one Duncan was sorry he had missed.

Ben came over to where his brother stood in the window. Physically, he took after his mother's family, the Speights, and was tall and thin with chestnut curling hair and tawny eyes to match, like marmalade, their mother always said. In the summer his hair would lighten and turn streaky and the hairs on his arms would glint gold in the light. He was in his way a very beautiful physical specimen, his brother thought; pity he couldn't find a decent girlfriend, but since his divorce almost two years ago he had been mostly single. There had been Marianne of course – but Ben had done what he always did when faced with something good – he screwed it up. As her employer, Duncan had a high opinion of Marianne Maclean. Ben needed a woman, a nice, sane woman (unlike Diana who was certainly not sane) to take him in hand. When Duncan asked him what he did for sex, Ben had said his system had 'shut down', whatever that meant. Duncan did not think his own sex drive was capable of 'shutting down'. He knew for a fact that it wasn't. When he asked Ben what he did instead he said he played the piano – which he did do very well as a matter of fact – but Duncan had not been sure if he was being made fun of or not. Ben was a quirky kind of fellow, a bit eccentric, and he couldn't have been particularly easy to have been married to his brother guessed, although the exuberant but rather cruel Diana Forbes had been an odd choice for such a gentle man; they had known each other since they were children and the Old Man had been pleased. He thought Diana had class for what it was worth; in Duncan's view the class was all very well but Diana was a perfect example of too much inbreeding: legs up to her armpits and a fine arse but she was a bit crazy; there was something wrong with the wiring in her brain.

People often commented on the fact that the brothers didn't look in the least alike, Duncan dark and swarthy and massive, with black hair and black eyes;

Ben so lean and springy, so somehow golden. Sartorially, they varied too. Duncan liked good tailoring: he enjoyed havering over the bales of cloth in his tailor's back room; the relative merits and demerits of different weights of wool engrossed him, and he loved to linger over the flamboyant linings he favoured – cyclamen pink, petrel blue, pistachio green – firework bursts of excitement inside a sober shell. He had his shirts and his shoes made for him and drove an old dark grey Porsche with a red leather interior, as lovingly kept as a favourite horse, and considerably cheaper. A Porsche did not eat its head off at livery. His house at number sixteen Ainslie Place, where he lived with Charles, was the most impeccably restored of all the family houses, even Luke's in Ann Street.

Ben was quite different. He drove a van for a start, useful for the dog and the gear, and rode a bicycle when possible. He restored buildings for a living and spent his life climbing in and out of roof spaces and belfries wearing a hard hat and boots. When asked, he described himself as a cobweb-and-birdshit man, not the Farrow and Ball expert, who assessed the structure of a building and regarded himself as a kind of surgeon, a flying doctor sent to relieve the ailments of Adam's structures and the great cliffs and canyons of the tenement landscape, so much a feature of Edinburgh life.

He also took on private clients for larger, interesting projects and was hand-in-glove with that smarmy bugger Andrew Murray at Barhill. At least he had got something right there. Murray was not only a native;

he was rich and influential and had friends who were likely to hire Ben. In fact Ben had recently been taken on by the Loebs at Castle Forbes, Diana Forbes' former family home (recently sold by her brother Hugo), on the say-so of Murray, who knew the Loebs. Indeed, it was Murray who had encouraged them to look for a suitable house in Galloway. Soon Galloway would have as many rich as 'Millionayrshire'.

Ben had briefly wanted to go into politics, but there was something irresistibly comic about the idea of Ben as an MSP, although it was something a lot of the less able were turning to. In the nineteenth and twentieth centuries, the bureaucracy of the Empire provided employment for the spares; now they had their very own parliament to take up the slack and waste good money on. Duncan, who believed in the power of the balance sheet, thought the new Parliament a piece of absurd window-dressing; a panacea to the vanity of his fellow countrymen.

There was no doubt the lad was passionate about his work and his problem with following through was one he was beginning to solve, not a moment too late. Life was a long race, but not that long.

Even Ben's clothes were improving, thought Duncan. He normally frequented charity shops for his clothes, favouring frayed collars and shattered-looking jackets worn with jeans and the ubiquitous boots that he bought in a fisherman's store on the harbour in Kirkcudbright. Today, however, he was wearing a suit of Duncan's together with a pair of black brogues, in deference to the sombreness of the occasion, no doubt sourced from what had become known in the family as 'Thomas Oxfam'.

'Hello, bro,' Duncan said, hugging Ben. He put his arm round his brother's shoulders and turned him to face the street so that what he said should not be heard. The doctor had arrived and was consulting with Jean. There was nothing either of them could do for the moment.

'Justine wants Eleanor to see her father,' he said in a low voice. 'She knows she can't see him herself but she wants Elly to.'

'How are we going to manage that?' Ben asked, pushing his hands deep into his pockets.

There had been a crisis meeting in Duncan's office after the Old Man's second heart attack, the one that had felled him. It was Duncan who had brought the subject up, taking an unusually coy Justine into his confidence. He'd been blunt with her but he could tell she preferred it that way.

'Father's not going to make it,' he had said, 'and my chief priority is to look after our mother. You will be taken care of; it's all in the will, but I'm afraid you won't be able to see him. I can't have mother upset.'

Justine had taken this well, or at least without fuss, which made Duncan admire her all the more, for he of all people knew she was a strong woman with views to match. It must be difficult for her; on the other hand, it was a situation that she had long ago assented to.

'Mother should rest in the day,' Duncan was saying to Ben. 'I'm going to get a nurse in from tomorrow onwards for the day as well; it was something that just occurred to me; I should have thought of it before. I'll call the agency on my way back to the office. We could smuggle Elly in when mother's resting. She'd be none the wiser.'

'Sounds risky to me,' said Ben, darting a look at his brother. 'I've got the press on my back too. Someone's writing a big piece about Dad, a journalist called Dan Mantle. I don't want him finding out about Justine, or Elly for that matter. He'll have to wait until Dad's dead before it's published of course.'

'I wonder why he contacted you and not me,' said Duncan. 'But he won't find out anything much, just bits of hearsay and tittle-tattle; no one will tell him anything substantial. He'll be pushed to make a story out of it.'

'No one will tell.' He thought for a moment. 'What about Diana?'

'She hates the press. She'd never split, I know that.'

'Do you?' Duncan's voice sounded sharper than he had intended.

'She has a sense of honour,' said Ben, 'of a sort.'

'A rather warped sort,' said Duncan, 'but on balance I agree with you. She would be with us rather than against us in this matter at any rate, and so she should be after father's generosity.'

Ben grimaced at this, yet another reminder that his family had viewed his marriage to Diana as if they were two toddlers in a playpen. His father had paid Diana off generously; all a part of his policy of keeping people who knew too much on side. If only

43

the Queen had followed his example, the Old Man was fond of saying, she wouldn't have had half the trouble she had had with that minx Diana Spencer.

'Have you seen her lately?' Duncan was asking. 'Charles says she came into the shop to ask if she could help out. She must be bored. I can't think what the hell she does all day.'

Ben frowned at the thought of Duncan knowing more about his former wife than he did, but Duncan had always been like that: a fixer, a know-all, absorbing information like a sponge, inferring things like a detective from what other people told him.

'Not for a while. She's been with Hugo. He's in a bad way after the move.'

Hugo was Diana's brother who had just sold up their family home, Forbes Castle, in Wigtownshire, to the Iowan industrialist, Kelvin Loeb.

'You know Loeb's retained me?'

'Yes, you said. A bit of a feather in your cap, my dear.'

'Diana won't like it.'

'So?'

'You know what she's like.'

'I do indeed. She's an under-employed menace.'

'You're awfully hard on her,' said Ben uneasily. 'She wasn't always like that.'

'That's because you're not tough enough, darling,' said Duncan. 'Better to have you doing the job at Forbes Castle than someone with no sympathy for the character of the place.'

'She's having an affair with Archie Maclean; did you know that?'

'Why does she have to tell you?' asked Duncan. 'Why can't she just do it and shut up about it? I hope for your sake she remarries,' he added, now in full cry as elder brother, 'but Archie Maclean is not a good bet. I can't see him getting married again; too much of a loner. I wonder why she's chosen him? But then she always did go for the wrong types like you, bro.'

'I seem to remember you thought it was a good thing at the time,' said Ben, not rising to the bait.

He wasn't going to give his brother the satisfaction of letting him know that he agreed. He didn't love her any longer as he had once done, but there was a part of him that was still susceptible to the thought of her in bed with another man. If you had loved someone once you carried him or her around with you in your head and your body; and there had been a point where he had thought she was the most meltingly lovely woman he had ever seen. But that had been before he had known and lost Marianne. The image of Diana had faded somewhat; he could only vaguely recall what she had looked like naked, but it was Marianne whose likeness he carried round in his head these days. He knew he had made a terrible mistake with her, but when he had called her she had made it clear she didn't want to be friends. He realised he had hurt her too deeply for that. What a fool he had been; what a blind, stupid fool! But he couldn't help wondering who she was seeing and what male company she was keeping. He had tried hanging around the Press but Marianne was canny and had her ways and means of avoiding him. He had written to her saying that he had been wrong, hoping that would be enough to sway her, but she had replied saying that she didn't think he was ready to love anyone; that the woman he wanted didn't exist in flesh and blood form and that she herself felt too vulnerable to go along that particular path with him. And that was where the matter rested.

In a way, Ben knew she was right about him. Diana had been a Procrustean experiment in love: find the girl and make her fit the vision he had, even when it hurt, even when she bled and he suffered. He had absurdly romantic, high-flown views about love that he kept to himself particularly in this family where love was, above everything, contractual: Duncan and Charles, his parents, his charismatic cousin Luke and his wife Alice with their so-called 'open' marriage: in each partnership, one or both of the partners was unfaithful to the other. Ben had a fair idea what his brother got up to sometimes when Charles was away. Diana had told him that.

'All those gay clubs have back rooms and that's where the ever-so-respectable Duncan is of a night, humping anything that moves.'

'How do you know?' he'd asked, unable to conceal his distaste. He knew his brother loved Charles and yet he did this!

'Because I do know, that's why,' said Diana. 'Don't

46

look so shocked, little brother,' she had said mock-ingly.

Their relationship had been in free fall by then, and she would have done anything to hurt him as a way of paying him back for rejecting her.

At the end of it all, Ben had had a vision of himself sitting in an aeroplane in crash-land mode waiting for the inevitable smash and wondering if he would survive. He had, but only just. After Diana had left had been a period of terrible blackness when he had found it hard to get up in the morning and harder still to force himself to do anything. Lolly, with the black splodge over one eye giving her an immensely rakish, piratical look, had been the antidote to that. There were times when dogs really were entirely preferable to humans.

He often thought of what Diana had said when he was with Duncan, but found it difficult to connect the sober-suited elder brother who had such presence, such *gravitas*, in every sense of the word, with the wild, sex-crazed man of Diana's story. Like so many things to do with other human beings, it didn't add up and yet it was a fact.

'At the time I thought you'd found yourself a hot little number and as it turned out I was right,' Duncan was saying.

'She just has a different set of rules to other people,' said Ben defensively, who found increasingly that he could listen to a conversation, even partake in it, but be somewhere completely different in his head. It was not a good habit, but one born of solitude. He didn't particularly want to defend Diana, but Duncan was needling him into it.

'Well, she'll have met her match with Archie Maclean,' said Duncan, 'he's a tough nut, make no mistake and he doesn't give easily either, according to father. They put the world to rights when he was working for the Old Man after he'd done Elly's portrait. Listen,' he added hastily, as their mother beckoned them back from the window, 'I'll have a word with Justine and we'll try and get Elly in, maybe at half term when she's back. It's only a day or so off, or so I believe.'

Another figure had entered the sickroom whilst the brothers were conferring at the window. This was Sandy's son, Luke, a professor of Arabic and Persian at the university, another swarthy 'black' Macarthur, a tall man like his cousin Duncan, but larger and more capacious, an impression accentuated by his clothes: baggy, threadbare cords, and a billowing jersey knitted by his mother years before with a hole in the elbow. On his feet he wore a pair of stained old brothel creepers.

'Lukey looks like a real mad professor,' said Duncan fondly, making a movement with his head to catch his cousin's eye. 'We need to warn him about the journalist.'

'I'll have a word with him, if you like,' said Ben, 'but he'll know what to do.'

'Of course he does,' said Duncan. 'Old Lukey is as safe as houses.'

'I think Auntie Jean wants us out,' said Luke,

joining his two cousins. He put an arm round each brother's shoulder and squeezed affectionately. 'Time for a drink, don't you think? I've been dreaming of one of the Old Man's malts for an hour at least.'

'I'm just going to have a word with mother,' said Duncan. 'You two go on down and I'll join you. Uncle Sandy looks as if he could use a drink too.'

'So, how are things?' asked Luke, standing at the sideboard under the portrait of Sir Walter Scott that was ubiquitous in Edinburgh dining-rooms, glass in one hand, decanter in the other. 'I hear business is booming.'

'Things are going quite well,' said Ben modestly. 'I've just got a commission from Loeb to do Castle Forbes for him. He liked what I'd done at Barhill and wanted me to wave my magic wand over Castle Forbes. It's a much larger project though; I just hope I can come up with the goods.'

'Of course you can,' said Luke, handing him a glass half full of Laphroaig. 'Don't doubt yourself; you'll do a fine job. It looks like you're on the up and up.'

'Thanks,' said Ben, wondering if Luke had meant what he said, or whether it was just another pat on the head to the little boy of the family. He sometimes wondered if his family would notice if he went round wearing a cow mask, so much did they take him for granted. He was just Ben, boring old Ben with his failed marriage and his passion for buildings. Even his political ambitions had made them smile as if he was a little boy walking round in his father's shoes like some sort of clown, although he'd taken his father's advice and given up on all that now. As ever, the Old Man had a point: stick to what you know. The project with Murray had gone, contrary to everyone's expectations, exceedingly well. Murray, for all his peculiarities, was an enthusiast who was interested in detail; he was a maniac for getting the small as well as the large things right and, as a result, Barhill was a consummate success. It had been talked about and photographed by architectural magazines as well as lifestyle ones, as a result of which Ben's office telephone had been ringing ever more often. He had even hired himself a secretary on the strength of it.

But beneath the *bonhomie* of clannishness and cousinhood and jokes about 'Macarthurtown' were the rivalries, subterranean rivers running corrosively beneath the apparently solid foundation of family. Luke and Ben were the same age. They had sat side by side in a double perambulator, attended the same kindergarten and the same primary and secondary schools. Luke had been an effortlessly clever child who with minimum effort had achieved maximum results. Ben had been able but vague and unfocused; a dreamer, a could-do-better sort of a boy with a wild mop of tawny hair like candyfloss and socks round his ankles.

To a certain extent these thumbnail sketches still applied. Ben envied Luke his laid-back cleverness, the ease with which he reached for prizes like plucking the ripe fruit off a tree – he was one of the youngest and most highly thought-of academics of his generation at the university – and Luke thought Ben was a bit of an idiot *savant* who had had it too easy financially. On the whole, however, they managed to keep these views to themselves and maintained, even worked at, their friendship. They were family and had been brought up to believe that family mattered more than anything. Ben quite often dined at Ann Street and occasionally had Patrick to stay when Luke and Alice wanted to get away.

He adored Luke, who could climb like a monkey, and thought his cousin Ben's limited repertoire of cooking (bacon and eggs and black pudding, or just bacon and eggs) was perfection, coupled with the fact that Ben seemed oblivious to bedtime; in fact they quite often fell asleep in Ben's staggeringly messy study with its crammed bookshelves and the drawing board in the window, in front of the telly like an old married couple, with Lolly draped across them.

'There's a journalist on our tail,' said Ben, sniffing the oily, peat-smoke aroma of the whisky before taking a mouthful. 'He's called Dan Mantle and he's been commissioned by some newspaper, I forget which, to do a big piece on Dad, once he's dead of course. Has he been in touch with you yet?'

'No,' said Luke, raising his bushy eyebrows as he gazed into his glass. 'But don't worry; I'll kick him into touch if he does. What does the bastard want to know?'

'Oh, he wants gossip, tit bits, juicy bits about us and the Old Man. Now he's dying, they smell blood.'

'Well, he's led an exemplary life; we all know that,' said Luke, winking. 'What's there to tell?'

'What indeed,' said Ben, clinking glasses with Luke.

'It'll be a blow though,' said Luke. 'Even long-expected deaths are. We'll none of us know what to do with ourselves once he's gone. The thought frightens me sometimes.'

'You? Frightened!'

'Why not?' enquired Luke, looking at Ben across the top of his glass.

'I don't know,' said Ben, at a loss. 'You're so wildly successful, I can't see what in the world you have to fear.'

Maybe Luke was right. The Old Man's death would loosen everything. It was hard not to think of him as a cornerstone. What would they all be without his vast overarching presence? As a child, his architectural analogy of his father had been the Pont du Gard: massive and magical, almost menacing, but also practical, a carrier of sweet water. Would there be a moment after his death when the edifice that was their family appeared to stand just as it always had done before collapsing with a shattering crash?

'Look,' said Luke, lowering his voice, 'I don't know if this is the right moment to ask you but I have a problem, a financial one. I was wondering if you might make me a loan of five grand.'

Ben looked at him startled. 'What do you need it for?'

'Do you mind if I don't tell you that, right at this moment? I'm in a pickle and I need help. Badly.'

'You can tell me, Lukey,' said Ben, 'I'll keep mum. What's going on?'

'Just a wee problem at work,' said Luke, trying and failing to sound light-hearted. 'A girl,' he added.

'She's blackmailing you?'

'You could say that,' said Luke, shifting his weight on to the other foot and fumbling in his pocket for the crumpled packet of fags he kept there for emergencies.

'But why are you going to pay her? Is she threatening to tell Alice, is that why? Surely you two can work something out? In any case, I thought you had an arrangement about such things?'

'Well, you know how it is,' said Luke conspiratorially, 'you think you do and then you don't. Or maybe you don't know.' He took a deep drag on his cigarette. 'I've fucked up and I need your help. Badly. I'll pay it back as soon as I can. I have a delivery advance coming, due on the new book.'

'It's not the money,' said Ben. 'I can't stand to think of you in this kind of situation.'

And he genuinely couldn't bear it. Compassion and love for a family member in a difficult situation overrode all other considerations. He had a bit of spare cash in a savings account that should cover it and Luke was welcome to it. The adrenaline rush of generosity made him feel quite dizzy.

'You're my brother,' said Luke. 'I'll never forget this.'

'You know I am,' said Ben, tears coming into his eyes. This was what family meant. If it disabled you, it also strengthened you. Nobody outside would ever understand.

The girl, Leila, half Syrian, half American, had been one of Luke's students to start with. Her Syrian blood, however, dominated her looks: she was tiny but voluptuous with a mane of long, lustrous, wavy hair that she allowed to tumble around her shoulders and that he could hardly keep his eyes, let alone his hands, off. Nevertheless, he had managed – his relationship with Alice, his wife, having gone through a difficult patch, was now in what Americans would call 'recovery': the previous emergency, yet another student, had been discovered and apologised for, and they had both agreed it was time to make a go of things, to consolidate, to hang in there – and yet, here she was: Leila, essence of temptation, *houri*, every guy's pathetic Oriental dream of beauty and sexual promise. He steeled himself not to touch her but then she had volunteered as one of his research assistants for his current project – a book on censorship in Islamic societies – and there she was, all the time, consulting with him side by side, facing him across a desk, picking up sheets of paper off the floor, lighting his cigarette for him and . . . oh God . . . he wasn't superhuman and she wanted it as much as he did.

To start with it had just been any student/professor affair: clandestine meetings, passionate sex in her room in some rented flat her family had paid for, but then Luke had decided to take a risk and crank it up a bit. Straight sex bored him after a while; he was a man who liked a little variety; nothing exceptionally kinky (in his view anyway), just a little recreational beating, a little bondage, the stuff he had never dared to ask Alice to do. Years ago, he'd hinted at what he would like, but she'd rejected him flatly and he hadn't pushed his luck in that department.

To start with, Leila had seemed to like it. It turned her on anyway. Then, one weekday when they were scheduled to meet, she had failed to turn up. He thought nothing of it and didn't even call her flat to see where she was. Students were like that; she'd probably been clubbing the night before and knocked herself out with booze and a tab or two of E.

After a few more days had gone by he tried to contact her but the number he dialled gave the unobtainable signal. He asked around the university, but no one seemed to know what had become of Leila. It wasn't an uncommon situation. Students, particularly foreign ones, came and went – maybe she'd had some family crisis – and Luke forgot about her because by this time he had found a new object, someone potentially much more exciting than Leila, someone he'd admired from afar for a while, and who suddenly appeared in his hand like a ripe peach, or some darker fruit.

He knew he was a hopeless case, irredeemable, unreformable, but if Alice didn't know, then where was the harm? He was back to square one with a vengeance.

Then, a week ago out of a clear blue sky, he had received a letter in Leila's handwriting addressed to him in his office, in which she said she was going to report him to the university authorities if he didn't pay her a certain sum of money: five thousand pounds to be exact. The letter stated that she had written to his wife, also at her office at the university, informing her of the situation. That had been a week ago. It was also a day that Alice didn't go into her office, but Leila couldn't have known that.

Luke had gone back to his house in Ann Street to talk to Alice. What else could he do? He arrived before her – she was collecting their son Patrick from some extra-curricular activity after school – and was, as ever, soothed by his house and its surroundings.

Ann Street was in Stockbridge, part of the New Town of Edinburgh, where development had crept over the Water of Leith two hundred years ago. It was a cold, blue May day with a cerulean sky swept clean by the east wind; late cherry blossom on the ground, great garlands of it, and hawthorn, white on blue. People, jealous people, said the street was twee. Luke adored it. The tranquillity, the sense of assurance and solidarity exuded by Raeburn's works, he also felt to be present in a street designed by that same artist. His house represented to him everything he admired.

Although Luke lived like a merchant prince in his magnificently beautiful house, he had no money, no spare money anyway. No thousands just sitting in the bank idly waiting to be used like dried pasta in a jar. He was an academic, Alice was an academic and they did not make enough money to pay off blackmailers.

Their child, Patrick, was eight and at a private school from where he would move to another private school. In spite of the fact that the house was a gift they had a huge mortgage, private medical insurance and a new but discreetly expensive Swedish car (Luke had a weakness for cars). They were also the proud owners of a marvellous new landscape by Sir William Nicholson that took up most of the wall above the sideboard in the dining-room that cost rather a lot more than the discreet Swedish car. It was one of the most beautiful paintings Luke had ever seen: a dark hillside, with the dawn light rising behind it – or was it dusk? – at any rate there was a kind of glow along the skyline that spoke of heaven and cost a great deal of dried pasta that Luke did not actually have. When he saw it in Cornelius Gibbons's gallery in Rose Street (next to Charles Murray's shop) he knew he would have to have it.

And now, as he waited in the dining-room for Alice to return, he had a thought amounting to a premonition, that there was something about the way the sunlight flooded the room, some impossible-to-define transcendental stillness that came with the quiet and washed blue of the sky, like the moment before the lava fell on Pompeii, which made him think that this was a last moment of ordinary happiness.

Patrick had come clattering in ahead of his mother, opening the letter box and letting the brass lip clang to – a favourite occupation – calling, 'Helloooooo, I know you're there,' and, 'It's me, Patrick,' as if it could be some strange boy who just happened to turn up. Luke's heart turned over at the sound of his son's voice and he cursed himself for being a fool, a daft fool.

'Hi,' he said, going out into the hall and clasping his son to him. 'How are you? How's my boy?' He covered Patrick's face with kisses.

'Fine,' said Patrick, pulling his father's thick, dark hair; an old habit from babyhood. 'Why are you home so early? You're never normally here at this time of day.'

'Well, I wanted to see you and I thought it would be good to give you a surprise, young man.'

When Patrick had gone upstairs to his room to start on his homework, Luke went into the kitchen in search of Alice, who was sitting at the table reading the northern edition of the *Guardian*.

'There's something here by Amos Oz,' she said, glancing up at him, 'about the illegal Jewish settlements on the West Bank: have you seen it?'

'Yeah, I saw it this morning, thanks.'

He put his hand on his wife's head, noting the grey hairs among the blonde. Poor Alice; he loved her in his way, his weird way. How could he say what he had to say? He wasn't amoral; he had a conscience – good, collapsed Catholic boy that he was – but it irked him that he would have to confess to something that no longer had any value. It was like paying good money for some dull but necessary item: the roof, or the building's insurance; only to maintain life as it was, not to enhance it.

'Look, we have to talk. How long's he going to be upstairs for?'

'An hour or so; he's got quite a lot of homework. What's so urgent?'

She was totally unprepared for it, which made him feel even worse.

'I'm in trouble,' he said, handing her the letter, and sitting in the chair next to hers. It was a bald way of doing it, but he couldn't think of any other and it seemed better to get it over with.

'I don't understand,' Alice said in a dazed voice, crumpling the letter down on the table after she had scanned it. 'You'll have to explain what you've been up to. What's all this stuff about? I don't understand. What is all this about beatings and you liking tying her up? What's happened to you? Have you gone mad?'

She put her face in her hands, but when he put his hand on her shoulder, she shrugged it off angrily.

'I think I must have done,' he said sorrowfully. 'I don't know what came over me.'

'What do you mean "you don't know"? It's obvious. You found someone who would pander to your sick perversions and now it's rebounded on you. How could you have been so stupid, especially after what we'd agreed? How could you? I thought we'd agreed to try and now you go and do this.'

She began to cry.

'I'm sorry,' he said, 'truly sorry.'

'It's no good being sorry. What good will "sorry" do? You'll lose your bloody job and it'll serve you right.'

'Unless I pay her.'

'What do you mean, "unless you pay her"? Where are you going to get that kind of money? From the bank manager? Huh! I don't think so. "Oh hello, Mr Erskine, I need a loan of five thousand pounds to pay off a tart. Could you give me a good rate, do you think?"'

'She wasn't a tart,' began Luke, but stopped when he saw his wife's face.

'You never learn, do you? You're a chronically unfaithful husband who also likes S&M. Well, why can't you keep your prick to yourself? It's not that much to ask!'

She got up and went out of the room, then the front door slammed.

'Where's Mum gone?' asked Patrick, coming into the kitchen a few moments later.

'She's just popped out for a while,' said Luke, hoping Patrick hadn't heard any of the terrible but true things his mother had had to say, 'but she'll be back soon. Shall I get you your tea? What would you like?'

'Macaroni cheese,' said Patrick promptly.

'OK,' said Luke, who enjoyed cooking. 'You grate the cheese and I'll make the sauce.'

When Patrick had gone into the larder to get the cheese, he picked up the letter from Leila that Alice had left lying on the table and put it back in its envelope. He felt exhausted. He also had no idea what Alice would do next. He had no idea what he would do next, come to that.

'Were you and Mum having a row?' Patrick asked, reappearing with a huge brick of cheddar in one hand.

'We were, I'm afraid. Did you hear us?'

'Not really,' said Patrick. 'I just heard angry sounds. She was crying, you know,' he added gravely, 'and that can't be right.'

'No, it isn't,' said Luke sadly. 'I sometimes get it wrong with Mum, I'm afraid.'

'Well, she's quite a handful,' said Patrick. 'That's what Grandma Hannah says.'

'Does she?' enquired Luke, astonished. 'When did she say that?'

'When I was with them when you and Mum went to the conference in London. They thought I was sleeping in the back of the car, but I wasn't.'

'Well, keep it to yourself,' said Luke, 'there's a good fellow. She's a good Mum and she needs your love.'

The offices of the Eglinton Press occupied the first and second floors of a graceful, pedimented building exactly on the curve of the crescent of Moray Place. For many years it had been possible to set one's watch by Jack Macarthur's progress from home to office, briefcase in hand, dog at foot. He was a local figure, a beloved fixture, a habit in a city that enjoyed acquiring habits.

Since his father's heart attack, it was Duncan who went to and fro in the Old Man's place, briefcase in hand, dog at foot. The dog, Theodore, was Bella's son, so that the clan was extended even into the canine world.

At about six o'clock on the same day that Luke had confronted Alice with his unpleasant news, Marianne Maclean, returning from a meeting, looked out of her office window conveniently located at the front of the building between two pillars with a view of the gardens, and saw Duncan returning to the office together with his partner, Charles Murray.

'Here's Duncan back again,' she said over her shoulder to Consuelo, the other editorial assistant with whom she shared an office. 'I wonder how the Old Man is.'

The Old Man had been much liked amongst his staff because of his habit of hiring people and allowing them to get on with their job with the minimum amount of interference. He occasionally pinched an intern's bottom but the staff were used to his ways and nobody particularly cared. Like Churchill, he had smoked huge cigars and was often found asleep on the sofa in his office, particularly after a good lunch, not that that affected his prodigious performance. Jack did twice as much as anyone else in half the time, which, as he was fond of saying, gave him more time to enjoy himself. His office in Moray Place was the nerve centre for all of his activities in the city, not just the publishing business, but the Old Man had enjoyed entertaining clients and cronies of whatever aspect of his business ventures in a bookish atmosphere. Books gave him intellectual clout, he reckoned and he liked playing at publishing. It beat the company of bankers any day.

'I think it's going to be crêpe armband time any

minute now,' said Consuelo, looking down at Duncan and Charles. 'Duncan looks very sombre.'

'They're amazingly close-knit as a family,' said Marianne. 'If you aren't used to that sort of thing, it can be quite off-putting; I certainly found it an interesting experience. And yet now, when I look at them supporting one another, I feel almost envious. It's a clan thing. I've never known it. Archie doesn't do clan.'

'More Mafia than clan, I'd say,' said Consuelo. 'They all look out for each other like crazy, which is what you were saying, I guess.'

'What's the difference?'

Consuelo thought for a moment. 'Clan is extended family; my house is your house and all that stuff, but Mafia is a code of silence, *omerta*, or whatever it's called, where you know stuff but you never ever let on that you know. For instance,' she added, lowering her voice, 'did you know that Justine is the Old Man's mistress?'

'What?'

'Come closer,' said Consuelo, 'the walls have ears in this place.'

'How do you know?'

'Hester told me.' Hester was one of the directors. 'I went in last week to get a script from Justine that's just come in and she was crying. When I asked her what was wrong she wouldn't tell me but it was obviously serious because she looked really unhappy. When I mentioned it to Hester, she said, "It's because the Old Man is dying and she can't see him. She's his mistress; has been for years. There's a child, a sixteen-year-old, as well; Elly she's called." It came out just like that – this huge secret. You could have knocked me down with a feather. They all know but nobody ever mentions it. Lady M is the only one that doesn't know apparently. Justine's flat in Howe Street is provided by the Old Man. He takes care of everyone; that's his motto. Didn't Ben tell you when you were going out with him?'

'He never mentioned a word,' said Marianne, 'but that's typical of the family, I suppose. The left hand knoweth not what the right is doing, or whatever the expression is, and I was an outsider. You only get full *confidante* status if you marry one of them.'

'He's kept two establishments going for years. I find that incredible in such proximity! They all know, but they never say. That's Mafia for you. There has to be an element of collusion somewhere.'

'Who put these flowers on my desk?' exclaimed Marianne, suddenly recognising the familiar roses, sweet-smelling, delicately striped, old-fashioned blooms that were shedding petals everywhere, that were a particular favourite of Ben's at Ardgay.

An element of collusion, she thought; of course there bloody was. In this city of surfaces where outward appearances mattered so much, what other fuel could the true life of the city run on other than collusion? I see but I don't see. I cannot see. I do not want to see. Nothing changes. Human beings always have something to hide. She thought with a guilty thrill of Luke, who had everything to hide.

64

'I don't know,' said Consuelo. 'I've only just got back myself. Maybe you have a secret admirer.'

'I wish,' said Marianne, glancing at her watch. These careless garden roses were not Luke's style; they were more Ben than Luke. He had probably brought them up from the country and got Duncan or someone to put them on her desk. She hadn't seen Ben around at all lately. According to Luke, her source of information, he was working hard and becoming quite successful. When she thought about him, she realised that she still loved him, but she couldn't wait her whole life for him to realise that he felt the same way. If there were a number of people one could truly love, say five or so, then Ben was definitely one of them. But what had suddenly impelled him to make such a gesture now? Was his father's impending death stirring him into thinking of his own future? Had he realised he'd made a terrible mistake in letting her go? Had he changed his mind about commitment, and if so why? And why had it had to wait until now when it was very nearly too late?

Nevertheless, Luke was providing a very satisfactory diversion; if he hadn't been a married man, she would have gone for him hook, line and sinker. For a moment, she wished there was a way she could convey to Ben that she was having a wild affair with someone; she still wanted to make him jealous, to have the satisfaction of knowing that he knew he'd made a terrible mistake. Then she would forgive him and fall into his arms. Unfortunately, life wasn't as tidy as that.

Luke, however, had certain advantages over Ben. Luke was good at women and knew how to deal with them. He was cosy, emotionally open, funny, cuddly and incredibly clever, although he never paraded it. She loved his style, or rather his lack of it, and she enjoyed the clandestine edge to their meetings that his marriage forced on them. Luke had told her that he and his wife had an 'arrangement', and that each allowed the other a certain amount of sexual freedom. There were certain things, he had said very early on, that his wife didn't like doing in bed, but Marianne hadn't enquired, thinking this was a euphemism for the fact that she didn't sleep with him at all.

Marianne, born and raised in Galloway, had chosen to live in Edinburgh because her father, the painter Archie Maclean RA, had been made painter-in-residence for three years or so at one of the city's famous art galleries.

She had found an apartment to share with her friend Nadia, a fledgling psychiatrist, whom she had met and been friends with at St Andrews University, and another friend of Nadia's, Jim, a solicitor who worked for one of the grand old law firms of the city.

Luke had been giving a lecture on Jerusalem at the Macarthur Foundation, an arts centre in Leith, set up and funded by Sandy and Jack (as she later discovered) as a joint venture with a handsome helping hand from the Scottish Development Agency. She had gone to the lecture because Archie, her father, had just come back from Jerusalem and had inspired her with

66

his tales of the beautiful stone alleys and fountains of the city. And anyway, it sounded romantic and mythical, a place that she could hardly believe really existed outside the imagination, like Venice or Samarkand.

It was initially his youth which had attracted her to him. He seemed so young to be a professor, though he was in fact thirty-five, around the same age as Ben. He talked passionately, without notes, of the history of the city and what he said was compellingly interesting. He even answered questions well. At the end she went up and asked him about the destruction of the city walls by the Ayubbid Sultan Muazzam to prevent their use by the approaching Crusaders; she had read this in a book somewhere and thought she could impress him with such an unusual question. She didn't want him to think she was just another groupie or fawning on him because she already knew him a bit. He answered her question as if he believed she had been serious in asking it, then he said, 'What are you doing next?' She'd known him slightly from her short time with Ben, and had always fancied his shaggy bear, shambling look. Some men, without trying at all, had sex appeal and Luke was one of them. Ben was another. Sartorially, they were both walking disaster areas but Marianne liked that. She'd always been allergic to spivs.

They had gone to a wine bar. Luke was wearing his usual uniform of terrible old combat trousers and a sweater reaching almost to his knees that had seen better days. His clothes were a matter of supreme indifference to him. She watched the back of his hands and then his mouth as he talked. Sometimes she looked at his hair and the way it fell over his collar or the skin on his neck that was still a shade darker than his throat from a summer holiday somewhere.

They had talked about her job at the family firm, gossiping about books and authors, though she noted that Luke kept well away from the subject of Ben, and they discussed her father, Archie, whom Luke admired enormously as a painter. 'I've got an early Archie in my office,' he said, 'one of the famous cow paintings. I get a huge kick out of it every time I look at it. You must come and see it some time.'

If it was an invitation, it was a pretty laconic one. He made no move on her at all.

He had driven her home to her flat in Marchmont, stopping outside the entrance to her building with the engine running.

'Thanks,' she had said, glancing at him to say goodbye.

He saw her looking but before she could turn away to open the door, he reached over and kissed her very passionately. And she returned his kiss equally passionately.

'I've been wanting to do that ever since I saw you,' he said, drawing back so that he could cup her chin in his hand.

'So pretty,' he said tenderly, 'so very pretty.'

'Go now, if you want.' He took his hand away but continued to look at her.

'I don't want.'

'You need to think,' he said, 'I understand that. I'm not a very good bet for a girl like you.'

It was only later on that she realised what a clever remark that had been. It suggested that he was thinking about her rather than himself; it also implied that he desired her, which was in itself hugely flattering. She was one of those pretty girls who could not believe in her own beauty for longer than a moment here and there. People told her she was lovely to look at but she couldn't see it.

Since her mother, Janet, had died it was as if she could no longer see her own reflection properly in the glass. Janet had been a very warm, bolstering figure who had put up with Archie's wild ways without complaining for far too long. Marianne had once asked her mother why she didn't leave him and Janet had said, 'Because I'm not myself without him. He's my other half. If you know that you're all right. I hope you find yours too.'

'What if there isn't one?' What if Socrates or whoever it was had been wrong?

'Oh, there is,' Janet had said sagely. 'He's out there somewhere. He'll turn up.'

'What if he already has and I've missed him?'

But Janet had just shaken her head at this piece of nonsense.

The first meeting at the lecture had taken place in February. He had waited for several days before telephoning her at the office. She hadn't given him the number but then she didn't have to. He knew exactly where to find her.

'Can you meet me for dinner this evening?' he'd asked. 'I must see you.'

It was the imperative that got her. It echoed her own feelings. She felt she had to see him too. She wanted to feel his warmth and see his lazy smile. She wanted him to kiss her again and to be folded in his arms where she had felt safe for the first time in a long while.

They met, romantically, by the Thistle Chapel in St Giles. There was a café in the basement where they went for a drink but didn't stay because Marianne saw Jim, her flatmate, with a whole gang of writers and advocates from the courts on the other side of Parliament Square. She wasn't sure whether Jim had seen her or not. She hoped not, but it was likely he had. Luke was a little too large to miss. It occurred to her that it was rather a foolish place to meet if one didn't wish to be seen, but Luke seemed indifferent to detection. Or maybe he was just careless.

His car was parked nearby, where he kissed her as passionately as he had done before until a tramp clutching a can of Tennant's Super banged on the window, startling them into fits of laughter.

'Where can we go?' she said, putting her hand under his shirt to feel his smooth, warm skin.

'I've the loan of an apartment in Comely Bank,' he said, looking at her, 'aptly named. A colleague of mine is away and I have the keys. Will you come there?'

'How very convenient,' she said gaily. 'Are you always so well prepared?'

'What do you mean "always"?' he asked, laughing. 'I don't know what my cousin Ben has been saying to you.'

'He never said anything about any of you. He was what my mother would have called first cousin to a clam when it came to the Clan Macarthur.'

'We're not that interesting,' said Luke. 'There's nothing much to say.'

'Oh, come on! You don't expect me to believe that, surely!'

She realised he was playing the same game as Ben, but in his own way.

'You're one of Edinburgh's first families,' she persisted. 'Of course you're interesting.'

'I'm much more interested in you,' he said, putting his hand on her thigh.

That first time had been very passionate and warm. They had made love in haste and then lay there in the tangled bed talking. Luke had asked her lots of questions about herself and her family and she had felt that he was really interested in her. Ben had talked so much about himself that she had sometimes wondered whether there was room for her in the relationship. Ben's greatest emotional involvement had so far been with himself. Diana had dented this self-preoccupation in a way that had scared him witless (she had been desperate for his attention, by all accounts) and Marianne had realised that his rejection of her had been part and parcel of this self-preoccupation. He couldn't face going through it again and so he had sent her away.

71

When she asked Luke about his wife, he was disarmingly frank.

'We have an open relationship,' he said, 'which means we both play away, from time to time.'

'I never understand "open" relationships,' Marianne had replied. 'What happens if you fall in love with someone?'

'It hasn't happened yet,' he said, stroking the inside of her thigh.

'"Yet" implies lots of girls. Have there been lots?'

'You do ask a bunch of questions,' he said. 'There've been a few, here and there.'

'And you're a cagey guy,' Marianne replied, turning towards him. 'What's wrong with your wife – Alice, isn't it? – that you can't have a complete relationship with her?'

'What's "complete"?' he countered. 'One man's meat . . . etcetera.'

'Well, you know, a full sexual relationship. Why do you both play away?'

'We married young,' he said, cupping her face in his hand, 'but we want to stay married. This seems one way of doing it.'

'Well, that's brutally honest, at least,' said Marianne. 'I'm always glad to help someone else's marriage along.'

'Do you always go to bed with a man expecting love and marriage?' asked Luke, teasingly. 'We've only just met.'

'No, I don't. I'm just nosy, I guess.'

'A very pretty nose,' he said, kissing it.

But she felt she was more to him than just a quick roll in the hay, in spite of what he had said on that first occasion. He was tender and warm to her. And a brilliant listener.

He represented deep sexual satisfaction and the calm, organising ear of the therapist. There was something about his bearishness that made her long to drown herself in his cuddly warmth when she lay with him in the tangled bed at Comely Bank. She talked to him at length about her mother's death and he understood her sadness, and the feeling she had that she hadn't shown her mother how much she loved her. He didn't appear to feel threatened by it, as Ben did. And so she had met him again and then again, so that after four or five times, he had become a habit to which she had become addicted and without which she began to wonder if she would be able to function at all.

Marianne's father, Archie, had been loaned a large and beautiful first-floor studio in the New Town in a neoclassical building completed in 1830 and paid for by the present government, as Archie was fond of telling his sitters. He was an ardent Scottish Nationalist for all the wrong reasons, a fact he was also fond of telling his sitters.

Bounty, such as a free studio in one of the most beautiful buildings in Edinburgh, was one of the many perks of what Archie called 'the great tit of the State', now sadly abolished by successive Tory governments in England (and he considered Mr Blair the natural heir of Mrs Thatcher), but in the process of splendid and profligate reconstruction north of the border and how glad and grateful he was for it. Others talked of the disappointment of devolution, the shabby unaccountability of a bunch of second-rate politicians, of the dangers of insularity and xenophobia towards the English in partnership with whom the Scots had flourished for generations, even running their government for them at Westminster, but not Archie.

Archie thought it was a great thing all round, including hating the English. The Scots had always hated the English, made a national sport of it indeed, and serve them right, silly buggers. At football matches between England and Scotland these days the chant went, 'If you hate the fucking English, clap your hands.' Archie was more than ready to do so. Anything for a laugh, really.

'So there is such a thing as a free lunch, darling – that's what you're really saying, isn't it?' remarked his sitter on this particular May morning: the former wife of Benjamin Macarthur, who now went by her maiden name of Diana Forbes.

The Macarthurs were sometimes known as the 'first family' of Scotland, by left-leaning journalists in various newspapers who regarded the royal family and the aristocracy as a spent force; doomed, if not quite to the guillotine, then certainly to oblivion. The Macarthurs were not only wealthy but clever to boot and prominent in almost every area of Scottish cultural life from publishing to the stage, where Ben's

Uncle Sandy, the well-known playwright, had staged a theatrical revival of the first order in Leith and turned down a knighthood on the back of it on account of the fact that he couldn't stand that namby-pamby Tory git Tony Blair.

Archie, as part of the 'New Enlightenment' portrait exhibition planned by the gallery for the year 2004, would be painting the portraits not only of Duncan and Benjamin Macarthur, but also their cousins Luke and Sukey Macarthur, as well as Sandy himself. These names had all been on the first list. He had ideas of his own about whom he would like to add. He had done some preliminary sketches of the Old Man in his office the previous year before he became too ill to sit for him.

He had liked Jack Macarthur finding him courteous and intelligent as well as intellectually formidable. The Old Man had also been one of his earliest patrons, buying the large oil, 'Cows at Carrick' (that now hung in the dining-room of his house at number twelve Ainslie Place) for a large sum of money when Archie was fresh out of art school. He was a polymath, a dying breed, Archie considered. He was especially intrigued when the old man revealed a mischievous side: 'I know I can trust you, Mr Maclean, with a secret. I have a daughter whom I would like you to paint as a present for her mother. Her name is Eleanor and she is presently at St Leonard's School in St Andrews. Perhaps you would get in touch with her mother, Mrs Justine Mackenzie, to arrange this. Please send the bill to me here in my office.'

'I suppose that's what I'm saying,' said Archie, whose mind had wandered from the sitter in front of him to her former father-in-law and his clandestine family. He had liked Justine Mackenzie very much; in fact he could quite see what had attracted the Old Man.

She was a woman of about fifty, he guessed, blonde, quite slender and with a large bosom – Archie had always regarded himself as a tit man – with a relaxed but slightly flirtatious manner. She was a senior editor at the Eglinton Press and hand-in-glove with Duncan Macarthur who seemed to accept that his father had a paramour, or whatever the expression was, without trouble. Families were really very odd things indeed.

'What's the news of the Old Man?' he asked. 'Is he still in the land of the living?'

'Just,' said Diana. 'I went to see him last night and he was so frail. Jean would only let me see him for a moment, just to say goodbye really. It made me very sad to see him like that. He was always wonderful to me, Jack, even when I broke up with Ben.'

She sniffed, moving her head slightly. Mention of her marriage still disturbed her; sad but true. Before she had married Ben she had been a light-hearted party girl; post-Ben she was sometimes depressed and quite often lonely.

'Chin down a little,' said Archie, wishing to God she'd sit still. She was like a piece of mercury on a slab the way she jittered about in her seat.

'Do you always talk to your sitters like that?' asked Diana, sticking her tongue out at him.

'I'm in charge in my studio, so the answer is yes I do. Sit still for God's sake, woman.'

'I need a fag, darling; can we have a break?' Diana rose from her armchair and stepped down lightly off the podium, without waiting for an answer. She enjoyed baiting Archie whose authoritarian ways amused her no end, particularly in bed when she was happy to play submissive maiden to his caveman or whatever he thought he was. In fact if Diana was truthful with herself, she enjoyed Archie's strength and the way he was prepared to shove her around without ceremony. Ben had been so careful of her that she had found herself bored. Dear Ben; he was a nice man, a good man, but he could be so tedious what with his architectural obsessions and his music, the falling asleep with the dog in front of the bloody telly, not to mention the monstrous self-obsession that took up all the other available space in his brain. But she had loved him and he had rejected her, and that rejection had turned her into what she was now: a self-loathing drunk, some of the time at any rate.

She wanted a lover who could perform the role of adversary as well, craved it in fact, somebody like her father whom she could push and shove against without them falling over, and had gone looking for it during the course of her marriage, when Ben had made it clear he wasn't interested. She had dallied with Luke Macarthur, the Lothario of Stockbridge, but had swiftly withdrawn when she realized what really turned him on. She liked kicks but found them in other ways, thank you very much.

Archie was authoritarian but he wasn't cruel; in fact he was a tender-hearted man when you knew him well as she was beginning to. She realized that she was rather falling for Archie Maclean.

'Go and put the kettle on, would you?' asked Archie, apparently unfazed. It wouldn't do to let her think she was getting her own way, however annoying she was. Women had to be kept in their place.

'I never heard of asking the client to do such things;' she said, looking in her handbag for her cigarettes and lighter. 'you need an assistant.' But even as she said it, he heard her footsteps going down the steep internal stairs to the galley kitchen.

He had asked Diana to sit for him because he wanted to put her portrait in the New Enlightenment series – that had been his initial reason at any rate (as a Miss Forbes of Forbes Castle she had a place as a glorious anachronism – her ancestor, Macneil Forbes, had been painted by Ramsay) but also because she was a handsome, sexy woman (crazy streak apart – she was a drinker who flipped her lid when she'd had a few too many; a bad habit in a woman (in anyone come to that, but particularly in a woman) and one Archie suspected would eventually terminate their relationship) whose company Archie enjoyed hugely, for the moment, particularly in bed.

Since his wife died he had been sexually lonely and he was determined not to live like some sort of bloody monk. He regarded Diana as a lover, not as wife material, a more permanent post that he was not interested in filling. After all, his kids were grown; why bother with marriage? One could choose when to see lovers, whereas wives demanded a more regular schedule. Now Janet was dead he could come and go as he wished between Edinburgh and Carrick, his house on the sea near Kirkcudbright.

He was not and never had been the kind of painter who slept with his working models, those little girls he used for life drawing, the Marias, the Katyas and the Basias, from Russia, Poland or the Baltic states, but instead preferred to bed his sitters, the grandees, as he put it to himself, not the servants. Not given to searching self-analysis, it did not occur to Archie that he was acting out through his work a gigantic chip on his shoulder and placing himself in a situation where as artist and lover he felt in total control.

Mrs Macarthur; Miss Forbes as she now was, was the latest in a long line of glamorous clients who had fallen prey to Archie's charms and his particular brand of 'blether', as the Scots refer to a touch of the Blarney.

'Raise your chin just a little,' replied Archie, when he had got her seated again after coffee, holding a long brush with a sable tip between the thumb and forefinger of his left hand as he assessed the planes of Diana's handsome face through narrowed eyes. He approached the podium where she was sitting in an armchair, examined her carefully for a moment, and then stepped back towards his easel where he would transfer the image seen close to onto the canvas as if she were sitting near and not twelve feet away. It was a technique known as 'sight size' used in the Renaissance and Archie was a passionate exponent of this technique. He always maintained that he reserved the right to shoot on sight people who suggested that he work from photographs.

Diana raised her chin and watched Archie watching her. It was an interesting business being painted, she thought, and bloody hard work too sitting still for hours; for she was aware that Archie looked at her differently when he was painting her to how he looked at her when she was naked in bed and she liked the contrast. It titillated her to think of him in bed when he was brandishing his professional persona; cut him down to size so to speak. Archie wasn't a good-looking man (although he was a marvellous lover), being small and fat with a nose like a potato (he had broken it boxing several times), but for some reason she found him terribly sexy. He was occasionally pugnacious in conversation and he had a huge chip on his shoulder, but he could talk brilliantly and nobody made her laugh quite like Archie. And she did so love to laugh. Sometimes he said things that were so funny that she positively ached with laughter. There were other matters too. She liked the way he cried out when he came; the great painter reduced to putty, and then the way he made her laugh again afterwards bitching about his other sitters – how a certain member of the royal family had offered to give him a blow job; the pop star who had kept altering her appearance with plastic surgery between sittings but wouldn't admit it; she loved the way he strutted off to the fridge later on to get the wine, nude but for a pair of urine-coloured Moroccan slippers. There was something highly sexy and comic about Archie Maclean. All in all, it boiled down to the fact that he was a life-enhancer; being with Archie made her feel alive.

'For God's sake hold still,' Archie said, 'or I'll never get this done.'

'You must make me look beautiful,' said Diana just to annoy him, 'it's extremely important that I do.'

'They all say that,' replied Archie, putting the finishing touches to Diana's wide, rather cruel mouth. 'You are beautiful anyway. You don't have to worry.'

'I bet you say that to everyone.'

'No. Not everyone. Not the dogs.'

'What are you doing this weekend?' she asked him, after a short silence.

'Going home,' he said, selecting another brush from the several he held in his left hand.

'Can I come?'

'Why?'

'Why not? I'm not doing anything.'

'No house party somewhere?' he jeered.

'Oh, shut up,' she said. 'Can't I come with you?'

Archie had a beautiful house overlooking the sea near Borgue in Galloway, rented from the National Trust for a peppercorn sum; a further subsidiary in all but name of the great tit of the State, and he loved to return to that place: the wide, grey sweep of the sea, the cattle wandering in the ocean on an incoming tide, the sense of sea-borne solitude. He would lie in his bed at night at Carrick House and listen to the low murmur of the restless tides on that inconstant coast. The melancholy he felt then was directly connected to his desire to paint, to capture what was there before it was gone forever. Diana had been there once recently when she was staying over in Wigtownshire with her brother, Hugo Forbes, who had recently sold up the family home, Forbes Castle. In Archie's view he was a hopeless case. Hugo was a good-looking man with a fine head, jug ears and bright blue eyes who sported, oddly in these days, a moustache. In Archie's view it was a wonder he'd survived as long as he had. His good looks concealed a weak character with a tendency towards self-pity. He'd made an almighty fuck-up of his business affairs but instead of admitting responsibility he droned on about how the Labour government's punitive taxes were to blame and so on and so forth. His wife, Rowena, had left him during the course of this débâcle, taking with them the one child of the marriage, Alec. A blessing in disguise for the child, Archie thought, to get out from under that cloud of doom-laden self-pity. He'd had enough after one lunch.

'I'm busy,' he said shortly, 'I've got people to see; my daughters for one.'

'What? That bossy Cressida creature?'

'I'll have you remember she is my flesh and blood,' said Archie. 'She's a good lass, Cressida is.'

'She lays down the law too much for my liking,' said Diana. 'Is the other one coming too?'

'Marianne? Yes, she is, unless that man of hers stops her.'

'What man?'

'She's got a lover, but won't tell me who he is.'

Archie was a little worried about his younger daughter, although he wouldn't have admitted it to Diana. She was cagey with him about what she was doing in her spare time, which she hadn't been in the past and she didn't telephone very much. He was keeping tally of the calls between them and so far had initiated the last four or five himself. He had got her to agree to think about coming home this weekend so that he could have a better look at her in a familiar setting.

'Well, why should she?'

'I'm only her father,' said Archie, 'that's all.'

'Oh, stop it,' said Diana. 'She's grown up. Why should she tell you?'

'Since her mother died, I feel I have to be more nosy. Janet always knew these things.'

'She'll tell you sooner or later,' said Diana. 'Please let me come.'

'Another time,' said Archie tersely. 'I'm working.'

'Please!'

'I told you. I'm going to be busy. I've got a lot of work to do as well.'

'Well, I'll go to Hugo's and then call you,' she said, trying her best to be conciliatory.

'How's he getting on?'

'Not very well.' For the first time during the conversation Diana lost her buoyancy.

'What's going on?'

It wasn't hard to guess. Hugo's wife had left him, he was drinking too much and it was probably only a matter of time before he had the good sense to take himself into the woodshed and shoot himself.

She shrugged. 'I think he's suffering from old-fashioned despair. Selling up after three hundred years is pretty awful. And no one is sympathetic to him either, poor darling; not these days. They all think he deserved it and in a way he did. He was a complete fool.'

'I'd agree with that,' said Archie.

'Don't be so beastly. It's hard to go from high estate to low.'

'Literally,' said Archie. Hugo was now living in a farmhouse on the estate.

'You've just got a chip on your shoulder; that's what's wrong with you. It's like a disease these days. You're a commissar at heart. You don't love democracy; you just want to be in charge. You think it's your turn.'

'He started off with a socking great silver spoon stuck in his gob,' said Archie inelegantly, ignoring the rest of what Diana had said, 'which is more than most of us do. I just can't find it in my heart to bleed for him.'

'You'd have adored the French Revolution,' said Diana acidly, 'cartloads of us going to the guillotine.'

'Aye, I would. A good purge; that's what we need.'

'Heartless bastard! The French Revolution tore everything apart; after that, anything was possible. We're still paying for it today.'

'Come on,' said Archie, putting down his palette and laying his brushes carefully on a table beside the sink where he would later wash them painstakingly, 'enough of this talk. Let's go to bed.'

'You hate aristocrats but it doesn't stop you wanting to go to bed with one, does it?'

'I don't hate them. I just find them pointless.'

'Do you find me pointless?'

'Obviously not and certainly not between the sheets,' he said, putting his arms round her waist.

'You really are a contrary bastard, aren't you?'

'Am I?'

'You know you are. Say one thing; do another.'

Archie shrugged. 'That's life, darling.'

The living quarters of the studio were down a flight of internal stairs: there was a small kitchen, ten feet by eight, containing nothing much more than some shelves and a Belfast sink, and here Archie, a talented cook, produced astonishingly delicious meals; a bathroom containing a vast claw bath and practically nothing else, together with a large bedroom containing a four-poster bed Archie had constructed himself. There was a chest of drawers that Archie had rescued and restored (he would have restored furniture for a living if he hadn't had a greater calling and had done so from time to time) and a large number of paintings, many stacked against the walls and some hung. The bedroom had the same smell as the rest of the studio: a potent mix of turps and garlic and linseed oil. Sometimes when Archie made rabbit's foot glue, the disgusting smell of boiled bones overlaid this smell, but it soon crept back. Diana noticed that her clothes smelled faintly of it when she had been with Archie, which she liked. For her it was the smell of freedom, the idea that she had understood so well from so early on that life was meant to be fun, and that had become obscured during the wreck of her marriage to Ben.

He made his mistresses undress slowly; it was a part of the erotic charge. Diana wasn't the Rubenesque type at all, but she was rounded with long limbs and a wasp waist. He had asked her to wear stockings and loved to watch her bending over to unhook the suspenders and then roll the stocking slowly down her leg. A cliché, but a good one. He was also unashamedly aware that this action echoed one he had seen his mother perform when he was a nosy little boy peering through the keyhole of her bedroom door, an experience he had logged as his first sexual thrill.

The hair between Diana's legs was a shade or two darker than the dull russet colour of her hair and her skin was almost tawny; not the milk-blue tone of the carrot top.

When he had told her she was beautiful, he meant it. He loved her body, her coarse mass of hair, her sensuous but rather cruel mouth. He knew she was a drunk – he had watched her mood flip more than once late at night when she was capable of turning from an amusing, somewhat waspish flirt into a harpy who talked vitriolic and embarrassing non-sense.

'I'd love to draw you like that,' Archie said, pausing to admire Diana's naked body before he climbed onto the bed. 'Your breasts are stupendous.'

'That's what having no children does for you,' she said. 'At least there are some advantages.'

'Do you want children?' he asked, in spite of himself. He made a point of not engaging childless women on the topic of children; there was invariably a can of worms in there somewhere: blighted hopes, blighted ovaries, blighted something.

'I did once, but we couldn't although we tried and tried.'

'Were you tested?'

'Oh God, yes. We both were. But they couldn't find anything however hard they looked up my insides or his for that matter. I think it's something to do with Ben. I think he has a low sperm count or something. I did get pregnant once, years ago, when I was about nineteen, so I know I can do it. I never told Ben that though. I didn't want to hurt his feelings. He's longing for babies. He'd be one of those really annoying hands-on sort of fathers who you see walking round with their babies in slings. I can't stand that! If we'd had children I would have had Nanny and tons of minions so that I could stay in bed in a satin nightdress and read novels all day. The Macarthurs are gagging for children. Duncan's a poofter so he won't have any. Jack and Jean are longing for grandchildren like you wouldn't believe and Ben is their only hope.'

'What about Eleanor?' asked Archie.

'Oh, so you know about her, do you?'

'The Old Man told me.'

'He is a bit of a blighter; really he is. I don't know how he's got away with it all these years. All that's going to come out when he dies, of course. Then the shit really will hit the fan.'

'Don't look so pleased about it,' said Archie.

'I'm not really,' said Diana, 'but they're all so middle-class and thrillingly pleased with themselves about everything. A little blood on the carpet won't do them any harm.'

'More than blood for Jean, nevertheless?'

'Poor old Jean. She's sweet but utterly frigid. He couldn't get a fuck there so he went elsewhere. He is half Italian, you know.'

'For a member of the useless upper classes you really do have a foul mouth,' said Archie.

'You like it though; it turns you on,' she said. 'I can tell.'

'You should be recorded and put in a museum,' he said. 'Soon there'll be none of you left in the Republic of Scotland. We'll be a meritocracy. We'll get rid of the royal family and enter the modern age, not before time.'

'Down a mine shaft, I suppose,' said Diana sarcastically. 'We were meritocrats once,' she continued, 'that's what aristocracy is. And I'd rather have the royal family than the Care Blairs or their claret-swilling ministers. They're all just as bad and a whole lot more corrupt.'

'Now you're just fossilised meritocracy,' said Archie, who was only half-listening, 'with the emphasis on fossilised, I might add. Why should I kowtow to someone who's descended from someone who once did something? The system has to keep fluid. I mean, look at your brother; he's a classic case in point. He's completely useless.'

'Leave off my brother!' she said in a mock-fierce voice. Hugo was her vulnerable point and Archie knew it, as he always knew these things by instinct. 'You love me because I'm a class act, darling. Admit it.'

It was true in a way. He adored her accent, thinking of it as pure Nancy Mitford. Hardly anyone dared to speak like that these days, especially in the Republic of Scotland where the old hatred of the Sassenach was now contemporary orthodoxy. In fact Diana's family were very Scottish and very ancient, but they spoke with English accents, as all their kind did, the most famous example being that Ancient of Days, the Queen Mother. Not for the first time, he found himself wondering when all that started; maybe it was when King James VI had gone to England upon the death of Elizabeth I and Scotland had lost her monarch to the southern enemy for good. Treacherous, cold-hearted James had never returned to Edinburgh, but then he had had a difficult upbringing, so maybe that explained it. The Prince Regent, he seemed to recall, had come north and pranced about Alan Ramsay-style in tartan, but until Queen Victoria, English monarchs had taken precious little interest in their northern kingdom and their northern kingdom had returned the compliment.

After they had made love, Archie went to fetch the bottle of champagne that Diana made him keep on ice for when she came to the studio. After they had drunk most of it they made love again.

'You really are quite something in the sack, aren't you?' she said, leaning on one elbow and looking down at him as he lay sprawled beside her, his flaccid penis lolling in his groin like some bizarre sea creature.

'You look like a Lucien Freud,' she said, flicking it gently. 'Vast belly, tiny penis; hideous really. The sexual organs really are God's way of having a joke; they must be.'

'Thanks a bunch,' he said, lazily unconcerned. 'What's the time?'

'Five thirty,' she said, consulting the tiny gold watch the Old Man had given her as a wedding present.

'I must go,' he said.

'Where to?'

'To see a man about a dog.'

'Can't I ask? Don't I have any rights of ownership? You do sleep with me, you know. Is that all I am, just a good fuck?'

'No.'

'Well then?'

'Well then what?'

'Answer the question.'

'I'm going out,' he said curtly.

'I want to know where!'

'Well, I'm not going to tell you. You're not my wife. I don't have to tell you anything.'

'You really are a fucking little shit,' said Diana, throwing the covers over his face. 'I'm leaving.'

She got out of bed and began to gather her clothes. 'You can keep these,' she said, throwing the stockings and the suspender belt onto the bed. 'Get the next bint you fuck to wear them.'

He pushed the covers back but said nothing; just watched her face.

When she was dressed, she waited just a moment to see if he would say anything. She was longing for him to stop her. Why didn't the bastard say something?

'So it's goodbye then, is it?' she asked.

'If that's what you want.'

'It isn't what I want.' She sat down on the bed and burst into tears. She was doing one of her flips, he realised wearily; swinging from A to Z of the emotional spectrum and back again.

'Then don't be such a silly,' he said, in what he hoped was a kind voice. He wasn't very good at being kind and tears repelled him, but he would have to get rid of her quickly because he was expected somewhere within the hour and the only way to do that was not to continue like this.

'Why are you so horrible to me?'

'Come on,' he said, taking her in his arms, 'come on now.'

It was working; the storm was ceasing. 'Have another glass of wine,' he said. 'There's a bottle open in the fridge; I'll fetch it.'

He wandered off naked but for his slippers, leaving Diana sniffing and dabbing on his bed. When he came back with the bottle in his hand, she was applying foundation from a compact.

'That's better,' he said approvingly, filling her glass and handing it to her. 'Do you want me to fetch your cigs for you?' She liked the caring touches: Nurse Archie she called it. He could be cosy when he tried.

'No, thanks.' She shook her head and gave him a brave little woman's watery smile. He preferred her when she was being a harpy to this version: Lady Jekyll and Lady Hyde, he had named it to himself.

'Drink up your wine now,' said Archie in his nurse's voice. She obediently drained her glass and held it out to be refilled.

'Where are you going really?'

'Just to see someone about a commission.' This was not untrue, except that he was having dinner with Justine Mackenzie to whom he had taken a damn great shine.

'Why didn't you say so?'

'Now, now,' he said, still in his nursy voice. 'I'll have to be away in ten minutes; do you think you can manage that, eh? Feeling up to facing the outside world?'

She drank fast. He wasn't going to give her any more, but she held out her glass anyway and he poured in a tiny bit. He hadn't touched his own glass. He looked at her appraisingly. 'Are you sure you're all right to drive?'

'Of course I am. I'm Scotland's best drunk driver, darling. I do it much better when I'm tanked. Anyway, you gave it to me. Don't give me so bloody much if you want me to be sober.'

There, he thought. Eureka! She was back again.

The bossy note in his voice infuriated her as he had calculated it would.

'I'm not sure you shouldn't go back on foot,' he said, in the same reproving, nanny tone. 'You can always get your car later. Why do you drive anyway? It's bloody lazy really.'

'Don't be ridiculous; I'm quite all right. And I can't get the bloody thing later; I have to be somewhere for dinner. I've just remembered.'

Christ, but where? More and more frequently, she had these blanks where, for all her efforts, she could not recall what the hell it was she wanted to. It was as if the compass of her mind, the rudder, had jammed, and the fact she wanted simply swam away out of reach.

'Oh? Who with?' She liked it if he took an interest; appeared to be a teensy weensy little bit jealous.

'I can't remember, but it'll come back to me. Some handsome hunk, I'm sure.'

Archie insisted on coming out to the car with her, no doubt to see that she was capable of turning on the ignition. Diana's car was a Range Rover, a present she had bought herself after her divorce.

'Why do you need a huge great thing like that?' asked Archie. 'It must guzzle fuel.'

'I know; isn't it disgusting, but I like looking down

on the hoi polloi. That's why people have these giant penises, so that they can shaft everyone else.'

'Is that so?' he said, in his best Morningside accent. 'And what about the environment, Miss Forbes?'

'Oh, bugger the environment. What difference will I make?'

She was pissed, he saw; much more so even than he had previously thought. That was the trouble with practised drinkers; they could knock it back and not show it until it was too late.

'Look,' he said, 'let me call you a cab if you're too idle to walk. You can always come back here later and get the damn car.'

'Oh, go to hell, darling,' she said lazily, starting the engine as her electric window glided downwards. 'Just leave me alone. I'm fine. I'll see you at the weekend,' she added. 'Do you want a lift?'

'No,' he said, frowning. 'Not with you at the wheel. I don't think you should drive tonight,' he added, 'you're not safe. You might kill someone.'

'If I kill anyone, it'll be myself,' she called, leaning out of her window, 'and that'll be a relief to some, I can tell you.'

She drove off with exaggerated slowness as if to show him how stupid he was being.

Rowena Forbes, Diana's sister-in-law, just happened to be looking out of the front window of her flat in Howe Street when that excessively vulgar car her sister-in-law drove hoved into sight. She watched as Diana parked, bang! into the car behind, and bang!

into the car in front, never mind the fact that she must have the very latest power steering; that was typical Diana riding rough-shod over everyone else, not caring a damn how much damage she did.

Rowena couldn't abide her sister-in-law (the feeling was entirely mutual) and it gave her considerable pleasure to see a policeman (and when did you ever see one of those when you needed one?) watching Diana's parking with interest. Whilst she was still sitting in the car, the policeman approached her, banging on the glass to get her to open the window. Rowena watched with fascination. She loved living in the city; there was so much to see and do all the time. If Hugo thought she was going to live in a dreary little farmhouse after the big house and all that that had meant socially, he had another think coming. Not on your nelly, as Mrs Bryce, her cleaning woman would say.

She hoped that the policeman would breathalyse Diana and take her away in handcuffs to the clink, but of course she got round him as she always did, climbing down out of her ridiculous wagon, smiling and laughing, the policeman joining in. There was no justice in the world, Rowena thought, freshening her rather lurid coral lipstick in the mirror and straightening the skirt of her Jaeger grey flannel suit. She was on her way out to play bridge with Jean Macarthur and two other ladies in Ainslie Place. It was Jean's turn to host the regular bridge four this evening and she had insisted in spite of the fact that the Old Man was so ill and the house was full of nurses squeaking about. Nurses always squeaked, irritating creatures that they were.

Duncan Macarthur opened the front door of his parents' house before Rowena had knocked; always a disconcerting thing to do.

'You're one of mother's bridge ladies,' he said, looking her up and down, placing her in an instant. 'Come through. She's just with father now, but she'll be down in a second. The others are here. I'm Duncan, by the way,' he added, holding out his hand.

Rowena knew exactly who Duncan Macarthur was. He was one of those homos. She didn't really want to take his hand; you never knew what you might catch. Who knew where his hand had been? What had Diana told her? Daisy chains; that was it: all buggering each other together in public toilets. Trust Diana to know that! Rowena had clapped her hands over her ears but she couldn't help hearing. She shook his hand as swiftly as she could and then let it away. She wouldn't eat or drink anything until she had washed it, she decided.

The big drawing-room was on the first floor of this grand house, but the room Duncan showed her into was a quiet back sitting-room looking over a secluded garden with a lawn and trees and a wonderful border Charles had helped Jean design. The bridge table was laid out with its packs of cards and scorers and the little onyx pencils with tassels that Jean always had. Rowena made a mental note to ask her where she had got them. Jean was one of those people who was always just so.

'Can I get you something to drink?' Duncan enquired politely.

'Oh, just a wee bit of ginger ale,' said Rowena. 'That would be lovely, thank you, Duncan.'

The other two ladies present were Polly Buchan and Margaret Buchanan who had their heads together in a corner when Rowena appeared.

'Hello, Rowena,' said Polly. 'That's a smart outfit. Have you been somewhere?'

Polly herself was wearing trousers and what looked like a very expensive cashmere sweater. She was the epitome of the expression 'smart casual'. Rowena instantly felt overdressed.

'Oh, I just hurried on from the afternoon,' said Rowena, 'no time to change, you know.'

'What were you doing, dear?' asked Margaret, who was about the same age as their hostess and married to a barrister friend of the Old Man's who had been made a judge, Rowena seemed to remember. They were now Lord and Lady Buchanan. Very grand. Hugo would be Sir Hugo at some point, but even that he couldn't get right. His father, old Sir James, lingered on at some vast age in a nursing home near Kirkcudbright. Apparently, he was a selling point for the nursing home and was trundled out for visitors to view, head lolling, dribble forming, as if to say, 'Look how good we are at preserving them.' So selfish, thought Rowena.

'Lunch and then a committee meeting,' said Rowena, 'you know how it goes.'

'Which committee was that?'

'Child Aid,' said Rowena, improvising. A flier had come through the front door of her building that morning showing the usual photograph of a beguiling dark-skinned child from the sub-continent. 'Giving Amira an education would only cost £3.50 a week,' etc. Rowena had thrown it straight in the bin. Charity begins at home, she reflected, thinking of herself.

'I don't know that one,' said Polly, 'but of course there are so many these days.'

'I think it's quite new. These charities spring up like mushrooms overnight.'

'I do the NSPCC myself,' said Margaret. 'There's enough child poverty in Craigmillar to keep us all going for a while.'

The other two listened respectfully while she spoke. Margaret sat on the bench and she knew what she was talking about. Bad housing, drugs, high unemployment, terrible schools. She might have been describing aliens from another planet for all Rowena cared; somewhere in her mind it was firmly fixed that those people deserved what they got.

Duncan came back with the ginger ale and then went out again. Someone else arrived. Rowena could hear the front door opening and closing, hushed voices conferring in the hall. Then Jean came in, immaculate as ever, but so thin. If you held her up to the light she would be almost transparent. There was a bandage on her left calf that Margaret spotted immediately. She was so professionally solicitous, Rowena thought resentfully.

'Have you hurt yourself, dear?'

'Oh, that,' said Jean in her bright way. 'No, I haven't hurt myself; I've got an ulcer that won't heal.'

'A rodent ulcer,' pronounced Margaret, shaking her head. 'That's bad, dear.'

'It's probably stress,' said Polly.

'How is he?' asked Rowena, as they shuffled their cards.

'A little stronger today, but he comes and goes. It's hard to say, really. The doctor can't say exactly.'

She meant the doctor couldn't predict how much longer this living hell was going to go on for, but she would never have spoken this thought aloud. Watching someone you loved die was like watching a familiar ship – a trireme with a black sail furled like one of those illustrations in the books about ancient Greece that the boys had read when they were children – sail further and further from land. Sometimes the ship would come nearer to the shore and sometimes it would recede again, with Jack on board, but always separated from her by the water. At the beginning of his dying he had reached down for her, but now at the end his head was turned in the other direction towards the horizon and the unknown regions that lay beyond.

'Who've you got?' asked Polly.

'Dr Jenner.'

'Oh, he's wonderful.'

Upstairs, Eleanor Macarthur, the Old Man's sixteen-year-old daughter, taken up by Duncan once his mother was safely seated at the bridge table (one of the few places she could be guaranteed to remain for hours) gazed upon the face of her father. He looked like some sort of ruined hulk lying there in his bed with his dry yellow lips and waxen complexion. The folds of skin on his neck made her think of the Nazis (whom she was studying at school) who had used human skin for lampshades. He was disgusting. There was a smell in the room, under the snow-white, clean laundry smell of the linen sheets in which the dying pharaoh lay, that caught in the back of her throat; a smell like no other, that reminded her of the dead cat she had once found in the summer house of a friend's garden, or rather a sack of putrefaction contained in the still-recognisable outline of a cat.

'Take his hand,' Duncan whispered, but Elly gave him an imploring look. The bones of the hand showed through the nearly transparent mottled skin; the half moons of his spade-like nails looked huge and unhealthily opaque as if some cloudiness from the murk in the depths had penetrated the extremities.

'Don't be afraid,' said Duncan. 'Just take his hand and say hello. Even if he doesn't appear to know you're there it makes a difference.'

Elly wondered how he knew but didn't ask. She was slightly afraid of Duncan although he had always been very kind, but there was something massive about him that intimidated her. Her mother had told her that Duncan with his black hair and swarthy complexion (his skin tanned in an instant even in Edinburgh) looked like her father had when she met him, but that had been years ago. Elly herself had fair hair but her skin had a tawny tint to it and her eyes were dark.

She wouldn't have said she knew her father. She saw him once or twice each holiday but he was a stranger to her, a powerful stranger whose word was law with her mother; a stranger who had sent her away to school for nine months of the year since she was five.

Elly did as she was told. 'Hello,' she whispered, but it made no difference, as she had known it wouldn't. She hoped he would die soon so that she could have her mother back.

As she took his hand and held it, he opened his eyes and gazed at her through a bloodshot haze. She wondered if he knew who she was.

His mouth framed a word that could have been anything and then his eyes closed again and he was gone. It was like being looked at by a corpse; the Lazarus look of one who had seen the unknown regions of ice and darkness.

As Duncan took her down the wide stairs a door opened somewhere off the hallway.

'Who's that?' said a female voice.

'It's only me, Mother,' said Duncan, grasping Elly's arm to stop her from proceeding.

'I thought there was someone with you.'

'No. Go back to your party; everything's fine,' Duncan replied, walking down the remaining flight of stairs.

'Why are you still here?' she heard his mother say to him.

'I've been sitting with father,' came the reply. 'Now go back to your game.'

The door closed softly.

Elly took off her shoes and crept down the stairs. Duncan opened the front door, beckoned her through it and then stepped out behind her, pulling the door to.

'You're a good girl, Elly,' he said, putting his arm round her. 'Sensible of you to take off your shoes, too. I think that was hard on you,' he said. 'I'm sorry.'

'That's OK,' said Elly, suddenly finding she felt tearful but not wanting to show Duncan. The air smelled of cold blossom and freshly cut grass; somewhere a motorbike made a dizzy whine like a fly trapped behind a shutter. She was alive and for the first time in her life completely conscious of it, a gift from the effigy in the upstairs room.

'I'll walk you home,' he said.

'It's OK,' she said, 'I'll take myself. Maybe you should get back.'

'You sure?'

She nodded. 'Here,' said Duncan, taking his wallet out of the inside pocket of his suit, 'take this. Young people always need cash.'

Elly looked at the note in her hand. He had given her fifty pounds; it wasn't the first time either. Impulsively she hugged him, feeling guilty for earlier having thought of him as intimidating. Duncan was a teddy bear, not an ogre. She kissed his cheek and then hugged him, inhaling a faint whiff of something evocatively clean and deep and dark that made her think of incense.

'Thanks,' she said gratefully. 'Thanks, Duncan. Will you ask Charles if I can work for him again in July before Mum and I go away on our holidays? I'd like to make some money.'

'I think he's hoping you'd come back,' said Duncan. 'I'll check and let you know, OK?'

'OK,' said Elly. 'I'd better be on my way. Mum'll be wondering where I've got to.'

Justine Mackenzie's flat was on the first floor of a building in Howe Street that had once been a single dwelling. Her drawing-room had tall mahogany double doors that Archie paused to admire as he followed her into the sitting-room.

'Nice,' he said, running his hand over the polished surface. 'Original?'

'Oh, yes,' she said. 'Period detail is all, as I'm sure you'd agree. What can I get you, Archie?'

Archie examined her from behind as she poured him a whisky; she had the sort of voluptuous figure he admired; he didn't like his women to be too skinny; he wanted something to get a hold of, not banister rails. She also exuded an air of calm that he found more attractive than any waist-to-hip ratio; unlike Diana, she was not reactive. You could say things to Justine on any topic, personal, political or whatever and she would consider them carefully before responding, whereas Diana was like an ammunition dump that any remark could ignite, amusing to bait but emotionally exhausting; he knew in his heart that he would have to put a stop to their affair shortly, however sexually agreeable it was. The price she exacted was too high.

'I'll join you, I think,' she said, handing him the glass and just allowing her hand to touch his as she did so. Archie was reminded of that phrase Evelyn Waugh had used about Mrs Stitch – 'the hypodermic needle of her charm' – for it applied to Justine Mackenzie with her honey-coloured hair in a chignon with a few wisps escaping, her waisted suit that showed off her figure, her high heels.

'Duncan's just spirited Elly round to see Jack,' she said, sinking into an armchair by the fireplace and kicking her shoes off. 'She'll be back in a moment.'

'How is he?' asked Archie, noticing that her toenails were varnished a bright red.

'Hovering over the edge, I think. It would be easier if he just got on with it and died but for Jack it's a challenge to hang on just like everything else. He's made being unpredictable into an art form.'

'How will the family cope?'

'They'll be just fine. It'll be a release for Jean, like cutting the string of a helium balloon; Duncan will become more and more like his father; and Ben . . . he's the most unpredictable of the family. It'll be make or break for him. I like Ben; he's a nice fellow with a good heart but he's lost his way.'

'And you?'

She shook her head. 'I don't know. I'll be a merry mistress, I expect.'

'It can't have been easy all these years.'

'Oh no, it's been fine. I'm lucky: I have Elly, I have

a job I like, and enough money. Jack gave me this apartment. We're taken care of in the will.'

'But you must have been lonely?'

'I'm used to it. As you must have been after Janet died.'

'Yes.'

Their eyes met and again Archie had a feeling that she understood him perfectly. It was such a relief, like sinking into a well-sprung mattress.

'I wanted to ask you about Marianne,' he said. 'I'm worried about her. How is she doing at work?'

'Oh, fine. She's excellent at her job; there's no problem there. Duncan likes her, she gets on with Consuelo, our other new recruit – when I say "new", I'm talking people recruited in the last five years. We have a very low turnover of staff at the Eglinton Press. What is it that worries you?'

'She never grieved for her mother properly, that's the first thing . . .'

'What do you mean?'

'I think she felt she couldn't let herself go in some way.'

'Why was that?'

He shook his head. 'I'm not sure. A feeling that if she did it might overwhelm her, drown her. So she buried it in busyness. I never seem to see her these days. She went out with Ben for a while, then that came to an abrupt halt for reasons she wouldn't specify.'

Justine raised her eyebrows. 'I could have predicted that,' she said. 'Ben's a darling, but he's a hopeless bet when it comes to women. People felt sorry for him when the marriage broke down, but I have a feeling it cut both ways. She had her work cut out and couldn't cope with him.'

'That's as may be,' said Archie, 'but I see her looking into space as if she's thinking of something that makes her unhappy. I don't know, just a father's hunch. She was a funny wee girl, always a bit fey and unhappy. Worrying the world might fall in.'

'You can't do it for them,' said Justine, 'or protect them from the world, the flesh and the devil.'

At that moment the buzzer went and Justine rose to her feet. 'That'll be Elly,' she said.

'I'll go.'

'No, don't go.'

The girl followed her mother into the room and, upon seeing Archie, stiffened slightly.

'How are you, Elly?' he asked, getting up.

'Cool, thanks. Can I have a glass of wine?' she asked her mother.

'If you want, yes. I'll get it.

'There's some in the fridge,' said Elly sulkily, 'I know where it is.'

She knew Archie and had quite liked him when he was painting her, although he was fantastically bossy in the studio, but finding him here now had been a bit much. He was like a wolf prowling round her mother. She'd seen it all before with Jack. Yet another man looking at her mother as if she had no clothes on. The king is dead, she thought, banging the fridge door shut so hard that it immediately sprang open again; long live the king.

When she went back into the room, Archie said once more, 'I'll go now.'

'I think you should,' agreed Elly. 'I need to talk to Mum and I haven't got long. I have to go back to school tomorrow.'

'There's no need to be rude, Elly,' said Justine, 'Archie understands only too well.'

'That's what bothers me,' Elly replied, undeterred by her mother's disapproval. She knew she was being rude and she was rather enjoying it. It was as good a way as any of making her mother pay for forcing her to go and see The Corpse, which was her new name for her father.

'What's eating you?' asked Justine, when she came back into the room.

'Nothing,' said Elly, her mouth turning down as it had done when she was a child.

Diana had decided to spend the entire weekend with Hugo whom she was more worried about than she cared to admit. At lunchtime she met a friend in Malmaison in Leith for oysters and champagne and to discuss the setting up of a decorating business. They drank one bottle of wine and then another; drinking and driving was not a subject Diana gave much thought to. She thought all the fuss about it was absurd and that the police ought to be catching rapists rather than tormenting poor motorists.

At five, Diana left for Hugo's. She had gone home

after lunch, thrown a few things in a case, had a sleep and set out feeling absolutely fine.

Somewhere, however, on the back roads of Wigtownshire she had fallen asleep at the wheel of her car and careered off the road into a dyke; the smash woke her and then there was silence, punctuated by the eerie cry of a lapwing drifting over the moor.

She got out of the car to investigate and found that she had done herself surprisingly little damage. The bull bars on the front of the car were scraped and she had smashed in a light, but otherwise it was fine. It was only a bloody car, after all. She climbed back into the driving seat and prepared to leave, but suddenly found that her hands were shaking and tears were threatening to overwhelm her. 'What is the point of it all?' she thought, leaning back in her seat and closing her eyes to stop herself crying. 'The point is that there is no point,' said a voice in her head, and when she heard that voice she felt that it was something she had always known.

Hugo's new house had previously belonged to the factor for the Forbes Estate. It was a handsome, whitewashed farmhouse with the window surrounds painted black, as was the tradition in that part of Scotland. The house was set back from the road and had a walled front garden and an orchard behind, separated from the fields by a drystone wall known as a dyke.

When Diana eventually arrived just in time for dinner on Friday night, Hugo was in the old-fashioned kitchen busily burning the food. Since Rowena had left him the previous year, he had deteriorated alarmingly in his physical appearance. This evening he was wearing an unironed and rather dirty checked shirt and some cavalry twills that weren't much better. On his feet he wore, to Diana's distress, a pair of red leather slippers of the kind that their father had once worn only between dressing room and lavatory. He was also unshaven and faintly bleary looking as if he'd been up half the night with a whisky bottle, which he probably had.

When he came out to greet her, still wearing his slippers, he said, 'Great God, sis, what the hell's happened to your bumpers? Have you run someone over?'

'I just had a little slip of the wrist on the back hill,' she said. 'Drove into a dyke.'

'How the hell did you do that?'

'Took a corner too fast,' she lied. 'You know how you do.'

'I'll get Willy at the garage to have a look at it tomorrow; he's good at panel-beating and fixing anything that's bent for a fraction of the normal cost. You shouldn't drive so fast, sis. I'm always telling you.'

'Oh, stop going on,' Diana said impatiently. 'There's only a little damage. I'm fine. Nobody was hurt.'

'That car's too big for you; you can't manage it. You should get something smaller. It's far too big for a town.'

'I like it,' said Diana. 'It's comfortable and it annoys people.'

'It what?'

'It irritates people. Men especially.'

'Is that a reason for driving it?' asked Hugo, puzzled. 'A car gets you from A to B in my view; that's what it's for.'

Hugo himself drove an ancient Land Rover with bales of hay in the back for seats.

'Cars are about sex,' said Diana. 'I should have thought you'd have worked that out by now.'

'I haven't an idea what you're on about,' said Hugo, going ahead of his sister through the back door.

'Darling, you look terrible,' Diana said, going onto the offensive as they went indoors, looking at Hugo and then at the kitchen. 'Haven't you anyone to clean for you? What happened to Mrs Mac, for God's sake?'

'She's not been well. Chill on the kidneys, or something,' said Hugo. He looked around him with surprise. 'Is it that bad?'

'Can't you see? Everything's filthy! I hate to find you like this.'

'Nice of you, sis, but I'm all right really,' said Hugo, taking the frying pan off the hot ring of the Aga. 'Have a drink, why don't you? There's some whisky in the drawing-room on the tray, and water, if you want. Glasses are there too.'

The drawing-room was reached by way of a dark stone-flagged passage and was crammed with furniture that Diana remembered so well from the big house. A full-length portrait by Alan Ramsay of Macneil Forbes took up the whole of one wall. There was a grand piano and two enormous sofas upon which several of Hugo's dogs were slumbering. When she came into the room one or two of them barked half-heartedly and then gave up, seeing who it was.

Diana helped herself to a large whisky and water from the decanters on the tray and then sat down in one of Hugo's armchairs for a moment. She had a kind of chill on her as if her vision was giving slightly. It had happened once or twice lately, but the way to deal with it was to pour another drink. She soon perked up then; it stopped the horrible thoughts too if one drank enough.

Looking round the room made her immensely sad, for she remembered every object in another incarnation. The portrait of Macneil Forbes had hung in the great drawing-room at Forbes Castle next to the portrait of his wife, Lady Hester Forbes, but there was no room for Hester in here, or anywhere else in this house come to that, and she was in store all in the dark, poor thing, with nobody to admire her. Diana had asked Hugo if she could take Hester for her own flat, but he had refused. 'It's for Alec, you see; primogeniture and all that. Can't have things vanishing into the distaff side of the family.'

'Alec's fourteen,' Diana had said. 'He won't want that portrait until he's at least thirty. Why can't I give it house room until then? Saves you having to pay storage.'

But Hugo had categorically refused. It was exactly that stubbornness that had capsized him financially. The stupid arse thought he knew how to do things so he would never take advice, or change his methods.

He was going to do it his way even if it meant financial meltdown, which was what had happened in the end.

Diana put her head in her hands, suddenly overwhelmed by a sense of the uselessness of her own life and that of her brother. What a fuck-up, she thought in spite of her resolution not to have any truck with this way of thinking; what a terrible, terrible fucking mess we've made of everything. We're a completely useless pair of duds.

And now look at him, she thought, silly old Hugo; he'd lost everything: his house, his wife, contact with his son; everything, poor darling. God, but the supper he was cooking smelled vile. She drained her glass and got up to pour herself another.

In the kitchen, Hugo was dishing something up onto plates she recognised as having been their mother's favourite Spode dinner service, but the knives and forks he was using could have come from Woolworths and, knowing Hugo, probably did. He adored Woollies, particularly enjoying the feeling of getting a bargain, never mind that most of the things he came back with were plastic tat of one kind or another.

'I've got some wine,' said Hugo, scrabbling in a drawer of cutlery, 'but I can't find the corkscrew. Oh, here it is! Thank God for that. Don't know what this is like but it was on special in the Spar.'

Diana glanced at her brother and then looked away.

'We're both cot cases,' she said sadly. 'Look at us.'

'What do you mean? What's wrong with us?'

'I don't know,' said Diana, gazing at her plate with distaste. 'What the hell is this, bro?'

'Spanish omelette,' said Hugo proudly. 'I got it out of my book.'

'What book?'

'*A Thousand Best Recipes.* It's brilliant. You should try it.'

'It can't be all that brilliant,' said Diana, poking at what was on her plate with her fork, 'this is inedible.'

'I haven't had much practice yet,' said Hugo, taking a mouthful. 'Anyway, what's wrong with it?'

'You don't know, do you?'

'Don't know what, for God's sake? What the hell is the matter with you tonight, sis? Is it that Archie Maclean fellow? I don't think he's your type, you know. He's not one of us for a start.'

'That's why I like him,' said Diana. 'Because he isn't a boring old fart like you.'

'Rowena used to say things like that,' said Hugo, pouring wine into Diana's glass. 'She told me I was an emotional cripple, whatever that's supposed to mean. I did my best to support her and Alec; she had a bloody good life when we were still up at the big house. But she couldn't take the fall from grace.'

'I never understood why you married her in the first place,' said Diana. 'She wasn't one of us either.'

'She trapped me,' said Hugo plaintively, 'you know that. She got pregnant with Alec. I had to marry her then.'

'The little scrubber probably had it all planned,' said Diana. 'Saw you coming a mile off.'

'Do you think so?' Hugo seemed genuinely shocked.

'Of course she did,' said Diana, putting down her fork. 'You're so dense you didn't notice.'

'You still haven't answered the question about Archie Maclean,' said Hugo. 'Are his intentions honourable?'

'Of course they aren't.'

'He could marry you if he wanted to.'

'He doesn't want to,' said Diana.

'Why not? You're a beautiful woman.'

'I don't know!' shouted Diana. 'How the hell do I know? I'm not a fucking mind-reader.'

'OK, OK,' said Hugo, taken aback by the sheer ferocity in his sister's voice. 'I was only asking, sis, because I care about you.'

'I know you do,' said Diana, wiping her mouth with the back of her hand. 'I'm sorry. I'm not feeling my best tonight. I think I might be going down with something.'

Luke realised that he had to be exceedingly careful that his liaison with Marianne remained a secret, which was difficult in a city where you were being watched even when you didn't know it. Countless times, people had said to him, 'I saw you today but you didn't see me.' That always sent a shiver down his back. Who was he with? What was he doing?

He couldn't risk Alice finding out, but neither was he strong enough to renounce Marianne and try and live the life he had promised to lead. She was such a promising little chick he couldn't quite bring himself to give her up at this stage, just when she was shaping so nicely. She was so responsive and willing that he had become quite besotted with her. When she had asked him at the beginning how he managed not to fall in love, he couldn't tell her that love never came into it, that love was nowhere near it. He didn't want love; he wanted something else.

The situation between him and Alice was very serious. She had come back later in the evening after he had shown her the letter from Leila and forced him to sit down and discuss what he was going to do.

It had been Alice's idea to get him to agree to go and see Gerry Lamont, the family lawyer, and get Gerry to draw up a document outlining exactly what the five thousand pounds represented. Alice's theory was that a stiff letter from a solicitor would frighten Leila. Luke had been reluctant. He didn't want Gerry's forensic brain at work over the detail of what had led up to the letter but neither did he want to lose Patrick and his house and his job.

The meeting had been excruciatingly embarrassing. Gerry, bland, smooth-jowled, sharp as a blade, was too well-schooled to betray any hint of surprise or reproach.

'Tell Gerry the story,' said Alice when they were sitting in Gerry's comfortable room, with the floor-to-ceiling bookshelves, adorned with busts of Roman sages and the obligatory photographs of Gerry's own happy family. Lawyers, Luke reflected miserably, always seemed to have happy families; it probably stemmed from dealing with so many people who had made such absurd fuck-ups, people like him who really ought to know better. The trouble was he did know better; he just couldn't do it.

Luke stumbled through the shabby little tale whilst Gerry listened and made notes. At the end, he said, 'You think it's better to pay her than to take the risk of putting the matter in front of the university authorities? At this stage, it would be her word against yours. Bruises fade, you know. You're a man with a fine reputation. Blackmailers are notorious for coming back for more.'

'If it comes out,' said Luke, 'and, believe me, it will, my name will be muck. You know how things are these days. You're guilty until you're proven innocent.'

'You are guilty by your own admission,' Alice interjected, 'so it's pointless making it into a contest. We need rid of her, Gerry, by whatever means. That's why we came to see you.'

She gave Luke a look that made him tremble.

'Very well,' said Gerry, whose shrewd, observant eyes took in every detail. 'Leave it with me.'

Thus, Alice had raised the stakes and Gerry wrote a stiff letter in which he not only threatened to have Leila's visa investigated, but also invited her to his office to collect the money in the form of a banker's draft.

'Why does she need the money?' he asked Luke.

'Who knows,' Luke shrugged. 'Her family seemed

quite wealthy – they paid the rent on her apartment when she was in Edinburgh – but there must be reasons we don't know about.'

'And don't want to know about,' added Alice. 'We just want her out of our life together.'

'Quite so,' said Gerry drily, making a further note.

This was Luke's last chance to rectify his behaviour. There were to be no more girls, no more dallying; instead, a regimen of marriage guidance and sexual counselling. The trouble was, Luke agreed with Alice on every point, and yet there was this other part of him that craved the kind of sexual kicks he was softening Marianne up for. Without it, life was grey and dull, hardly worth living. All the things he valued were dross. It was like an illness, but an illness he pined for. He was an addict and this was his fix.

The apartment in Comely Bank belonged to an academic friend of Luke's at the university and was in a Victorian tenement block very similar to the one Marianne herself shared in Marchmont with Jim and Nadia, Edinburgh being a tenement city; people packed into flats and apartments, whole lives and histories separated by only the most trifling walls.

The academic and his wife had decamped to a foreign city somewhere for a few months and had not wanted to let their apartment for so short a length of time. The long, narrow corridor that led to the kitchen at the end was lined floor-to-ceiling with books – that was all right – but the bedroom with its walls the colour of lightly cooked liver distressed Marianne.

The one beautiful object in the room was a picture: a reproduction of Vermeer's *Lady Seated at a Virginal*, a beautiful domestic interior with an otherworldly atmosphere. Marianne stared and stared at this picture so hard that she came to know every detail. The window that looked out into a dank well had shoulder length curtains in a William Morris print that Marianne could see imprinted on the inside of her eyelids and that she grew to hate. The furniture was a generic type of blonde Scandawegian pine in boxy utilitarian shapes of such astonishing ugliness that Marianne couldn't understand how a classicist, for one of the couple was clearly that (she could tell from the books), could live in such unclassically hideous surroundings. Luke agreed but said that it needn't bother them. It was available to them and that was all that mattered.

The first time in that room had been in the evening and Marianne had not really noticed her surroundings. They were in the bedroom and Luke, seeing her hesitate, had started to undress her, slowly undoing the buttons of her shirt and then with practised ease slipping his hand round her back and undoing her bra without fumbling; then he had eased her skirt over her hips and taken her knickers off, making her step out of them so that she was naked whilst he was still fully clothed. He then carried her to the bed.

After that he had begun to kiss her body all over very slowly and romantically so that by the time he had swiftly taken his own clothes off she was more than ready for him. Undressed, his body was more muscled than she had thought it would be for such a big, cuddly man. He had quite a tummy on him but she liked it for some reason. He wasn't fat but he was large and strong, and he made her feel quite tiny and feminine and exquisite. His little doll, he called her.

And when they made love on the Scandawegian bed that was so badly constructed that Marianne felt it might collapse at any moment, it had been beautiful and romantic.

Those romantic, passionate liaisons continued for some time. They would meet and make love and talk. Sometimes, Luke brought wine and delicious things to eat: pâté, smoked salmon, and once a tiny pot of caviar. For Marianne, it was a kind of picnic love affair, a game, her own secret. She wasn't in love with him – he made no secret of his marriage and his child – but she trusted him in some strange way as her mentor, her guru. Luke appeared to possess a kind of wisdom that she craved. When she talked about her life and her ambitions, particularly her desire to write, he seemed to understand. He encouraged her and strengthened her; he was almost a father figure, her sugar daddy, with whom she had sex. It all seemed so cosy, so secure, a place where she could discover herself safely. He was a wonderful lover, patient, tender, who taught her about her own body, gradually allowing herself to discover her potential and to get over Ben whose image had grown fainter with time and the attentions of Luke.

One evening towards the end of May, she agreed to meet him as usual at Comely Bank. She had her own key by this time (the affair had been going on for some months by now) and let herself in. Luke was already there, sitting on the sofa in the living room drinking a glass of white wine. He had poured one for her too and handed it to her when he had kissed her hello.

For some reason, he seemed different this evening; less relaxed, almost distant, not his normal, friendly, jolly self.

'I bought you a present,' he said, holding up a carrier bag.

'What is it?'

'Look and see.'

Marianne took the bag from him and looked into it. She took out a black lace suspender belt and a packet of fine nylons of the kind that ladder as soon as you look at them. There was a black lace bra at the bottom with holes where her nipples would be.

She looked at him. He was tense with the effort of trying to conceal his eagerness.

'You want me to put these on?' she asked him lightly.

'Will you?'

'Why not? If you want me to.'

She was surprised but she couldn't see any harm in it if that's what he wanted.

In the bedroom, he had closed the curtains and put lighted candles on the chest of drawers.

'Everything is different this evening,' she said, turning to him.

'I want to play a game with you if you'll let me,'

he said. 'I want you to go out and come in wearing the bra and the suspender belt and your heels. Will you do that?'

'Then what?' she asked lightly. It still didn't occur to her that this was something that meant a lot to him. To her it was just a rather silly little erotic game, but whatever turned you on, baby.

Luke took off his own clothes while she was out of the room and put them tidily on the chair by the chest. He looked at his face in the mirror and saw the desire mingled with fear. As a boy he used to take all his clothes off and try on his mother's shoes, mincing about in front of the long mirror in his parents' bedroom naked but for the shoes (fawn-coloured stilettos). Looking at his reflection he was reminded of himself as he was, naked but scared, aroused by his own fear. Once Sandy had found him doing this and belted him on the buttocks with his domine's belt that he had held onto from his period as a schoolmaster in a school in the Borders. A terrible row had followed about 'no son of mine does things like that' and 'you'll grow up a Nancy boy like your cousin Duncan and if I catch you doing it again, I'll fucking kill you'. The Gorbals method had endured behind the façade of the well-to-do intellectual, the left-leaning liberal, the Colossus of Scottish letters and pillar of Edinburgh society.

When Marianne knocked and came in, he was ready for her.

'There's one more thing,' he said gently, admiring her.
'What's that?'

She wiggled her hips to make him laugh but when he didn't, she suddenly realised that he was deadly earnest, that this was more than a titillating little game. His eyes were almost glazed. For the first time she felt a little frightened of him.

'I want to blindfold you.'

'Why?' He was holding her arm but when she tried to take it away he resisted.

'It's all right,' he said, gentling her, 'it's OK. It's just a little game.'

She had allowed him to do what he wanted, submitting to the blindfold and then allowing him to lay her down on the bed on her tummy. He had tied her legs together with something that wasn't rope but which she couldn't wriggle out of and then he had started to beat her with what felt like a wooden paddle, gently at first and then harder until she cried out to him to stop, that she was frightened.

He had stopped at once and untied her legs and taken off the blindfold. Now, he was no longer the stranger but the sugar daddy, tender, conciliatory and amazingly passionate. They were back to normal, the violent little interlude was over, but in spite of his subsequent tenderness she felt betrayed by him. She allowed him to make love to her, but afterwards she cried and asked him why he needed to do those things. Because he was back in his tender, cuddly bear persona he seemed confused and uncertain as to the answer to her question.

'I adore you,' he had said, stroking her hair. 'You're the only woman who's all there for me sexually.'

'Alice won't do those things?'

'No.'

'Why not?'

'Because she considers them demeaning. Alice is a feminist.'

'So am I,' said Marianne.

'But you're also a woman who likes to please a man, no?'

This was also true but it didn't necessarily preclude the first condition.

At the same time – and she didn't want to admit this at first – it excited her. She wanted more. She wanted to see how far he would go.

Increasingly, she found herself thinking about the things they did in that ugly room in Comely Bank, going over them in her mind and brooding about them. It was their secret, something they shared and that separated her from the other people in her life, although she had mentioned it to Nadia, her flatmate, whom she had known for several years and trusted.

The previous Sunday morning they had been sitting in Nadia's bed under her duvet drinking coffee and eating croissants together in the chaotic tenement apartment they shared with Jim in Marchmont.

'You're in an abusive relationship,' said Nadia predictably, when she had heard what Marianne had to say. 'You need to ask yourself why and why it started when it did. Did that father of yours abuse you when you were a child?'

Nadia had met Archie once or twice; the second time he had come on strong to her. Marianne's mother had been dying by then; Nadia thought Archie's behaviour stank and told him so.

'No, never.'

'There're plenty of different kinds of abuse, mind you. And Archie is into power. Maybe this man's got something you recognise. Why are you attracted to someone who does that to you?'

'I didn't know what his bag was when I met him. I found him incredibly attractive; that seemed enough at the time.'

'But why continue now that you do know?'

'I'm not sure. I suppose that's why I'm talking to you. I'm not in love with him; I think I'm addicted to him.'

'How can you want to be with someone who hurts you? You need to ask yourself why him and why now? Your life has changed a lot over the last two years. Your Mum is dead, your Dad is playing the field himself – as he always has done, mind you – your elder sister is involved with her own family, Ben rejected you. All of which leaves you a bit rootless and vulnerable, my dear. I've thought you'd lost a bit of your sparkle, my glittering friend. You were always such a crazy kid when we were at St Andrew's. I hardly recognise the girl who lit up the room by the sheer force of her presence. You're so lovely, kid,' she said, putting her arms round Marianne. 'Don't forget that. Don't let this man take you over. You haven't even told me his name.'

'Luke Macarthur.'

'The academic?'

'Do you know him?'

'I know of him,' said Nadia, frowning, and pushing her fine fair hair out of her eyes. 'Bit of a risky ploy for an academic, isn't it? I mean that kind of thing could get a guy into trouble, particularly if he's picking on his students too.'

'I'm not his student.'

'I know you're not. But you may not be the only one. Guys in these kinds of relationships often have a number of sexual partners. You should probably get some help. Do you want me to organise it? I can if you want.'

'Can I think about it?'

'Don't leave it too long. It's like cancer; the longer you leave it, the worse it gets.'

The following Monday, Luke was sitting in his office at the university, checking the proofs of his new book biked over that morning from the publisher, when the telephone rang.

'Luke Macarthur,' he said in an irritated voice. The script was full of ludicrous errors; that dimwit sub must have run it through the spell check, fatal to any manuscript, let alone one as full of strange place-names as his.

'Oh, hello,' said a nasal Antipodean voice. 'Is that Professor Macarthur.'

'Speaking,' said Luke. 'What can I do for you?'

Some idiot who needed the admissions tutor put through to him by mistake.

His eye fell on Archie's cow painting, which was strategically placed on the wall opposite his desk.

'My name's Dan Mantle; I'm a freelance journalist. A national daily newspaper has retained me to write a piece about your uncle, Sir Jack Macarthur, and about the family in general.'

'Why?' asked Luke, scratching his nose with his pencil. 'Because he's about to snuff it?'

'Your expression, not mine,' said Mantle. 'But yes, if you want to put it that way.'

Luke thought about what his father Sandy had said, 'Difficult as his dying has been, his death will be worse.'

'Why do you say that? We're all prepared for it, aren't we?'

'We may think we are,' was Sandy's response, 'but we're not. People think of death as an end, which it is for the dying, of course – but for the rest of us it's a corner to be turned, more of a hairpin bend, and we don't know what to expect. We may all of us plunge off the end.'

'Why are you ringing me?' asked Luke.

'Because, to be quite frank, I haven't succeeded in getting much information out of the rest of your family.'

'That's because there's nothing to tell,' said Luke. 'My uncle has led an exemplary life.'

'Nobody has led an exemplary life, other than Jesus Christ, if I may beg to differ,' said Mantle, 'and your uncle Jack is no exception.'

'Why's he of any interest to you?' Luke asked,

wondering how to get rid of this reptile as quickly as possible.

'Oh, come on,' said Mantle, 'it's obvious. It's a great story: rags to riches, child of an immigrant made good, famous playwright for a brother, instrumental in saving Edinburgh's world heritage in the shape of the New Town, and countless other buildings all over Scotland, and then of course there's the colourful private life. That's where you come in, I guess.'

'What do you mean "that's where I come in"?'

'Well, I hear there are certain irregularities in your own life.'

'What the hell are you talking about?'

'A certain Miss Marianne Maclean, for instance?'

'What?'

'We've got pictures of you coming out of an apartment in Comely Bank with her.'

'Pictures!' Luke simply couldn't take this in. 'How?'

'Look, there's always someone who'll talk, someone who'll tell you who to watch.'

Someone, but who?

'Look, you can't print those pictures. My wife will leave me. I'll lose everything.'

'Should have thought of that before, mate. Got an awful lot at stake it seems to me, but I tell you what; I'll swop you. You tell me what I need to know and I'll send you the nice pics of you and Miss Marianne. How's that?'

'I need to think about it,' said Luke. This was the first of the hairpin bends Sandy had predicted.

'Tell you what; I'll call you back in half an hour. That gives you time to review your options.'

Luke put the phone down and put his head in his hands. He groaned aloud. He had betrayed his wife on many occasions (the 'open' marriage had worked entirely in Luke's favour, and in fact had been his idea; Alice had acquiesced because she had thought it a prudent way of hanging on to her marriage in earlier times, but Luke had pushed his luck too far, ending with the Leila incident) but he had never betrayed the family as a whole; if asked, he would have said he drew all his strength from his family and now he was about to shop them to save his marriage.

His uncle, who had been kindness itself to him, Justine, who had never done him any harm, his aunt Jean, whom he was exceedingly fond of, Duncan, Ben, Elly . . . the litany was endless, and all because his 'perverted' desires (to him the sex was normal, exciting; he couldn't see the problem. The 'problem' was what other people thought about it, like so much in life) drove him on and on recklessly towards the brink of disaster.

For a moment, he was tempted to say to the Australian reptile, 'Publish and be damned,' and trust that Alice wouldn't follow through. But he knew she would. The thought of losing Patrick stopped him from going down that path.

When Mantle called back, Luke told him what he needed to know about the Old Man as the dying Caesar, the exposé of the Caesar's private life with particular reference to Mrs Justine Mackenzie and their child, Eleanor Mackenzie, now a schoolgirl at an exclusive Scottish girls' public school in St Andrews. Photographers would stake out Justine's apartment and Elly's life at St Leonard's. They would go down to Ardgay. Duncan would be shadowed. He went out into the inferno of Edinburgh's gay scene on the weekend, Luke told Mantle.

'Where are the best gay clubs?' asked Mantle.

'For God's sake get a guide book,' said Luke contemptuously, 'it's all in there; don't ask me.'

'Not your scene?' enquired Mantle. 'There must be S&M joints in a town as diverse as this, surely?'

'What?' exclaimed Luke. 'What are you talking about? Who told you that?'

He had to hide his feeling of panic, the feeling that he had just supped with the devil, the sensation that everything was slipping out of his grasp.

'Oh well, then,' the Australian reptile was saying, 'don't worry about it, mate. Not my scene either. There're a lot of perverts out there, man; what's one more or less?'

'I think you may need to call the priest, m'lady,' said Mrs Guthrie, the bottle-blonde, plump night nurse who, like Jack, had been born in the Gorbals, Glasgow's notorious slum, following Jean out of the room. Mrs Guthrie was nosy and garrulous and wore desert tan coloured stockings, a white overall and white shoes with crêpe soles that squeaked, but Jack liked her because he had been born and raised amongst women of her type who were both motherly and brutal at the same time.

'I think he'd like it now while he's still in the land of the living,' said Mrs Guthrie, folding her fat arms and planting her feet apart like a bouncer in a nightclub, Jean thought; hardly appropriate body language considering the subject under discussion.

'I'll go and ring Father O'Connor now,' Jean replied politely, 'thank you, Mrs Guthrie,' and would have liked to have added as her mother would have done without a backward glance, 'That will be all,' but didn't have the nerve. Life was so tiresomely democratic these days, even when one was paying through the nose for the privilege of help. Mrs Guthrie was a bit of a bully in her way and Jean's good manners were so ingrained that she found it difficult to say what she meant, which in this case would have been, 'I think that's my business and my husband's, thank you.' She wished Duncan were here; he wouldn't have allowed Mrs Guthrie to look at her like that. She was such a great big blonde pudding of a woman with her fat, pink forearms and her determined calves. Very Beryl Cook, as Duncan had commented dryly when he had first seen her.

Jean went into her bedroom and locked the door behind her to keep Mrs Guthrie out. Once or twice she had followed Jean into the room she regarded as her sanctuary and made comments about the furnishings as if she were some sort of bailiff with a pencil behind her ear. 'Lovely settee; that must have cost a bit. Those curtains would keep even an Edinburgh wind out.'

If death was a play, Jean thought, then it brought with it an astonishing cast of grotesques of whom Mrs Guthrie was one. The priest whom she was about to telephone, Father O'Connor, was another. She very much hoped she would get his deputy, the nice, young and rather handsome Father Sean, who talked about 'the internal forum', and thought that love was more important than rules although he was clever enough to appear to play by the book, as one had to do with the Roman Catholic Church. Love was more important than rules and as she had discovered there were many ways of loving, some of which would astonish the people who thought they knew her, the Pollys and the Margarets; even her children.

She picked up the telephone by her bed and dialled a number. She had no truck with these memory buttons that deprived the mind of its need to limber up; memory was like a muscle and needed exercise.

The housekeeper in the presbytery answered the telephone but when Jean asked for Father Sean she was told that he was at a Guild of Mary meeting but she would fetch Father O'Connor, seeing as it was you, Lady Macarthur. Jean could hear her footsteps as she tip-tapped across the parquet floor of the hall; in her mind's eye she could see the crucifix in its niche and smell the odour of sanctity: a combination of cigarette smoke, overcooked vegetables and Mansion House furniture polish.

She had raised her children as Catholics but she had not converted to Rome when she married Jack. She had a residual distrust not so much of the Papacy itself but of the Irish who for centuries had been Rome's representatives in Britain. The Irish were dirty, treacherous vermin who had murdered her great uncle Desmond, the lepidopterist, in his bed at Carolstown during the Troubles by the simple expedient of burning his house down at night when he was asleep.

'Lady Macarthur, Father O'Connor speaking. What can I do for you?'

'I'd like you to come and see my husband while he's still conscious.' She had to stop herself from using Mrs Guthrie's phrase, 'still in the land of the living.' She did not want to speak to the priest in Mrs Guthrie's voice or to use her expressions; it was like wearing someone else's clothes.

'I'll come now,' he said.

'Thank you,' Jean answered. She couldn't bring herself, even after all these years, to call him 'Father'. 'The sooner the better, I think.'

'I'll be with you right away,' said Father O'Connor, who had been half-way through watching *The Bill*. As soon as he had sat down he had known he should have videoed it. It was tempting Fate not to, like going out without an umbrella.

The photographer who had stationed himself opposite number sixteen Ainslie Place so that he could be in the middle of the three family houses should anything happen, was stirred from his apathy at about 8 o'clock on this Friday night by the front door of number sixteen opening. Consulting his notes, he logged the fact that this was the house that belonged to the heir apparent; the poofter. A barefoot man (the partner?) wearing a striped apron over a pair of jeans and a tee shirt stood framed in the doorway under the fanlight for a moment looking up and down the street as if waiting for someone. He was either suspicious or anxious or both. The photographer took his picture anyway.

Ten minutes later, a car drew up outside HQ at number twelve. A Roman candle got out holding a black bag like some sort of bloody doctor, thought the photographer, taking his picture too for good measure, just as the door was opened by Lady M herself, a tall, angular old bat, the sort that looked straight through you at parties as if you were made of glass. He took another shot but she didn't appear to notice, although you could never tell with her sort.

'Come in, Father O'Connor,' said Jean Macarthur, holding the door wide. The priest was wearing a clerical suit with a Roman collar and policeman's shoes. She had often thought the shoes must be special Vatican issue; all priests wore them, even the nice young ones, but you never saw them in shops.

'He'd like to see you now,' she said, when the door was closed again. 'Shall we go straight up?'

'Yes, indeed,' said Father O'Connor, looking round him, taking in the bust of Augustus wearing a straw hat that looked as if it belonged to Lady Macarthur. She was a strange woman, he had always found; he would not have said that he knew her. In fact he would have said that she made a point of not allowing him to. She kept him at a distance; very polite, very formal and yet somewhere he sensed her distaste for what he peddled; her word not his. She was too polite, too well trained to denigrate his calling other than secretly in her heart. Nevertheless, he could almost hear her saying 'mumbo jumbo'. Father Sean on the other hand said he found her amusing, almost playful, but Father Sean had charm; women liked him as they did not like Father O'Connor. In the old days a priest had not needed charm because he had authority. Now God's word had to be made palatable for this generation of vipers, the ones who thought – as they all thought – that you could cut corners with God.

Mrs Guthrie was sitting on a chair next to the bed.

'Thank you, Mrs Guthrie; you may leave us now,' said Jean in her grandest manner, paying homage to the shade of her long-dead mother. 'Take Mrs Guthrie's chair, if you would like, Father O'Connor. I'll go round the other side.'

The priest did as he was told, opening his box of tricks to find his stole and his other instruments of absolution.

'Jack,' she said, bending over her husband, 'the priest is here.'

Jack opened his eyes. Jean could hear him trying to find his breath. She visualised it lying coiled in him somewhere like a wisp of coloured silk forgotten in a corridor.

'Mrs Mackenzie,' he managed to say eventually in a whisper. 'The child. I feel guilty about the child.'

'What is he saying?' asked Father O'Connor, looking at Jean for corroboration.

'He has a mistress, a Miss Mackenzie. She has a child. He feels guilty about the child. He wants you to forgive him.'

Father O'Connor, who considered himself experienced, was astonished.

'And you know about this?'

'Evidently,' said Jean. She was tempted to say, 'I found her for him,' just to shock him, but didn't. The poor little man had no conception of what he was dealing with. She felt quite sorry for him.

'He wants absolution, Father.'

There, she had said it, and instantly felt that it diminished her. There was something wheedling about it, something dishonest.

'But is he sorry? I can't absolve a man who isn't sorry for his sins. He must earnestly seek pardon for the great wrong he has done to you and your family, let alone his . . . this other . . . arrangement.'

Jean looked at the priest. She was tempted to say, as Mrs Guthrie would have done, 'Can't you see he's on his last legs?'

'He is sorry,' she said, glancing at Jack and then looking back at the priest again. 'It's about love. Can't you see that? Love and tolerance.' I had to find it in my heart, she thought, so why can't you, man of God?

A way of not tearing everything down, a *modus vivendi*.

'I beg your pardon, Lady Macarthur,' said Father

135

O'Connor, 'but I cannot absolve your husband of his sins or administer the last rites under these conditions.'

He was taking off his stole as he spoke. It was clearly hopeless to argue with him. Somewhere in her heart she had always known it would turn out like this if she got Father O'Connor. He was God's prosecutor with his spade-shaped face, his burning eyes, and his lack of love.

'We all make a mess of our lives in one way or another,' she said quietly. 'Can't you give him a blessing?'

'I'm afraid not. Not under these circumstances.'

'On your own conscience be it,' said Jean. 'I'll show you out, Father O'Connor.'

He knew as soon as he had put his key in the front door that Duncan had not returned because both the bottom and the top locks were still locked. Instantly, Charles felt the desolation of the empty house; of course there was Theo in the kitchen, but even Theo's nose along the edge of the door, normally something that made them both laugh when they came back from a night out somewhere, was not salve enough for this evening's wounding absence.

People who knew Charles quite well would have said he was an easy-going man, tolerant, good-humoured and affectionate; those who knew him better knew that he was all of those things but that he was also an intensely principled man, almost rigidly so. Duncan's disappearance on a night such as this began to seem to him not so much a needy man behaving according to instinct but the behaviour of a man who ought to have exercised some self-control. Tonight of all nights it seemed to Charles absolutely vital that Duncan should be available, but no. Duncan had decided otherwise; and Duncan was always right. He was incredibly like the Old Man in that respect. It was fantastic if you happened to agree with him; tough shit if you didn't. In fact, Charles thought to himself, as he took Theo out round the railings, Duncan wasn't always right and what was more, Duncan was a bully, just like his father before him.

They had lived together for twelve years; the passion of their early relationship had declined and now they were a solid married couple with a dog and a house and holidays in Tuscany with other similar couples.

Duncan and Charles; never Charles and Duncan, were a fixture, like the railings or the lampposts or one of those fucking Adam fanlights. Well, thought Charles, pulling firmly on the lead, that might be about to change.

As Theo (as headstrong in certain respects as Duncan) continued to linger lovingly over one of the back wheels of Duncan's Porsche, the flash from a camera went off again. Charles swore and went in the direction of the light, dragging Theo behind him. Theo, interrupted during a very important task, responded by employing the blocking tactic of stiffening his paws so that the photographer saw a man striding towards him trailing what could have been a sledge or a sack behind him but which turned out to be a rather large liver-and-white spaniel with its collar practically over its ears.

'Stop taking pictures,' said Charles, leaning down towards the car window, 'or I'll smash that fucking thing.'

'All right, all right, keep your hair on,' said the photographer. 'Don't want to upset you, mate. Nice dog.'

'Yes, isn't he,' said Charles, forgetting instantly that he was supposed to be angry. 'Very stubborn though.'

'I saw you dragging him along like that and I thought it was a sack or something.'

'He doesn't like being interrupted when he's having a pee, poor boy,' said Charles, bending down to stroke Theo's curly head. 'Sorry, Theo.'

'Here, give him a crisp,' said the photographer. 'That'll make him feel better. Dogs love salt and vinegar.'

'He's not supposed to eat things like that,' said Charles. 'He's such a greedy pig that the vet's put him on something called the Science Diet.'

'Science method of making money, if you ask me,' said the photographer. 'Want a dog to get thinner then give it less to eat, just like us, mate.' He paused to give Theo another crisp. 'I couldn't take a leak and a freshen-up in your place, could I? I've been here for hours.'

'Yes, OK,' said Charles. 'I'm just over there. Number sixteen.'

'Nice place,' said the photographer, as Charles unlocked the front door and let him in. 'How much would this set you back these days?'

'A few hundred grand,' said Charles, knowing perfectly well it would be more like a million. The Old Man, who knew a thing or two about property, had bought these houses in Ainslie Place for about fifty grand a piece in the early seventies when nobody had wanted them and the whole place was falling to bits. Duncan had been given this house as a twenty-first birthday present but with no money to do it up with. That was the task the Old Man had set him. Some task.

'Who are you taking all these pictures for?' he asked, when the photographer came back from the lavatory.

'It's an agency job,' said the photographer. 'Don't know who's ordered them, but there's quite a lot of tabloid interest in your family. They commission the pics and then flog them wherever they can. A lot of the broadsheets buy in too and just pretend they're reporting a story run by a downmarket paper. In fact the interest is across the board.'

'Not my family,' said Charles. 'My partner's family.'

'Where is he then, your other half?'

'Good question,' said Charles, remembering his anger. 'But you could try this place.' He gave him the name of a certain club. 'You could probably get a good picture there if you're patient.'

'Can't be too patient. I'll have to get them down the wire soon.'

Duncan would never know and it would serve him bloody well right.

'OK, my friend,' said the photographer. 'Thanks a bunch. Good luck with the dog.'

Charles had known it was a futile exercise to open the front door and look up and down the street for Duncan's familiar shape, but he couldn't stop himself doing it after he had spoken to the photographer. It was a nervous tic, part of a package of displacement activities that he engaged in when Duncan did one of his disappearing acts. As he usually chose a Friday night, Charles knew that he should have been prepared; like the approach of a trough of low pressure, he could feel the climate change before it happened: Duncan's anxiety about his father coupled with his desire for sexual variety meant that tonight was as likely a choice as any for it to happen. Charles's masochistic reaction had been to shop for the ingredients for a delicious dinner (spending a fortune in Valvona & Crolla) and then to cook it, having been unable to get hold of Duncan on his mobile.

As he went back into the house and closed the door, it occurred to Charles that he should walk up the street and ask Jean if she would like to join him for dinner. It was all ready, she had a nurse *in situ* for the Old Man and he would like the company. It might stop him going mad.

When she opened the door to him, she put her face on his shoulder for an instant, a gesture of surrender and a confession of pain that he instantly recognised for what it was. She felt as thin as a paper fan.

'How is he?' asked Charles, taking Jean's arm and steering her by the elbow to the hall chair.

'Slipping away, but still taking his time over it: I think it'll be another day or two,' said Jean, raising her face to Charles. 'I've just had the priest in. He refused Jack absolution. I wanted it while Jack was still just about *compos*.'

'I didn't think you could refuse,' said Charles, pulling up a chair for himself.

'Well, he did. It was my fault really. I shouldn't have let on that I knew about Justine. That tore it with Father O'Connor. It was all too much of a can of worms for him.'

'I didn't know that you did know,' said Charles, trying to conceal his astonishment. 'Duncan doesn't either.'

Or does he? wondered Charles. Has he always known but decided not to know? It takes a death, he thought, for us to know one another, peeling away the evasions and pretences, but possibly only to reveal more beneath. The Old Man's passing would radically alter the *status quo*; the prospect made Charles feel faintly seasick.

'I wanted it to be that way,' said Jean. 'It suited me. If I'd made a fuss, it would have got out somehow; these things always do. It was bearable because it was a family secret. I would never let on to an outsider that I knew. My idea, my one big idea, was to preserve the *status quo*.' She paused for a moment as if considering her achievement.

'Where is Duncan by the way?'

Charles raised his eyebrows but said nothing.

'I see,' said Jean, leaning forwards in her chair to take his hand. 'Poor Charles. That must be hard.'

'You should know.'

'She was a good bet,' said Jean. 'At least I knew where he was. You don't have that comfort. I taught myself to bear it. You can imagine how painful it was in the beginning, however. And she wasn't the first, either.'

'Did you mind?'

'Of course. You always mind if you love someone. You must mind too?'

'Yes.'

'Aren't you tempted to do the same?'

He shook his head. 'It's not my scene. I was always one for love. Terribly dull, really. When I met Duncan I knew I'd met the love of my life. That was it. What about you? How did you cope?'

He could never have discussed these matters with his own mother, a doctor's widow who lived in Bruntisfield, who even now coped by pretending that one day, sometime, Charles would meet the girl of his dreams.

'By pretending I didn't know anything about it. If you play a part for long enough you come to believe in it. If I hadn't done that I would have lost him and that I could not have borne. Duncan and my husband are very alike: they are intensely loyal people with a very strong sex drive. I couldn't cope with him. He needed somebody younger and stronger than I. I was proud of myself because I managed to be able to go on loving him. She's really a very nice woman, Miss Mackenzie. I couldn't bring myself to hate her; in the end I was grateful.'

'You're amazing,' said Charles. 'I don't know how you do it.'

'In the end it's about love, I suppose,' said Jean, sipping her wine. Darling Charles really was the daughter she had never had. She could talk to him as she never could to her sons or even her husband. 'Love has to be stronger than hatred. You have to work at it. It's not just warm, happy feelings; it's damn hard work. I mean look at Jesus and what love did to him. It left him dying in agony, but he was still able to love. That's what poor Father O'Connor couldn't understand.'

'I feel rather sorry for Father O'Connor,' said Charles. 'He was obviously completely out of his depth. Pity you didn't get the other one, Father Sean. Duncan goes to him and he lets him off the hook on a regular basis.'

'What else can he do? I always understood that Catholicism was about being a sinner. It's Calvinism that insists you become purer and purer and all that means is that the sin is compartmentalised. You don't have to look at it but it's there. I must go back upstairs,' she said.

She met Mrs Guthrie on the landing. 'He's going,' she said. 'I think you'd better call your family.'

Ben arrived to find that Charles had beaten him to it which displeased him greatly. He'd been considering going down to Barhill and then on to Castle Forbes, leaving on this Friday night, but had felt too tired to face the traffic and so had put off his journey, thank God. He was dozing on his sofa when the phone rang and came at once, pausing only to lock Lolly in the kitchen.

His mother was seated on one side of the bed watching the Old Man. Charles hovered behind Jean and was massaging her shoulders. This picture of togetherness gave Ben a shock. What business did Charles have being so intimate with his mother at such a time? And where the bloody hell was Duncan when he was needed?

He kissed his mother and nodded coolly at Charles, unable to keep his anger from showing.

'Where's Duncan?'

'I don't know,' said Charles, glancing at Jean, who in turn looked at Ben and shook her head slightly.

'Sandy and Hannah are coming,' she said, 'and Luke and Alice. I told them to put Patrick in one of the spare beds. Sukey's away at the moment on an assignment.'

'What about Father Sean? Shouldn't there be a priest here, for God's sake?'

When Jean told him what had happened, Ben was furious. 'Why didn't you call me then? I would have given Father O'Connor what for. When I think of all Father's done for that church, it's outrageous.'

'I know it is,' said Jean. 'I'm sorry, darling. I should have called you. It was the bit about Justine Father O'Connor couldn't take.'

'What bit?' asked Ben, flabbergasted.

'Later,' said Jean, making a movement with her head, indicating *'pas devant les domestiques'*.

Mrs Guthrie was doing something with the medicines, which were kept on top of the Old Man's chest of drawers and had her broad, fleshy back to the room like a priest in the old rite. She had very pronounced calves, Ben noticed, like an athlete's, that seemed to speak a reproach to the room and this unorthodox gathering, as if to say, 'This is not the kind of thing I am used to.' Before the Old Man, Mrs Guthrie had nursed some dying grandee in the north of Scotland and she had let it be known that it was a house in which everything was 'properly' done, unlike this one in which nothing was quite what it seemed.

The Old Man appeared to have almost given up breathing altogether but every now and again a bubble of breath would break over his face in a kind of ripple. Ben went to the foot of the bed and gazed upon the effigy of his father. He was angry and upset and knew he should calm himself and that he would regret it if he remembered this scene through the prism of his anger and, it had to be said, his great fear.

He wanted to feel the right sorrowful kind of emotions, but found that all he could think of was that it was time the Old Man just got on with it and left them in peace; and he didn't feel guilty about this.

His relationship with his father, often difficult in the past, had mellowed latterly, particularly after his marriage had broken up, when the Old Man had been supportive and solicitous. He had seemed to understand and sympathise in a way that Duncan, although very much on Ben's side, had not. But in these last days the relationship between the dying man and his son had deepened further and unexpectedly. Somehow Ben had the feeling that he, without meaning to, 'measured up', in the Old Man's view; how this had been communicated he couldn't quite say, but it was something he was conscious of and that gave him strength. The Old Man had finished his task and was ready to leave.

Suddenly, however, everything seemed to happen at once. His mother was kicking off her shoes and climbing on to the bed to take the dying man in her arms, her tartan skirt rucking up over her knees revealing her excellent, slender legs. She put her arm under his shoulders and pressed her cheek to his. Mrs Guthrie turned round quickly and knocked over several bottles, just as Bella, who had been biding her time, jumped on to the bed having been skulking underneath it.

The Old Man coughed and then vomited a little; he took a final, shuddering breath and then was gone. For a moment there was silence and everyone froze, then it was as if the reel moved on again. Bella, sensing the tension, suddenly barked; a sharp, slightly hysterical woof. Ben tried to get her off the bed but Jean said, 'Leave her. Your father would have liked it. You know what he was about that dog.'

'Would you like me to clean him up a little, my lady?' asked Mrs Guthrie, who had moved to the bedside, looking down at the dead man appraisingly as if she were measuring him for his coffin.

'No, thank you, Mrs Guthrie,' said Jean firmly, sliding her arm out from under her husband's head, and laying him gently on the pillow. 'What I would like is that we each spend some time with him on our own.'

As she spoke, the door knocker thundered.

'I'll go,' said Charles, sensitive to the fact that he needed to play the servant's role in order to appease Ben. At the same time, it occurred to him that anger and its corollary of authority rather became Ben.

When he had gone, Ben said, 'I can't believe Duncan's not here. Where on earth is he?'

'Out somewhere,' said Jean. 'Please don't dwell on it now. I don't want your father's death sullied by it.'

'Very well,' said Ben. 'Now, Mother, I'll leave you for a few minutes with him, then I'll bring up the rest of the family.'

'Thank you, darling,' she said. 'You're my tower. Open the window, would you?'

Ben glanced at his mother and went to the window, which was already open a little, and pushed it up to its full extent. Luckily, it was a still evening for once.

Downstairs, Sandy and Hannah and Luke and Alice, plus Patrick, had all arrived at once and were standing in the hall with Charles. When Ben came down the stairs they all looked up at him, as if waiting for some authoritative statement. He was aware afterwards that it had been one of his life's defining moments. In the absence of Duncan, he was the head of this part of the family.

'Mother wants to be with Father for a few minutes,' he said, greeting everybody in turn and hugging Patrick who was wearing a sweatshirt over his pyjamas and holding a very tattered-looking teddy bear.

'I'll put Patrick to bed,' said Alice, glancing down at her son's tousled hair.

'No, I'll do that,' said Luke, taking his son's hand.

Watching him, Ben had a feeling that this was a set piece, performed for the family's benefit. Good father puts small child to bed. He glanced at Alice, but her expression gave nothing away.

'Put him in Father's old dressing-room,' he said. 'The rest of you come into the dining-room and help yourselves to drinks. Then we can go up one by one.'

'Shall I get some food?' asked Charles. 'Is anyone hungry?'

'We've all eaten,' said Ben, who had got over his earlier and rather unfair fury with Charles, whom he loved, 'but thanks anyway.'

As the others filed into the dining-room, he took Charles aside.

'Is there no way we can get hold of Duncan?' he asked.

'His mobile's switched off,' said Charles. 'It always is when he's out on the razzle.'

'Why do you put up with it?' asked Ben, putting

his arm round Charles's shoulder to show that there were no hard feelings.

'Because I love him, I suppose. Your mother asked me the same thing.'

'Just wait till I get my hands on him,' said Ben fiercely. 'I'm not going to let him get away with this. He's always lecturing the rest of us about how to behave; now it's his turn.'

The Old Man's death took place on Friday night but was not officially announced until Monday by Mr Gerald Lamont of Lamont & Lamont, WS, whose office dealt with announcements to the newspapers, the death columns and all other journalistic enquiries. Request for interviews with the family were refused. The funeral would take place on Friday at St Patrick's Cathedral.

Duncan returned from wherever it was he had been at about six a.m. on Saturday morning. Charles, who had got to sleep at four, was not particularly pleased to see him.

'Where've you been?' he asked, sitting up in bed and turning on his light.

'God! Don't ask!' said Duncan, who was already tearing his clothes off. 'Didn't mean to wake you,' he added.

He was clearly far from sober.

'I've bad news for you,' said Charles, getting out of bed.

'What?' said Duncan, who was now naked. 'Can't it wait until the morning?'

149

'Oh, shit!' he said, seeing Charles's expression. 'It's Father, isn't it? He's snuffed it. That's what you're about to tell me.'

'I'm afraid so,' said Charles. 'I tried to call you but your mobile was off.'

'Oh, fuck!' exclaimed Duncan.

'I'm sorry, darling, so sorry.'

To Charles's horror he began to cry. He sat on the end of the bed and waited for Duncan to get a hold of himself. Duncan hated any show of weakness. Charles had never seen him cry before even when he was as drunk as this.

'What possessed you?' Charles began gently, looking round for his glasses. 'You knew it was going to happen any minute. It wasn't a good moment to choose for a bender.'

'I realise that,' said Duncan bitterly. 'I don't need it pointed out to me.' He sniffed and then got up and went into the bathroom to find something to blow his nose with.

'How's Mother?' he asked, when he came back out again. 'She must have been horrified that I wasn't there.'

'Well,' said Charles, unwilling to sink the knife in any further, 'Ben took charge and dealt with everything very well.'

'He couldn't organise a piss-up in a brewery,' said Duncan, 'much as I love him.'

'He acted with great dignity,' said Charles, 'and was a stalwart to your mother. The family came, Hannah and Sandy, Luke and Alice and Patrick. Patrick's staying over. Your mother said it would be nice to have a child in the house on such a night.'

'So I'm not only derelict; I'm a derelict prat to boot,' said Duncan.

'You weren't there,' said Charles shortly. 'What did you expect everyone to do? You make such a goddamn play about being head of the family and yet when you're needed you fuck off and don't leave a number.'

Duncan looked at him without speaking. 'I'll go and sleep in the spare room,' he eventually said.

On the following Tuesday morning, a tabloid national daily ran a double-page spread on the Macarthur family, following the death of the Old Man.

The headline read: 'Tycoon's Death Reveals Truth Behind Perfect Façade' and went on to list in excruciating detail the history of the Old Man's love affair with Justine, complete with blurry pictures of Elly walking along a street in St Andrew's and Justine entering the portals of the Eglinton Press.

'For years,' it said, 'Sir Jack Macarthur seemed to exemplify an immigrant's rise from rags to riches, from Glasgow boy to Edinburgh grandee. He had made enormous amounts of money speculating in property in several British cities, but chiefly in Edinburgh, and had married into one of Scotland's oldest and most aristocratic families. He had two vigorous sons and an estate in Kirkcudbrightshire, plus a handsome neo-classical town house in Edinburgh's New Town. At the same time,' the piece continued, 'he was leading a double life and had for years kept a mistress just round the corner with whom he had a child, sixteen-year-old Eleanor Mackenzie, now a boarder at one of Scotland's most exclusive academies for young ladies. His wife, Lady Jean,' the article continued, 'had NO IDEA that her sainted husband was leading such a brash double life, under her very nose.'

The piece was lavishly illustrated with photographs, not only of Elly and Justine, but also of Duncan kissing an anonymous man in the street.

Ben was at home and working at his drawing board on the new plans for Castle Forbes when the telephone rang.

It was Duncan. 'Have you seen the *Daily Mercury*?' he said, sounding positively menacing.

'No. Why should I? I read the *Guardian*; you know that.'

'Well, I suggest you go out and buy a copy. Someone has shopped us big time and I intend to find out who. I'm going to put a call through to Gerry now.'

'Is it by Dan Mantle?'

'Yes.'

'I told you he'd contacted me. You obviously don't remember.'

'You didn't tell him anything, did you?'

'What do you take me for?'

'I'm sorry,' said Duncan, suddenly and uncharacteristically humble, such a violent change Ben wasn't sure he could cope with. He preferred his Duncan in character rather than out of it in sackcloth.

'I'll go out and get a copy.'

'Do that and then come round. I'm at Mother's.'

'Mother's'. How odd it sounded. 'OK. I'll be along in twenty minutes or so.'

'Have you seen this?' said Consuelo, coming round the door of the office she shared with Marianne and brandishing a newspaper at her.

'What is it? The *Daily Filth*?'

'Yes. But there's a huge piece about the Old Man in it, giving away everything: Justine, Elly, the works. There's a picture of Duncan kissing a guy in the street.'

'My God!' said Marianne, snatching it from her. Together, they spread it out on Marianne's desk and read avidly.

'She's not in, is she?' asked Consuelo, referring to Justine.

'Not yet,' said Marianne. 'Duncan isn't either, surprise, surprise. I mean it's one thing to be in a gay couple but another to be caught snogging some Albanian in the street. It won't look too good at those Holyrood garden parties he gets so excited about.'

'The Royal Company of Archers,' said Consuelo, striking an affected pose, 'get you luvvie.'

They burst into fits of giggles.

'The Germans won't like it,' said Marianne. There was a German delegation from their new office in Bonn expected the following week, whom Duncan had been planning great things for.

'His laurel wreath has slipped badly, I'm afraid,' said Marianne. 'Poor Duncan.'

'He'll get over it,' said Consuelo. 'Duncan's a survivor. He's not built like a brick shithouse for nothing, mentally as well as physically.'

'He might, but will Justine?'

Consuelo shrugged. 'And what about Lady M? Horrible for her.'

Duncan handed the newspaper to Jean. 'I'm sorry, Mother,' he said.

Jean took it from him without comment and read.

'I knew about her,' she said. 'Did I not tell you?'

'No, Mother, you didn't,' said Duncan. 'It must have slipped your mind somehow.'

'As it slipped yours that you might be needed, my son.'

'As indeed it did, Mother.'

'I'm disappointed in you, Duncan. You could at least have covered your tracks.'

'Like Father, you mean?'

She nodded. 'I suppose that's what I do mean.' She got up – they were sitting in the back room where they gathered for bridge – and went to the window. 'Who told the journalist about this?' she asked quietly. 'I want you to find out, Duncan. I don't care how and I will sue the newspaper for defamation of character.'

'You can't if it's true, Mother.'

'Of course it's true,' said Jean, wearily. 'It's just the way it's put. It makes it all sound so sordid. I don't know how I'll hold my head up on the Victoria League committee now, or any of my other charities for that matter. They'll all be gossiping.'

'Polly, is that you?' Margaret Buchanan lowered her voice as Mary, her cleaning lady, came back into the kitchen to get the Flash, before she washed the hall floor.

'You've seen it, then?'

'I have, yes. To think of Jack perpetrating a lie on that scale. Poor Jean. What a humiliation for her.'

'And Jack such a pillar of society. I wonder if they'll withdraw his knighthood.'

'They can't if he's dead, surely?'

'They did with Jack Lyons.'

'Yes, but he'd committed a fraud. Jack Macarthur just kept a mistress.'

'Just?'

'Well, not "just",' said Margaret. 'It was a terrible thing to do. Such a betrayal of all he purported to stand for. Donald says everyone in chambers is talking about it. There's a feeling about that if Jack pulled the wool on this, then what else did he manage to conceal? Manny Jamieson is very disappointed. He always claimed that Jack was his best friend and Manny didn't know. He feels betrayed.'

'So do any number of other people. That poor child!'

'The poor, wee thing. Teenagers are so quick to feel humiliated.'

In the kitchen of his farmhouse, Hugo had opened

the *Daily Telegraph* at the scandals page and didn't notice that his sister was slopping orange juice into a glass already half full of something else. Diana had decided to stay on for a day or two to help Hugo straighten out the house. His rooms were chaotic and pained her with their disorder, particularly as he still had a number of beautiful things left from the sale that could be displayed to advantage. If he could sit in a tidy, handsome room she reckoned he might start to climb out of his depression quicker, for it was obvious to her that Hugo was chronically depressed. A pity that bitch Rowena hadn't noticed and done something for him instead of kicking him in the balls.

'Have you seen this?' he said wonderingly. The best days were when the scandals concerned someone one knew or knew of. There had been a terribly satisfactory case only recently when someone he had been at school with had tried to run his wife down with a lawn mower. The case had gone to trial and had lasted several glorious *schadenfreude*-laden days. As a sufferer from the impertinence of newspaper reporters himself – the *Daily Telegraph* had run a big spread on his own débâcle when he had sold one of Scotland's most historic houses to an Iowan industrialist – it was a just reward when something equally good came along and today it had, with knobs on.

'What?'

'Huge item about your ex-father-in-law, the Old Man. How he's been running a mistress for years and . . .'

'I don't consider that news,' said Diana scathingly. 'Men of Jack's stature always have mistresses; it's *de rigueur*.'

'Hang on though, there's more. Illegitimate child at St Leonard's – pretty little thing I must say – mistress who works at the Eglinton Press . . .'

'Everyone knows this,' said Diana, taking a swig of her gin and orange. 'It's not really news.'

'Not everyone, sis. I didn't and neither did half the world by the looks of it. What a shit Jack was.

'I say! There's a picture of you, sis,' he continued. 'Not a very good one. You look a bit dishevelled. Actually, you look a bit pissed if you don't mind my saying so.'

'Let me see,' said Diana furiously, coming round to Hugo's side of the table.

'And Duncan Macarthur too kissing a man in the street. That's disgusting!' exclaimed Hugo. 'I'd have never have sent him Pa's memoirs if I'd known he was a poofter. Thank God he turned them down, although I was terribly cross at the time.'

'Fuckers!' Diana said vehemently. 'The fuckers! How dare they lie in wait for me like that.' They must have taken that picture on Friday when she returned to get her stuff after lunch with Corinne. She never even bloody noticed. Bastard arseholes!

'Your Ben is the one who comes off best, other than poor old Lady Macarthur,' said Hugo. 'He's just throwing sticks for his dog in this photograph. Nice-looking dog, I must say. Reminds me of Jip.'

'And Jean letting the priest in,' said Diana. 'I know

that priest. He behaves as if he has a knitting needle up his arse most of the time. Not a particularly Christian character.'

'Where did you learn to speak like that?' asked Hugo, gazing at his sister. 'Mother never used a swear word in her whole life.'

'She lived on a different planet; that's why,' said Diana. 'Mother never needed to swear. She only had to lift her little finger and there was someone to do her bidding. She only had to smile. We have to shout to get heard.'

'Maybe you're right,' said Hugo sadly. 'The world has changed an awful lot; much too much for my liking.'

He looked at his sister and to her horror she saw his eyes were filled with tears.

'I don't really understand anything anymore,' he went on, reaching for the packet of cigarettes on the table. 'When I realised I'd have to sell up I thought of killing myself. I felt I'd let down generations of the family, not to mention Alec. It's so hard on him.'

'He'll be all right,' said Diana, putting her hand on Hugo's. 'He's young. This generation are different. They don't look back to the glories in the way we were brought up to. He'll never have known it and they say you can't miss what you don't know.'

'But I wanted to pass it on to him,' Hugo said. 'I wanted to pass it on to him enhanced, as a good custodian would want to. I wanted to say, "Here you are, my son." I'm pathetic, I know.' He made a grimace and dashed the back of his hand across his eyes. 'I see how people look at me and I know what they're thinking. They think, "Poor old Hugo; there he goes, hopeless old git who couldn't read a balance sheet properly; wife's left him, son hardly knows him anymore," but I can't help it; I can't adapt to this brave new world. I am what I am; I'm an anachronism. Do you know the dictionary definition of an anachronism?'

Diana shook her head. He was making her want to cry herself and she hated that. Hugo's pain made her all too aware of her own.

'It says "a person or thing out of harmony with the time"; well that's me all right. Sometimes I can't see the point of going on; most of the time in fact. I think to myself, "Why bother?" I've buggered up what I had and now there's nothing left. And I go up and look at the house when the Loebs aren't there and I see they've turned it into a hotel, with Ben's help. They're putting in a swimming pool, for God's sake; an indoor one, in the old servants' hall. Can you imagine? The soul's gone out of the place.'

'I told you,' said Diana. 'Don't go up there. You should really move away from here, bro. It's not doing you any good. And don't blame Ben; he's just doing his job. He has to do what the client wants.'

'You're right,' said Hugo. 'Can't be here; can't not be here. There is no answer to the problem. Just got to endure it, I suppose. Trouble is, sis, it's my landscape. I look out of the window in the morning and I see it waiting for me: the hill, the way the fields fall, and I think, "Oh, hello there." It soothes me.'

'You need a holiday,' said Diana. 'I'm going to try and arrange something, bro. I've got a friend who's got an apartment in Nîmes, a nice hot southern city with oodles of wine and marble pavements and good food. Let's bugger off there for a few weeks and relax. Archie's always telling me what a marvellous place it is. He's painted there a lot. The Romans liked it too, apparently.'

'Well they usually knew what they were doing,' said Hugo, looking more hopeful. 'That's a great idea, sis. Do arrange it if you can. I'm sorry I let the side down just then.'

'You didn't,' said Diana, slopping some more orange juice into her glass. 'I just don't want you getting depressed here on your own. I'm worried about you. I'm going to have to go in a minute if I want to go and see our father before I get to Carrick.'

Hugo and Diana's father, old Sir James Forbes, lived in a nursing home on the outskirts of Kirkcudbright. He was a hundred and five and the oldest resident. Born in 1895, he claimed to remember the funeral of Queen Victoria with absolute clarity; other events were also firmly ensconced, in particular the Great War in which he had fought for four years on the Western Front without so much as a scratch. Hitler he still had opinions about and Uncle Joe, but post-war memory had become increasingly selective. Mr Attlee, for instance, had vanished into a deep abyss.

'So you are going to see him?'

'As I'm passing, yes.'

'Does it make any difference, do you think? I went twice in a week for various reasons and he couldn't remember anything about the first visit. In fact he got quite shirty about it and more or less accused me of lying.'

'I don't know if it makes any difference to him,' said Diana, 'but it makes a difference to me. It reinforces my desire to be culled if I live beyond the age of ninety. He's outrageous. He's just doing it to spite us.'

'You are awful,' said Hugo admiringly. 'Do you have to go so soon, sis?'

'I have to go back today, yes, but I'll come back at the weekend if I can – how about that? I don't want you getting depressed.'

Marianne rang Luke when Consuelo had gone to see Hester about something, but his line was engaged. Then, after some deliberation, she tried Ben's mobile and got him just as he was leaving the house.

'I'm sorry about the Old Man – I'm writing to your mother,' she said, 'and very, very sorry about the piece in the newspaper. That must be hard for you and your mother; for all of you. How are you coping?'

'We're more or less under siege. Everyone's either furious or hurt.'

'How's Justine? She's not in the office. Is there anything I can do in that department?'

'Thank you, Marianne,' said Ben. 'I really appreciate that.' He sounded tired but curiously undaunted, she thought, almost as if the crisis were strengthening him rather than the other way round.

'You want me to go round?'

'I'd love you to. She's OK, but could do with some support. We've got our hands full here: I'm on my way to Mother's; Duncan's phoning lawyers. There are a whole lot of photographers hanging around outside number twenty,' he said, lowering his voice. 'Fucking vultures.'

'Don't let them know you think that,' said Marianne swiftly. 'Be gracious; then they won't have anything on you.'

Ben never used to swear. Clearly, there were changes afoot.

'No, you're right.'

'I'll go and call on Justine,' said Marianne.

'Same advice applies to you there,' said Ben. 'She tells me the place is infested with press, poor woman. Elly's hysterical. The headmistress rang me to tell me. I'm going to fetch her later today.'

'Wouldn't she be better to stay there?'

'Yes, probably. But I feel it would be kinder to have Elly here in the heart of her family. It's tough on her, all this, and she's a really sweet kid.'

'Do you want me to go?' asked Marianne. 'Nobody knows who I am.'

Thank God, she thought, wondering how Luke was coping.

'That's an incredibly kind offer,' said Ben, 'but I think I'll go because she needs to feel included and I am her brother. Andrew Murray called, by the way.'

'This won't go down well with the born agains.'

'Oddly,' said Ben, 'he was quite nice about it, about the Old Man anyway. It was the homosexual element that got him. He's so fundamentalist he's practically alight, but he was very kind. He offered mother sanctuary at Barhill. I was touched. I'm going to go down next weekend to Ardgay – I've got to get to Castle Forbes to see the Loebs and Barhill too; Andrew has a whole raft of new plans for me there – maybe I could see you. We could meet in Kirkcudbright or something? It'll be some light relief after the funeral.'

'I'd like that,' said Marianne, feeling her spirits lift. 'I'd like that very much.'

'Gerry?' said Duncan. 'I need a word with you. You've seen the paper, I suppose.'

'I have, yes,' said Gerry. 'I'm very sorry, Duncan. It's hard for you all. You have my sympathy.'

'Thanks,' said Duncan, pausing to allow Gerry's sympathy the appropriate space, 'but there's something I want you to do for me, Gerry.'

'Go on,' said Gerry.

'I want you to find out who shopped my family. And when I know who told that little rat, Mantle, what he needed to know, then I'll deal with him myself.'

'Newspapers never disclose their sources,' said Gerry.

'In theory, newspapers never disclose their sources,' said Duncan, 'but you and I know better than that, Gerry. I know you're pally with the editor of that rag and I'd appreciate a favour.'

'I'll see what I can do,' said Gerry, making a note of the conversation on a yellow legal pad, 'and I'll call you back. It may not be today.'

'However long it takes,' said Duncan. 'Thanks, Gerry. I appreciate it.'

All week, the press interest grew. There were photographers outside all three Macarthur houses in Ainslie Place, as well as the offices of the Press and in Howe Street, where Justine was attempting to lead a normal life. Each day the story sparked a fresh conflagration of interest in a different newspaper and refused to die down.

On the day of the funeral, the family arrived in a fleet of black limousines; Jean and her sons in the first with Justine and Elly bringing up the rear. A family council of war held by Jean, Duncan and Ben had agreed that Justine should be grouped with the family, a solution both dignified and kind, and to hell with what anyone else thought about it. The ushers were still going to and fro even as the service was about to begin.

The church was packed to the gunnels with Jack's friends and colleagues from the judiciary, the city council, the new Parliament itself – the first minister's deputy was there – from the worlds of publishing and finance, plus the chief officers of his favourite charities, not to mention the hosts of friends he had made during his long and colourful life; country gentry from Galloway; Glasgow cousins on his mother's side. A sense of excitement prevailed in the church as if this was a circus, not a funeral. A hum of conversation was barely concealed by the organ music.

Jean, in black, with a veil concealing her face, emerged from a limousine and walked between her sons into the church, followed by the rest of the family: Sandy and Hannah, Luke and Alice, and, bringing up the rear, Justine Mackenzie and Eleanor. Charles, who was an important part of the family group, had been in the church for several hours already, putting the finishing touches to the flowers that he had arranged two days before so that they should be open, and was waiting for them discreetly in one of the front pews. The sudden percussive clack of the cameras' lenses penetrated deeply and intrusively into the thick fug of holiness that was beginning to coalesce around the altar.

The clergy, (excluding Father O'Connor at Jean's request – she wasn't going to have a priest who had refused a dying man absolution showing off his hand movements at a society funeral) fronted by a real live cardinal complete with mitre and crosier for rescuing lost sheep, were lined up in the sanctuary in their white and purple funeral robes; the white damask-draped coffin already in its place on a bier with one wreath on it from Jean – white roses (from the garden at Ardgay) and lilies – and one from the sons containing, Marianne noted, some of Ben's stripy roses. She liked the way he had chosen such simple flowers; she saw that the petals were already beginning to drop and lie like scattered sweets round the coffin.

The organist was playing a sonata by Bach that was so moving that she didn't understand how anyone listening to it could do anything but weep. She was having trouble controlling her own tears but when she looked down the row she saw that her colleagues had somehow mastered the secret of Bach resistance. 'You've always been a weeper,' Cressida had once said crossly. 'You're just a portable fountain; it's not fair.' And it didn't have to be Bach; just the sight of the Queen Mother in a petal bath cap could bring on the tears. 'Manipulative,' Cressida said. 'You were a manipulative little girl. You ran rings round everyone. You were the apple of Mum's eye of course.'

As Ben walked slowly past he glanced down to his left where Marianne was sitting and made a very slight gesture with his hand, hardly noticeable except to her, but she was touched that he had acknowledged her at such a time.

Luke, walking with Alice and holding Patrick's hand, looked neither to right nor left. Today he was wearing a dark suit and a black tie like his cousin, but even in a suit he managed to look somehow shambolic. Patrick walked beside his father wearing his school blazer and a very tightly knotted tie, managing somehow to look like a little old man.

Marianne glanced up at Luke quickly and her heart went out to him as he passed. He looked haunted. There were black circles under his eyes and new furrows running between nose and mouth that she didn't remember seeing before. He looked like someone who had been torn to pieces and rather inexpertly reformed which puzzled Marianne. She knew that he was fond of his uncle, but not that fond. Why did he look so ravaged? They had spoken during the previous frantic week but had not considered it safe to meet, particularly as the Old Man's story grew and grew.

Behind Luke and Alice came Justine and Elly. Elly's thick fair hair lay down her back in a great flaxen plait; her colouring was mostly her mother's but she had a look of the Old Man about her in the shape of her head, and the Italian blood showed in her great dark eyes. She looked slightly afraid, having had her photograph taken outside the church where the press were lying in wait like hyenas.

'Hello Elly,' they called, 'give us a smile then, sweetheart.'

She both liked and didn't like the fact that these men with their great phallic lenses knew her name. It felt like a violation of some sort, as if she'd been fingered, but it also felt titillating, as if she were both inside and outside herself. Before her father died there had been a photographer hanging about outside school who had taken several pictures of her before she ran for cover. But it also meant that everyone knew about who her father was and what was going on in the family. The interest at school had been intense and Elly had hated the feeling there that everyone was whispering about her.

In particular the picture of Duncan kissing some foreign-looking guy in the street had torn her heart. She loved Duncan and she loved Charles and she couldn't understand what had gone wrong or what it meant. Her mother just said that was how gays were – that the poor things couldn't help themselves but be promiscuous from time to time – but Elly, who knew Charles well from working with him in the shop, not only knew that Charles was not like that but that he was easily hurt. Everyone wondered who had told the photographer where to look for Duncan, just as they were wondering who had told the journalist about her and her mother.

Rowena Forbes had taken her place among the over-excited mourners on the basis of her slender acquaintance with Jean over the bridge table, all bright lipstick, black linen and a black straw hat so large that her neighbours reluctantly had to make extra room to accommodate her. For Rowena a funeral was as good an opportunity to see and be seen as a wedding; and of course the *crème de la crème* of Edinburgh society were present. She looked round her with bright eyes counting judges and doctors and merchant bankers. Banking wasn't really what she called a profession as such but she wouldn't mind the money, ha ha. Eying Elly, Rowena thought she might do for Alec if the Old Man ran true to form and left her a fat chunk of his estate, which he was highly likely to do according to her sources. Illegitimacy no longer bore the same stigma these days and she was a nice-looking girl.

Diana had wanted to sit with the family but Ben wouldn't let her.

'Mother doesn't think it would be right,' he had said, 'now that we're divorced.'

'I suppose his tart will be there,' said Diana. 'At least I was married to you. I'm legit. I want to come. Your father loved me.'

Diana had a clever trick of harnessing a rude remark to another less rude, which allowed her to get away with it.

'You can come, of course,' said Ben, 'but you can't sit with me. Please don't argue about it.'

'OK,' said Diana in a small voice, 'I'll come with Hugo or someone. Can I send flowers or would that excite the press too much?'

'Of course you can send flowers,' said Ben, wearily.

'I've never known you so pompous. The king is dead, long live the king,' said Diana.

'What's that supposed to mean?'

'You're getting very authoritarian now the Old Man is gone,' she replied. 'I hear Duncan's marriage has collapsed. Can't say I'm terribly surprised. He's been humping anything that moved for years. I know you never believed me.'

'It's only temporary,' said Ben. 'We're hoping for a *rapprochement* when things have quietened down.'

'God, you're so grand! We, indeed!'

Just as the cardinal announced the number of the first hymn, Archie slid in beside Marianne followed by Diana Forbes, causing every single person to shift up two places in their pew. The organist stumbled over the introductory bars of the hymn – 'Dear Lord and Father of mankind, forgive our foolish ways' – as the congregation turned round to see who was causing the disturbance. People were still talking even though the service had begun.

'Sorry I'm late,' whispered Archie, who smelled strongly of Trumper's Essence of Limes and slightly less strongly of linseed oil mingled with cigar smoke. 'I meant to get here earlier, but Diana suddenly appeared and forced me to drive her. She's pissed,' he added as an afterthought. 'She was like that when she arrived.'

'Why didn't you stop her coming?'

'I'd have had to have shot her,' whispered Archie, 'and I didn't have a silver bullet handy.'

Marianne glanced at Diana who was wearing a black sleeveless dress, very large dark glasses and only one diamond and pearl earring. Diana was burrowing in her handbag for something; a receipt fluttered to the floor, followed by a Tampax.

'Is this a non-smoking church?' she asked suddenly in a very loud, upper-class voice, extracting a packet of cigarettes and lighting one before Archie could stop her.

'Yes, it is,' Archie said, deftly removing the cigarette from between Diana's fingers before grinding it out on the stone floor.

'I say,' Diana announced, still in the same loud voice, 'what did you do that for?'

'If you don't shut up, I'll fucking kill you,' said Archie calmly, picking up the cigarette and putting it in his pocket. The Tampax had rolled away out of sight.

Consuelo was shaking with laughter beside Marianne. The other people in the pew were trying not to notice what was happening. The cardinal, however, used to congregations in Italy who talked on their mobile phones and walked round the church during services, scarcely appeared to notice the commotion.

Ben, sandwiched in the front pew between his mother and his aunt Hannah, could do nothing. He had suggested a bouncer to Duncan in case there was trouble but had allowed Duncan to overrule him.

'The Old Man wasn't a mafia don, you know,' he had said waspishly, 'and if your ex-wife decides to turn up there's sweet Fanny Adams we can do about it. I'm not having some fat boy in dark glasses standing on the door at my father's funeral just so that we can gratify Diana's theatrical urges.'

Ben got up to read the first lesson, which was something bloodthirsty from the Old Testament – ignorant armies clashing by night – but he read well in a calm, clear voice and the congregation began to settle again into a kind of holy stupor. Marianne watched him but didn't really listen to the words; the light from the clerestory window suddenly intensified and flooded the sanctuary, altering Ben so that he was suddenly all outline with the light round him like a nimbus; a mediaeval painter would have surrounded his figure with a thick line of gold paint, adding one of those soup-plate halos to the top of his head. He was admirably calm, Marianne thought, for such a nervous, highly-strung man. Standing up in front of a congregation like this one couldn't have been easy and yet he made it look easy.

As Ben took his seat, Diana suddenly snored very loudly and Archie smirked as if she was some kind of dangerous circus animal on a chain, a dancing bear perhaps, that only he could control.

'You shouldn't have come,' Marianne whispered. 'She's in no fit state to be here.' She suddenly understood why he had done it. He liked being the keeper of the unpredictable because it made him the only possible interpreter of someone else's behaviour. What more powerful position could there be than that? Archie was playing God where Diana was concerned: a cheating, perfidious deity of the kind that Greek myths were composed about, just as at the same time he loved to decry her and to pretend that he found her intolerable. Marianne found herself feeling sorry for Diana. Behind all the glamour and the wit was a truly lost soul.

'What was I to do?'

'You know bloody well what you should have done. You always did.'

'What's that supposed to mean?' he enquired, all mock innocence.

'Work it out for yourself.'

Marianne turned and faced straight ahead, deliberately ignoring Archie. He was a person she could no longer trust because he derived more pleasure from harm than from healing. It had taken her all this time to realise that her father was a cruel man, without heart.

* * *

After the interment, the family returned to number twelve Ainslie Place for the wake. A striped awning with a scalloped edge had been erected from the front door to the street over a strip of red carpet. The police had cordoned off the street, allowing passengers to be dropped outside number twelve by their drivers but not allowing anyone to park. Because of the presence of so many dignitaries, the press were penned in on the other side of the street. Tomorrow the story would undoubtedly return to the front pages, particularly the picture of Lady Macarthur accompanied by Cardinal Vasari, his massive and colourful bulk contrasting starkly with Jean's bone-thin, black-clad figure. One of her long bird legs was still bandaged and this wounded elegance made her more striking than ever. She wore two pieces of jewellery: the double string of pearls with the magnificent diamond clasp Jack had given her when Duncan was born and the great starburst diamond brooch he had presented to her after Ben's birth.

When she had discovered about Justine he had given her a pavé diamond bracelet once owned by the Duchess of Windsor but Jean had never worn it, considering it ugly and debased, rather like the Duchess of Windsor. It had been a rare lapse of taste in a man who usually had a good eye.

Now Jack was dead she would sell the bracelet and give the proceeds to one of her charities, a nice unfashionable one like Action for Arthritis, that was unflashily dear to her heart. The thought of one of Mrs Simpson's revolting gew gaws helping someone with sore joints seemed to Jean to have considerable poetic justice.

The house was so packed with people that it was hard to move to start with. Jean, Ben and Duncan stood in the hall shaking hands and accepting condolences, whilst waitresses offered champagne to guests at the foot of the stairs to encourage them to move upstairs to the drawing-room.

As Marianne arrived, she saw the deputy first minister shaking hands with Jean, saying something appropriate and then moving on down the line with his aides. There was a condolence book on the hall table which people were being encouraged to sign so that the family would know who had been present.

'Poor Jean,' said a voice behind Marianne, 'this must be a terrible ordeal for her. For Jack to sully his record in such a way must be very humiliating. It trivialises all his other achievements, very unfairly in my view.'

Glancing round, Marianne saw that the speaker was an imposing, heavily built man whom she vaguely recognised as a Lord Justice someone-or-other whom Archie must have painted at one point.

'There's talk about Duncan Macarthur too,' put in the person the judge was addressing. 'He's just been appointed an Archer. How can you have among the so-called élite one who kisses men in the street?'

'Hmmm,' said the judge. 'It's a bad business. Makes a laughing stock of everyone, but he can't help it presumably.'

'That's the latest theory – cooked up by homo-sexuals, if you ask me,' said the man he was talking to, a Tory Westminster MP of Edinburgh extraction, who had held a Cabinet post in a former administration.

Marianne looked round the gathering in the upstairs drawing-room for Luke and eventually spotted him in a corner talking to a man in dog collar whom she recognised as the Moderator of the General Assembly. She caught Luke's eye but he gave no indication that he had ever seen her before in his life. She didn't expect him to kiss her passionately in public, but a wave or a nod would have done and would have excited no suspicion. The thought of the secrets they shared made her shiver, but at the same time she was aware of feeling impatient with Luke, angry even. Why should she be relegated to a compartment in his life, one he couldn't even be bothered to acknowledge by so much as the flicker of an eyelid, the twitch of a nostril? Who did he think he was?

As she turned away, Ben came up to her and took her arm.

'Come and say hello to my mother,' he said. 'Poor thing, she's exhausted. I've got her to sit down on a sofa round the corner; she could do with some congenial company.'

In fact, he was guarding his mother carefully and filtering whom she saw and didn't see, although he didn't want to point this out to Marianne, as he didn't want to frighten her off. He'd treated her so badly once, that he felt he had to proceed with her as if she were as fragile as a piece of old silk. However, he had made up his mind that he wanted to try again with her.

He had realised that he could no longer drift through his life. He was thirty-six and had no wife and no children.

He longed and longed for a family and often found himself staring moonily at fathers with children in the street as if he were some kind of lovesick lass. He didn't know if other men felt this way about children or not. Duncan certainly didn't but then Duncan wasn't as other men. His best friend from school, Marius Morgan, now lived in a large Edwardian villa in Morningside with his wife and their four children. When Ben went there for dinner evidence of children was everywhere from the photographs in the living-room to the occasional appearance of a small person in rose-sprigged pyjamas at the dinner table. Watching Marius holding his baby daughter in his arms made Ben's insides contract with yearning.

Marius and Fiona had invariably dredged up some 'suitable' girl for Ben to dally with but as his yearning for children grew so did his list of what he wanted or didn't want in a woman. He wanted a sensitive, tender beauty who would take care of him and bear his children effortlessly. When he mentioned this to Duncan, Duncan had said in his blunt way, 'Well why did you marry a crocodile, my dear?'

'Mother,' he said. 'You remember Marianne, don't you?'

'Of course,' said Jean, patting the seat beside her. 'I'm awfully pleased to see you again, my dear; sweet of you to come to this bun fight. Jack wanted a huge wake, but this is ridiculous; it's more of a bacchanal than a wake.'

'Dad would have loved it,' said Ben. 'You've done him proud.'

'It's not been an easy week,' murmured Jean to Marianne, 'as you can imagine.'

'I can,' said Marianne. 'The Press has been besieged. And you can't lose your temper so you have to wave every time and smile. It's like having permanent builders in residence, only these ones have cameras.'

'I don't know when it's going to end, I'm afraid,' said Jean. 'The world has got very silly indeed that it's interested in such a rather sad story. The trouble is these days that if you're in any way a loyal wife or not prepared to spill the beans, people can't leave you alone. They refer to me as "brave" and "strong". I may be both, but what do they expect? I'm not about to tell the intimate secrets of my marriage. Why should I? I'd rather rot in hell.'

She was pleased to see Marianne again, having liked her the first time round. Girls could be recycled and why not? And there was something awfully sweet and fresh about this specimen; she so much wanted Ben to find somebody to love him comprehensively, otherwise she felt he was in distinct danger of becoming like her father, a mixture of naivety and brilliance that eventually mulched down into a form of eccentricity that bordered on insanity.

177

'It must have been hell this week,' said Marianne sympathetically, 'but at least you have the family.'

'I do indeed. Ben's been fantastic; Duncan somewhat less so, for obvious reasons.'

'Poor Duncan,' Marianne said. 'He's been very down this week in the office.'

'Self-inflicted wounds,' said Jean. 'I'm more worried about Charles, if you want to know. Duncan can cope. Duncan's made of cast iron, always was as a child. Couldn't dent him, whereas Ben . . .'

Their eyes met and both women laughed. Jean was deliberately being indiscreet with Marianne. It was her way of encouraging Marianne and at the same time telling Ben that he should seize the opportunity with this girl. Men were so stupid sometimes; they couldn't see what was under their nose.

Jack had seen himself so exactly reflected in Duncan's abilities that it had been difficult for Ben, who was essentially a dreamer, to compete; but Duncan's sexual proclivities meant that there would be no grandchildren forthcoming there; that was Ben's job and one he'd singularly failed at so far. Diana, who knew so very well how to wound, had hinted that Ben was infertile or had a low sperm count or one of those modern afflictions that no one had ever heard of before, so perhaps this pretty, dark, smiling girl was the answer to all their prayers.

In the dining-room, Archie found Justine standing by herself. There were plenty of people around her but she was still alone.

'How are you?' he asked.

178

'Bearing up,' she replied, holding out her glass. 'I'm tired, Archie. Get me a refill, would you?'

'Must be a strain for you, all this,' he said, when he came back bringing fresh whiskies for both of them. 'Are people not talking to you?'

'Not quite, but I feel as if I'm being held at arm's length so that they can examine me. It's been terrible all week. Have you ever felt as if you were having the flesh picked off your bones bit by bit in public?'

'No, I haven't. But I imagine it must be exhausting. Brave of you to come.'

'Not brave. Foolhardy, maybe, but I have my pride. I was a part of his life.'

'And Jean has hers.'

'Jean Macarthur is an extraordinary woman. Jack was lucky to be married to her; I see that now.'

'Not the kind of comment mistresses normally make about wives.'

'No, Archie,' Justine said, 'but this is no ordinary situation, as you yourself would be the first to notice. The Macarthurs are remarkable people, of course.'

'Will you have dinner with me tonight?'

'Oh, come on! How could I? To be seen having dinner with a new man on the evening of Jack's funeral would give the press even more ammunition.'

'You can't let your life by ruled by what other people think.'

He minded that she had rejected him but was damned if he was going to let it show.

179

'There's such a thing as prudence,' said Justine. 'Not a word you're familiar with, Archie Maclean.'

'And why not?'

'Because you strike me as a man who does what he wants when he wants and bugger everyone else.'

'Do I?'

'Marianne tells me it was you that brought Diana to the funeral drunk.'

'I couldn't stop her.'

'And you expect me to believe that?' she said. 'Jean was mortified. So was Ben.'

'She wanted to come,' Archie blustered. 'I'm not her keeper.'

'But you sleep with her?'

Archie took a swallow of his drink. He was getting angry now. 'So?' he said aggressively. 'So what if I do?'

'So what indeed?' Justine replied coolly. 'But if you sleep with someone, that implies a measure of involvement in their life.'

'Not necessarily,' said Archie. 'We have an arrangement.'

'Where you take what you want and leave the rest. That's not an "arrangement"; that's called taking advantage.'

'The Old Man took advantage of you when you were young.'

'And I was stupid enough to allow him to. With hindsight, I was wrong, but by the time I'd decided I was wrong it was too late to rectify the mistake.'

Justine turned away from Archie to put her glass

down. She was tired and there was no point in fighting, particularly with Archie who couldn't bear to lose.

'Goodbye, Archie,' she said.

The mere sight of Marianne had made the public Luke feel utterly petrified. He felt that if he betrayed he had ever set eyes on her in his life, all would be lost: his status, his career, his home and family. He had spent a week of terror in the face of the massive press interest in their family.

At any moment, Leila or any of the others might come out of the woodwork. Alice was unusually jittery too as if she had somehow picked up something from him. He felt she was watching him. Even from across the room, she was keeping an eye on him, monitoring his progress and whom he was talking to.

In another part of his being, however, he was screaming with frustration. How could he live the rest of his life in the fishbowl of his wife's accusatory attention? How could he manage to see Marianne again? He needed her now more than ever to defuse him, to provide the serrated garnish he had come to crave in his outwardly perfect-seeming life. He made up his mind that he would somehow manage to call her later and arrange to meet. He had to see her. He clenched his fist secretly in his pocket.

When Ben came up and took her arm, he wanted to cry out, 'Leave her; she's mine!'

He tried to attend to what the white-haired, humorous Moderator was saying; something about share prices, and that he should buy BT now, but his mind kept sliding off the subject and on to the thought of Marianne, naked except for a suspender belt and black stockings. He felt so desperate for her that he could tear something with teeth. He wondered what the Moderator would do if he knew what kind of thoughts were going through his mind.

Gerry Lamont was in another corner of the large upstairs drawing-room of number twelve, talking to Duncan; both men had their solid backs to the room so that no one could see their expressions. What Gerry had to say was highly explosive.

'I've found out what you needed to know,' he said. 'I know who your mole is. The problem is, you won't like what I have to tell you.'

Duncan glanced at him balefully. 'The person in question won't like what I have to tell them either.'

'Very well,' said Gerry, squaring his shoulders. As a young man, he had had various nervous tics, but he had trained himself not to scratch his eyebrow or turn down the corners of his mouth or, heaven forfend, do what the Prince of Wales did and twist his signet ring.

'The person who fed the press their information was your cousin Luke.'

'You can't be serious!'

Duncan was astounded. He was expecting to hear that it was Hester, maybe, or someone at the Press, someone he would have to ritually sacrifice to let the blood, to heal the wound. But Lukey! He loved Luke;

always had. And yet Lukey had done this to them. He simply couldn't begin to understand what had driven him to do such a thing.

'I'm afraid it's true. I had the same reaction as you. I checked and checked again. It was Luke all right.'

Gerry glanced at Duncan and wondered what he was going to do next. He was reminded of a cobra about to strike. He didn't want Duncan to ask him if he knew why Luke had done such a thing. He just wanted to hand him the fact on a plate, like a ham, and retreat. The treachery was undoubtedly linked to the earlier and rather sordid little matter that Luke and Alice had consulted him over but he couldn't possibly indicate by so much as a flicker that he had any idea of this at all. Being a lawyer meant playing many different parts. He knew nothing. He wondered what Duncan would do.

Marianne had driven down to Carrick with Archie a week after the Old Man's funeral. She'd taken the Friday afternoon off from her work and had gone round to Archie's studio after lunch and found him lying on the huge sagging studio sofa smoking an enormous and pungent cigar of positively Churchill-like dimensions.

'Have you had lunch?' he asked, not appearing to notice as he spoke that a large piece of ash had fallen off the end of his cigar onto his trouser leg. He was wearing a faded pair of his favourite blue French workman's trousers that he bought each summer on his annual painting trip to France.

'There's some pâté in the fridge. Help yourself to a glass of wine.'

'I'm fine,' said Marianne. 'I'm not hungry.'

'Are you eating properly? You look awfully thin.'

She could see that he was examining her with his painter's forensic eye. He practically had the callipers out.

'I'm fine,' she repeated, bored by the idea of going into detail about what she ate or didn't eat.

Archie frowned but restrained himself from saying anything further. He was determined to find out from Marianne this weekend what was going on in her life, but he knew that he had to be delicate about it and he was not famous for delicacy. Janet used to say that he had all the tact of a blunderbuss. Now was not the time. He had talked to Cressida who had warned him to be careful.

'You know what she's like,' Cressida had said. 'If she thinks you're interfering she'll clam up.'

'I think she's still grieving for your mother,' Archie went on.

'Why do you think that?'

'She's all eaten up with loss; you can see it in her face. Maybe she blames herself in some way.'

'For what?'

'Your mother's death.'

'Why would she do that?' Cressida asked. 'Although it would be just like her to be so silly.'

'I think she still misses her.'

'Come and have supper with us on Friday night and I can tell you what I think. I haven't spoken to her for a while,' said Cressida, who sought practical solutions for emotional problems.

'What time are we leaving?' asked Marianne, turning the painting on the easel the right side up so that she could examine his subject. Archie always turned his paintings upside down when they were work-in-progress; something to do with the way the paint settled but also, Marianne suspected, because he hated people commenting on what he was up to.

'Quite soon. I don't want to sit in the traffic. Leave that picture alone, will you?'

'Are you going to finish it?' The portrait was of Diana.

'Maybe,' said Archie cagily, getting to his feet. 'She's coming for the night tomorrow, by the way.'

'Why?'

'Because I asked her.'

He had given those kinds of answers when they were children: 'Where are you going?' 'Out.' 'What to do?' 'See a man about a dog.' 'Why do you do it like that?' 'Because that's the way it's done.'

'Are you still sleeping with her?' she asked, still with her back turned.

'What business is it of yours?'

'I'm asking you.'

'On and off,' he said, rolling up his sleeves at the sink to wash his brushes. He thought of Justine at the funeral and sighed imperceptibly. He had bungled that one good and true.

Consuelo, Marianne's colleague at the Press, had heard Duncan and Justine discussing Diana Forbes, and had reported back to Marianne some juicy tale of Diana throwing her glass of wine at someone during the last week in one of the New Town's numerous wine bars.

'I'm glad Ben's shot of her,' Duncan had said. 'She's a disaster area.'

'She was drunk at your father's funeral,' said Justine. 'I see her sometimes in that car of hers and I'm tempted to shop her for drink driving before she kills someone.'

'Diana needs to go into rehab,' said Marianne. 'Have you suggested it?'

'You don't suggest those kinds of things to Diana,' said Archie, without looking round.

'I think you should settle down again, Dad,' said Marianne, 'but with the right person and I don't think she is the right person. This bohemian life you lead isn't good for you.'

'Why? I'm doing fine on it, thank you very much – and by the way I've no intention of marrying Diana Forbes – but I could say the same about you,' he added, turning to face her, his hands dripping. 'Time you settled down, young lady. I wanted to talk to you about it.'

'You sound like some Victorian paterfamilias,' said Marianne, putting on a cartwheel straw hat that was being worn by a bust of Beethoven (one of Archie's favourites) and looking at herself in the long mirror. Since she was a child, she had loved the atmosphere of the studio – all of Archie's studios were very similar – with their amazing mixture of strange objects: the busts on plinths, the stacks of canvases, the jar after jar of brushes of different sizes, the great containers of pigment that she had stared and stared at as a child, feasting on the beautiful colours, stacked on a long shelf above the huge old Belfast sink, the costumes hanging up to be worn by sitters. Diana Forbes's incredibly beautiful evening dress that she wore to be painted in was hanging behind the door at that very moment: a copy of a costume worn by one of Sargent's sitters, all ribbon and gorgeous silk tulle; a king's ransom of a dress that would have cost Marianne a month's wages.

'Who are you seeing at the moment?' asked Archie as casually as he could manage.

'Why?'

'Just asking,' he said, pulling out the plug from the sink and bending down to help himself to one of the pile of old newspapers that he kept handy for dealing with his brushes when he had washed them. He would tear the paper into strips and wrap the end of each brush in a paper curler to dry before laying them out in rows on the draining board. Washing his brushes was part of his religion, a ritual he had learned as a young apprentice in the studio of a famous Italian painter in Florence where he had gone after he first left art school all those years ago.

'No one.'

'Is that true?'

'Yes.'

It was now anyway. Luke had called her at work during the week. He had been in his office.

'I have to see you,' he said. 'Can you meet this evening?'

'I can't do this evening,' she had said.

'Why not?'

'I can't, I'm afraid.'

'You're offended about the funeral,' he began, 'is that it?'

'You could have smiled. I'm not just an object, you know.'

'Last week was a terrible week for all of us. We were all traumatised. I thought you'd understand.'

'Not so bad for you, surely? Terrible for the Jack Macarthurs and for poor Justine. Why was it so hard for you? We were besieged at the Press too. They weren't press outside your house, were they? I mean you were the only one who didn't get much of a mention, you and Alice and Patrick. What about poor Elly, for God's sake?'

'OK,' he said, 'OK. But it was stressful,' he paused, torn between his desire to win the point and the need to see her. 'I have to see you.'

'I can't do tonight.'

'Tomorrow then?'

In the beginning, she had always fitted in with him, knowing it was more difficult for him, but now she was changing. Like all women, she thought she could get the upper hand.

'Please,' he added.

'OK. What time?'

'Six.'

He could make some excuse for being late home for dinner when the time came.

He had been there when she arrived at the ugly apartment in Comely Bank. He had poured himself a glass of wine and had drunk half of it. He offered her a drink too, but didn't seem to have his mind on the matter. She noticed that he didn't kiss her but just looked at her, as a farmer might look at a prize piece of beef walking past in the ring. She didn't like his look and didn't like the way he appeared to have forgotten his manners. She felt he had only asked her there for one reason alone and that made her angry, although she had been a willing enough player before this in the drama between them. But tonight she felt was somehow different, as if the Luke who looked at her as just a piece of meat was the 'true' Luke and that all the other stuff, the affection, the listening ear, had been a blind, a lure. She was suddenly not at all sure that she wanted to be there. It occurred to her with a sudden shock of clarity that the only reason she *was* there was to assuage her feelings of anger and rejection over Ben, and that those were not good enough reasons for getting herself into something increasingly complicated, even physically dangerous.

She drank half the glass of wine and then put it down on the table.

'I won't stay,' she said. 'There's no point. You seem so gloomy.'

'I'm not gloomy. I'm tired.' He looked up at her

from the sofa. 'You don't seem to understand how difficult everything has been.'

'We've already had this conversation,' she said. 'You tell me I don't understand and I don't agree. There doesn't seem to be much point in having it again. I'm going to go.'

She began to look round for her handbag.

'Don't go,' he said, getting up and putting his arms round her. 'I'm sorry; you're right, it is me. I need you.'

He tried to kiss her, but she turned her head away. It wasn't enough; it wasn't working.

'What is it?' he asked, tightening his grip on her shoulder. 'Have you gone off me, then?'

'I'm tired too, I suppose. It's been a long week.'

She didn't add that the whole thing again seemed to her suddenly ridiculous: his need, her absurd compliance. What was she doing here in this ugly place with a man who only wanted one thing? And why had she only just realized it? It wasn't as if it was the first time, for God's sake! And why couldn't he go to a specialist in such things? She knew from reading the newspapers that such women existed. Why had she allowed herself to get into this situation? It was like awaking from an exciting but dangerous dream and finding it was not a dream after all.

'You haven't answered the question,' he said, taking her by the wrists and looking at her. 'Have you?'

Dextrously, he moved his hands down to her waist as if they were dancing and she felt it then, felt the pull of his charm, his sexuality.

'Let's go to bed,' he said, putting one hand under her chin so that he could look into her face. He picked her up and carried into the bedroom as he had done the first time, and undressed her and then himself. It was a clever move. She was willing by now, ready for him, pleased with herself in a way for having turned him tender by making her point. For the first time, she felt as if she had some power over him and it exhilarated her.

They made love tenderly, beautifully. He was all he ever had been at his very best: masculine, direct, curious, warm. He said all the things he knew she needed to hear, the things all women needed to hear about their beauty and their charm and their wit.

Then they made love again and this time she dressed for him. As soon as she came into the room she knew the stakes had been raised dangerously high. When he beat her he hit her so hard that she screamed. And then he did it again, and again. When she had first come to the apartment, she had noticed the sounds around them: the person upstairs who listened to the television very loudly, the individual next door who she could hear putting the kettle on, but by then she was worried about the noises she and Luke made. But nobody had ever come to see what was going on. They might have been the only people in the building.

This evening, however, someone banged on the door and a male voice called out, saying, 'I'll call the police if this goes on.'

Luke appeared not to notice, as if he had entered a place where nothing from the outside world could touch him, but Marianne froze in shame and terror. She had the feeling that Luke might kill her with one of his blows and not even notice.

She tried to get off the bed but he restrained her, holding her down with his considerable weight. She struggled but even with the strength born of fear she knew it was useless. He pushed her back down on the bed, putting his hand over her mouth. She took her opportunity and bit him as hard as she could and then she screamed very loudly.

For a second, nothing. And then, thank God, the male voice was back in the passage banging on the door.

'I'm calling the police right now,' he called. 'What's going on in there?'

Luke withdrew his hand and cursed. His body had gone slack. Marianne seized her opportunity and tumbled off the bed, almost falling over in the process. Luke made no effort to follow her. She was no longer afraid of him but of discovery, of the humiliation of being discovered by the police and the interrogation that would surely follow that would spare no detail.

She tore off what she was wearing and tried to dress, half-sobbing to herself. She found herself for some reason thinking of her mother and what she would think if she could see her beloved daughter now in this weeping and degraded state. What had brought her to such a point? Had it been a desire to debase herself after the failure of her relationship with Ben, a relationship she had set such store by? Maybe. A way of getting at the great Clan Macarthur, of mocking them through exploiting their weakness and her own? A sense of disgust and shock at her own behaviour threatened to engulf her as she hurried to get out before something worse happened.

As she was putting her shoes on Luke came into the room.

'I'm going now,' she said shakily, watching him. He was wrapped in one of the mauve sheets from the bed next door. She was no longer frightened of him. She could tell by the very look of him that the devil that had possessed him had vanished for the time being. He seemed almost confused that she was leaving.

'You need help,' she said, 'before something worse happens. You could hurt someone.'

'What are you going to do?' he asked. 'Are you going to tell someone?'

'You need help,' she repeated, taking a step back. 'I don't know how you've got away with this for so long.'

'Help?' He seemed not to understand what she meant.

'Yes, help. You should see a shrink.'

'Are you going to tell someone?'

'I will if you don't get help.'

'I sold my family to the devil to prevent some photographs appearing of us together,' he said, adding, 'I wanted to protect you.'

'You what?'

'There were some photographs of us. I couldn't risk them being seen.'

'You sold the press the story about Justine and Elly? You?'

'Yes.'

'I can't believe you did that. It was you.' She shook her head.

'To protect you,' he said.

'Yourself, more like,' she retorted. 'You don't give a toss about anyone but yourself. I have to go now.'

She had run out of the apartment and down the stairs and out into the fresh air, feeling as if she had escaped some catastrophe. She realised that she had been playing with fire and that she was lucky to escape without further injury, whether physical or moral. She thought with a sudden and dreadful pang of what Ben would say if he knew. For the first time in a long time, she found herself praying for help.

'And there was I thinking you had a secret man you were keeping from us,' Archie was saying.

'Us? Who's us?' she asked, turning round to face him. 'You've been talking about me to Cressida, haven't you? Admit it.'

'Aye, I do admit it,' he said, looking up from his brushes. 'I've thought you looked so sad lately, darling. Are you able to talk about it or is it something you'd rather keep to yourself?'

Marianne paused. The 'darling' from her father, a man of sparse endearments, had rather undone her. Archie had a very abrupt, somewhat austere manner a lot of the time, a way of not tolerating fools he claimed, but it made him formidable.

'There isn't anyone,' she said. 'There was, but it's over and I don't want to talk about it.'

As a child, Marianne had feared his ironic tongue. Her mother had excused it saying it was just his way but Marianne felt that her mother was too quick to explain away what she herself saw as harshness; and she had resented the way that he never used endearments to her mother, seeing it as a kind of cruelty or a deliberate withholding of himself and his affection.

On the same Friday afternoon, Ben Macarthur was down on the waterfront at Newhaven throwing a stick over and over again for his insatiable stick-fetching collie dog, Lolly. He had been along to Madeira Street to have a look at the roof of the North Leith Parish Church at the request of the minister. When he had finished his job in the heights, he remembered poor Lolly sitting patiently in the driver's seat of the van waiting for a swim, and decided to knock off before he went to fetch Patrick who was going with him to Ardgay for the weekend. He would then return to Ainslie Place, pick up his stuff, and change cars as he was also taking his mother and Charles to Ardgay. He had site visits to make at the weekend to Barhill and Castle Forbes, but he also intended to find time to see Marianne. Increasingly, she was entering his thoughts as someone who was just right, someone he felt he knew, a warm, reliable figure who had crossed with him from the old order into the new.

He watched the dog's head for the nth time as she swam out after the bobbing stick and thought, not for the first time, that there was something very tranquil about throwing a stick for a dog; an occupation that could be seen as dull and repetitious was made bearable by the dog's enormous pleasure in what they were doing.

'That's enough now,' said Ben to Lolly, who was watching his face with such trembling eagerness that she had forgotten to shake herself. He took the stick and ran for cover as Lolly shook what seemed like the entire contents of a washing machine-full of water in his direction. When he opened the back door of his van she jumped in and then jumped over onto the driving seat so that by the time he got to Luke's house in Ann Street where he was going to collect Patrick he had a huge wet patch on his trousers that Patrick who opened the front door to him thought was hilarious.

'I'm ready when you are,' said Patrick, putting down his bag at Ben's feet. 'I've got swimmers, flippers, goggles, snorkel and boots. Will I need a wet suit?'

'And probably no pants or sweaters or spare trousers for when you fall in the water,' said Alice, coming down the stairs behind her son. 'Let me look in that bag.'

She smiled at Ben. 'You've time for a cup of tea, surely?'

'I should think so,' said Ben, looking round him as

he invariably did when he entered any house, whether it was one he knew or not.

'No, please!' exclaimed Patrick. 'Can't we go?'

'Not until your cousin Ben has had a cup of tea,' said Alice. 'Have you done any of your homework?'

'Some of it,' said Patrick indignantly. A weekend with Ben at Ardgay without his parents – Ardgay was the house that Ben's mother, Jean Macarthur, had inherited when her father died – had been one of the highlights of Patrick's summer since he was about six.

Ardgay House was a middling-size Georgian house near Kirkcudbright in south-west Scotland that had been owned by Jean Macarthur's father, an eccentric baronet called Sir Benjamin Speight, after whom Ben was named. After Jean's mother died in the late nineteen fifties, Sir Benjamin had lived at Ardgay by himself with his spaniels (Bella's ancestors), growing increasingly antisocial and generally peculiar. He had kept a shotgun by his bed which he used to fire out of his bedroom window at seagulls and once opened the back door to the district nurse stark-naked, a story which caused much amusement when it was disseminated locally. The young Jean Speight had been rescued from her Rapunzel-like seclusion by Jack Macarthur who, always curious about property, had just turned up one day to have a look at a house that he had been told nobody was ever invited into. He married Jean three months later and when the old boy died, barricaded into his bedroom by great tunnels of yellowing newsprint, the young Macarthurs kept the house for holidays, doing it up as they went and it had long since been restored to its original pleasing austerity. Ben and Duncan and their cousins Luke and Sukey had loved the place as children and now it was Patrick's turn.

'How've you been this week?' asked Ben as he followed Alice into the kitchen.

'Frazzled,' said Alice, 'but thank God the story seems to have died away. Are the press still parked outside your house?'

'No; they've faded away as quickly and abruptly as they appeared, leaving a trail of wreckage behind them of course. Mother's taken to her bed since the funeral, although she's consented to come down to Ardgay with us; Duncan's in a furious rage about something and won't speak to anyone; Charles has moved out and is living with Mother, whom he insists on looking after himself.'

'And you?' asked Alice.

'Me? I'm just trying to get on with my life. Sorting out the Old Man's affairs is going to take a while, however, and I'm pretty busy professionally at the moment.'

'I'm pleased for you,' said Alice. 'The business seems to be building up nicely, I hear.'

'I've just had a bit of luck this last year,' said Ben.

'You shouldn't be so modest,' said Alice. 'It's your skill that's made it happen.'

'How's Lukey?' asked Ben, to change the subject. He never felt he deserved praise.

'Very down,' said Alice, 'I'm not quite sure why. He . . .'

She stopped talking and Ben saw that Patrick had followed them into the kitchen. Ben knew that he was the kind of child who reacted like a piece of litmus paper where his parents' relationship was concerned. Being an only child was hard sometimes. He had watched Patrick monitoring his parents like a spectator at a tennis game, head this way then that, weighing and checking, constantly taking the emotional temperature.

It was known in the family that the Luke Macarthurs had had difficulties in their marriage, but it was hoped that they would manage to stay together for Patrick's sake, particularly as he was the only child in the next generation. There were rumours about Luke's infidelities with his students – the temptation must be fairly strong, Ben had thought, particularly if one wasn't getting on with one's wife – but he had never mentioned the subject to Luke or discussed it with him at all until the other day when Luke had asked for money. Even then he had been spectacularly unforthcoming.

It was a family pattern, or so it seemed, to remain married but to look elsewhere for sexual satisfaction. His father did it, Luke did it, Duncan did it; only he, Ben, felt distaste for such arrangements. When he had found that Diana had been unfaithful to him he had not been tempted to do the same himself. He had just felt a great cold wave of disappointment and tiredness at the wreck of all his hopes.

'What are you two doing this weekend?' Ben asked, hoping that Alice would lighten her tone and at least pretend that all was well for Patrick's sake.

'Nothing much,' said Alice, sounding fed up, when she had finished asking Patrick to get the cups down off the dresser. 'Luke's working on his book and I've got stuff to catch up with too.'

'You could go out to dinner and enjoy yourselves,' said Patrick, putting a cup on its saucer and pushing it towards Ben. 'You won't have me to worry about.'

'Thank you, darling,' said Alice, smiling at Ben over Patrick's head. 'That's very thoughtful of you.'

When she smiled, Ben thought, she really was a very attractive woman. Duncan had always said she was tough and that was why Luke had chosen her, and Diana had always referred to Alice dismissively as 'the gym mistress', but there was a fresh, athletic look about her.

She had very shiny shoulder-length fair hair and an attractive rather than a pretty face; when she was tired or depressed she looked washed-out but as soon as she smiled she gleamed again. The Old Man had liked her; he had always liked blonde women; Ben's mother had been a delicate blonde as a young woman, a little on the thin side for the Old Man, he had once told his younger son; but Justine displayed all the physical characteristics the old wretch had admired: blonde, shapely but not in an exaggerated Dolly Parton sort of way. Justine was also motherly and calm, a bit of a northern Madonna figure after her own fashion. A few months ago when the Old Man could still string a sentence together he had told Ben that he had had everything in life a man could want in a material sense, 'But now,' he had said in a wondering way, 'I can't even have a glass of water. That's dying for you.'

When Ben had blustered about recovery, the Old Man had said, 'I won't recover; I don't want to; I'm tired. It's up to you now.'

Had he any idea, Ben wondered, how those words made him feel? The answer was probably yes. It was his way of passing the baton.

'Is your mother well enough to go to Ardgay?' Alice was asking.

'I felt it would do her good,' said Ben. 'She needs the change after all she's been through.'

'I think it's a good thing she's collapsed,' said Alice. 'It's the body and the brain's way of saying, "Enough!". One of the problems your mother has is being wonderful all of the time.'

'You're not going to have one are you?' asked Patrick. 'You often say you are.'

'That's just a figure of speech,' said Alice, smiling again at her son.

'What's a figure of speech?'

As Alice explained patiently, Ben thought that children were not only exhaustive but exhausting too. When Patrick was with him he asked questions all the time about everything from the way the van's engine worked to more abstruse things that puzzled him about the Roman Empire or Ancient Egypt. Once he had asked Ben on a particularly tricky stretch of road which was the greatest in its time, the Roman

Empire or the British, but there was nothing he liked more, Ben reflected, than seeing that great mop of fair hair and that determined profile strapped into the passenger seat beside him, with Lolly either at his feet or breathing doggily down his neck.

At the end of the drive to Carrick, after all those big roads with service stations and huge important signs directing travellers to borders and airports and the centres of cities, there was a tiny road on the map of rural Galloway, a lost trail as Marianne thought of it, a road of enchantment that led towards the sea. The landscape undulated gently, forming hummocks and tree-topped hillocks; there was the flaming gorse and deep heather and rocky outcrops cascading into scree paths where the sheep came and went mysteriously, and look-out points where beasts, great slow Herefords or Belted Galloways, gazed luminously towards the horizon and the sea. It was the coastline from where the poor Queen of Scots had departed to Cumberland and captivity; sometimes, Marianne thought, one might not be surprised to find her again bobbing about in her rowing boat, as if the reel of time could be reversed; or herself aged seven, weeping, having fallen off her bike, her knees bleeding, the contents of her satchel spread across the dung-encrusted road.

'You're quiet,' said Archie, slowing behind the last of Carrick Mains' herd of dairy cows as they trailed obediently into the milking parlour, a great gaggle of maiden aunts, dewy-eyed, incurious, followed by a boy and a collie sloping along behind sullen with the tension.

'I'm thinking,' Marianne replied. 'It's exhausting. Put me out here, will you? I'll walk the last bit. I could do with the exercise.'

'Cressida's expecting us at eight,' Archie said, 'so don't get lost, will you? It's half five now. I'll go and open up.'

The sound of the car's engine vanished abruptly when Archie had turned the corner, as if he had vanished through a baize door that had slammed shut behind him. The lie of the land did that, Marianne reflected; there was something cosy and companionable about it, both beautiful and familiar; the kind of landscape that an angel might suddenly appear in, an Italian angel with coloured wings and a dull gold soup plate for a nimbus, startling a sheep or a grazing cow, getting her banner of proclamation tangled in the gorse.

She had wanted to walk through this familiar and somehow prophetic scenery to think about her last encounter with Luke but found she couldn't attend to it; its potency was dissipated amongst the scenery of her childhood, or, rather, it lay poisonously elsewhere, somewhere ahead, a place towards which she would come.

She kept thinking of herself as a child here, the solitary days spent meandering sometimes inland amongst the woods and the scree with the smell of gorse in her nostrils and the drone of the wild bees feeding on the nectar, sometimes at the water's edge amongst the rock pools (the pink and vulnerable anemones had fascinated her) or the treacherous slippery rust-coloured stones and the salt-smelling bladderwrack, or following the tide out to the horizon, past the salmon nets and the clusters of rocks, bare and ugly as skinned knuckles without their covering of sea.

But behind all these memories lay fear. Marianne stopped dead in her tracks as this thought occurred to her. How could one forget? How could she have forgotten? To her left was the entrance to a field with a gate across it. She climbed the gate and found herself looking across another field beyond which lay the sea.

Fear. She had always been afraid as a child. Once there had been a snake by the studio door at Carrick, or had she dreamed that?

'Born anxious,' her mother had said. When she was a baby, her mother, Janet, would go out and she wouldn't close her eyes until she returned. Cressida was four years older than Marianne and there had been a baby after Marianne, another girl, who had died shortly after her birth of an infection. She remembered a black-and-white snap (surely they had colour photographs in 1977?) of her father holding this child, Anna, in what must have been the maternity hospital in Dumfries. He was seated on an upright chair wearing, for some reason, a white linen suit with a waistcoat; very Archie; always having to be different. White linen and Dumfries were not natural companions. His expression was one of studied indifference. He might have been holding a puppy or a prize marrow. Marianne would have been four then. The baby died of meningitis from an infection picked up in hospital.

Janet had been ill afterwards, mentally ill, Cressida had told her. She had spent some time in the local loony bin, the Crichton. Jessie, Janet's mother, their grandmother, had looked after them in Garholm, a village very near Carrick but inland, a dull place with a main street lined with sullen pebble-dashed cottages, with a pub at the end of the main street, the Star of Garholm. Then to the right, a steep street that led down to the river rising again on the other side to be crowned by the sandstone church where the elders sat like a prosecuting jury under the pulpit every Sunday morning.

Marianne remembered the church vividly and singing 'By cool Siloam's shady rill' and 'There is a green hill far away without a city wall'. How could a hill lack a city wall? Nobody ever explained. The minister was called Mr Wright, and Mrs Wright, small and solid and as densely effective as a cannon ball, taught in the primary school.

Jessie's house was near the church, an old white cottage with a front garden full of flowers and a back garden where their grandfather, Andrew, grew vegetables, wigwams of beans, and rows and rows of onions and leeks.

But she had wanted her mother with an ache that had been so powerful that it had prevented her from eating or sleeping. The doctor had been called but he had not known what to do either. 'The child is fading away,' Marianne had heard him tell Jessie in a low voice as he stood on the path by the front door with the door ajar. 'Her weight is dangerously low.'

'I cannae get her to eat,' Jessie had said. 'She won't touch a thing, other than the occasional sardine.'

'That's a start,' said the doctor. 'Get her to take some milk if you can.'

'She never touches milk. It makes her retch.'

Milk. Even now the smell of it made her gag; and the memory of compulsory milk at breaktime at Garholm School had almost the same effect. The smell of the milk bottles combined with the disinfectant used to swab the corridor after hours was a part of the ache; the smell of pain.

Then Archie reappeared suddenly. 'Where had he been all this time?' 'It was only a few weeks,' said Cressida. 'You exaggerate everything. He had been on a big commission – some duchess or other – we had to eat, you know. I remember thinking you were just doing it to get attention. And you certainly succeeded. You had the doctor and the minister and God only knows who else all talking to Jessie about you in the front room or on the path by the front door where the lavender grew.'

But then Archie came back and took them home to Carrick and she had her room again with its view of the bay and the stone buoys, two stone phalli planted there by the Edwardian draper who had built Carrick in 1904, and the sound of the sea as she lay in her bed waiting to sleep, trying not to think of the snake by the studio door.

And then Janet had come back. 'She was only away for a month,' said Cressida, 'and Gran took us to see her.' 'I don't remember that.' 'Well, you don't remember a lot of things.' And Archie came back and everything was all right again. Except that it wasn't. The fear was there like the memory of the snake by the studio door; something you might put your foot on at any moment, in the dark perhaps or half asleep. It never left you but was coiled close.

Archie and Janet went on with their life, but what had happened – the death of the baby, the fact that Archie had been sleeping with the duchess or the countess or whoever it was he had left his girls with Jessie so that he could paint – meant that like a canvas that had been attacked with a knife (death, madness, a coffin the size of a shoe box are all an attack on a domestic situation), the rent was still there; the scar of the invisible mend lay across their lives. And the scar tissue of childhood can continue to ache and even sometimes to grow, one old wound running into a new: Luke, for instance. Love and pain inextricably mixed. Being with Luke had opened old wounds; maybe that was why she had stayed – to become conscious of what ailed her that had sunk beyond reach.

The marriage survived but Janet became heavier and slower. She no longer went to parties or up to Edinburgh with Archie. They had separate bedrooms. Archie slept in the studio a good deal and was often away. Cressida, brisk, bossy Cressida, put on more mental armour training as a psychiatric nurse and became a calm person unfazed by the woman in reception with a knife or the drunken wife-beater who threatened to give her one. She found Archie's posturings and costumes absurd and nursed Janet competently when she was discovered to have untreatable breast cancer at the same time as looking after her own family: Pete and the twins, Jessie and Will, now aged four. Marianne thought of Cressida as a crab, secure and confident in her armour, and of herself as the anemone in the rock pool, pink and vulnerable, dangerously available to predators.

And Luke was a predator who had seen her coming. That last time in the bedroom of the apartment at Comely Bank, his desire to tear into her had been obvious from the start and he had been unable to conceal it. This was what he had been leading up to all along and this was what it would become more and more. All the other stuff, the tenderness after making love, the talk, the yearning looks in crummy wine bars; those things had been the tenderiser or whatever hormone it was they applied to meat to make it more palatable before they sold it on slabs in the supermarket. The tenderiser had been applied; the softening-up process was in Luke's view well under way, so that the real business could begin, only he had misjudged the timing. The Old Man's death had got in the way, he had panicked and done something so incredibly stupid that as an act it would drag him under. He had told her that he had sold his family to protect her, but that was not his real reason. The truth was that it was to protect himself. Luke wanted to have his cake and eat it but as even small children knew, that was not possible.

Nadia had asked the question: why do you seek pain? But it was never as simple as that. She couldn't have known what he was like before they began as lovers. Or was there something subliminal in it, some calculation that lay beyond the reach of consciousness, a form of synchronicity that drove certain kinds of lovers together, like the high-pitched whistle that dogs can hear but not humans?

The Volvo was parked in the courtyard by the back door with its boot open. Archie had made himself special boxes to transport oil paintings in so that they could dry without him having to fold them if he was in a hurry, and one or two of these containers had been taken out and stood with their lids open by the back of the car. The quarry-tiled passage that led past the studio to the kitchen stairs was dim after the bright sea light and smelt of oil paint and rubber boots and linseed oil.

He was in his studio but he wasn't really doing anything constructive; he was just fiddling and turned guiltily to face her when she came in unannounced.

'I thought you'd be longer,' he said, putting down the Stanley knife with which he had been cleaning his nails, a habit Janet had always abhorred, but Archie had gone on doing it anyway. He never really cared what other people thought about things like that. He picked his teeth and cleaned his fingernails with a

Stanley knife and cut his toenails by the side of his bed and left the remains for someone else to clean up like mouse droppings.

'No, just a little saunter,' she said. 'Just checking to see that everything was in order.'

'And is it?'

'So far, so good. What were you doing when I came in?'

'I was thinking.'

'And what were you thinking about that made you look so guilty?'

'Did I?'

'Yes.'

'We could walk out to your mother's grave,' he said.

He had a way of not answering questions directly that was a part of his armoury. He had not admitted that he looked guilty but his proposal of a walk to Janet's grave was a kind of oblique answer to her question. It was always like this with Archie: you were shadow-boxing with someone whose footwork was exceedingly nimble. He could never admit to anything or be wrong about anything. He was always Archie in charge, Archie in control, Archie setting the scene. No wonder he earned his living by making formal representations of other people. What greater controlling feature could there be than that?

Archie had obtained special permission from the National Trust to have Janet buried on the island that lay opposite the jetty and the ruined summerhouse, a place that could only be reached at low tide. She had particularly wanted to be there in solitude, the only grave on the island. Like Archie (whose father and grandfather had been blacksmiths) she had grown up on this coast; the sea with its capricious tides and mists (the haar thick as a membrane); the crashing, foaming tides of winter and spring solstice had formed her and now, little by little, deformed her, each tide taking something back.

'Were you thinking about Mum?'

'Kind of.' He gave her a look.

'Is the tide right?'

'According to the newspaper.'

'It must be right then. OK. If you think we've got time, let's go.'

The nursery at Ardgay was where Patrick made for as soon as Ben had opened the front door. He didn't wait to ask. The nursery was where Auntie Jean's father was a boy a hundred years ago before the wars. Patrick thought in his mind of wars as walls – towering things behind which crouched people and events in strange costumes, intent on killing each other; in the same way that he had misheard the Creed and thought of Pontius Pilate as Pontius Pirate with a cutlass and a gold earring and a hankie over his hair.

Uncle Jean's father, Uncle Ben, was born before the First World Wall and spent, as far as Patrick could tell, an entirely idyllic childhood in this room at the top of the house; not the attic floor, but the one next to it. There was a huge rocking horse called Bucephalus which Patrick knew was the name of Alexander the Great's horse, because Ben had told him so. Ben had also told him that Alexander had wanted to conquer the known world and was engaged in a lot of walls along the way including the Great Wall of China. Bucephalus had dappled sides and glaring eyes and flared nostrils and a moth-eaten tail because he had not been ridden enough and loved enough for a long time. Patrick immediately remedied this by climbing up into Bucephalus's saddle and beginning to rock. From his vantage point he glanced round the nursery, taking in the bookcase with its volumes and volumes of the *Children's Encyclopaedia* with their dark blue coverings and gold-stamped lettering edited by a man with a strange name, Arthur Mee. Arthur You, Arthur Them, thought Patrick frowning, Arthur Us. He shook his head. Arthur Mee sounded strangely right. He liked to linger with a volume in bed of a night, opening whichever one he had at any page and reading about things he had never dreamed of. There were other books too of which he was fond; volumes of the adventures of Sinbad; fairy tales with hypnotic and frightening illustrations that made their way into Patrick's dreams sometimes. He was particularly fond of a volume of New Testament Bible stories showing the bearded Jesus in a white nightie with long, bony, bare feet going around being good and blessing people and turning water into wine at weddings, a useful trick, Patrick thought – to be able to conjure up another Coke when you felt like it or an extra packet of Monster Munch.

Ben, knowing exactly what Patrick was up to, let him tear up the stairs without bothering to ask him if he wanted a pee or something to drink. Alice told him that Patrick was sometimes so engrossed in what he was doing that he wet his pants, but that was too bad, thought Ben; he's happy, let him be. The poor fellow had such an organised life when he was at home in Edinburgh that Ben felt time at Ardgay was time out from the endless labour of being Patrick Macarthur, aged eight. The poor little sod not only went to school (which was bad enough in Ben's estimation) but he had all kinds of extra-curricular activities including tennis, riding and even judo, for God's sake! There seemed to be a conspiracy that modern children should never have a moment in which to stand and stare and this was where he came in. When Patrick was at Ardgay or with him in Edinburgh at a weekend with no school day ahead, then he could read all night for all Ben cared and sleep half the morning.

He let the child go and turned back to the car where Charles was helping his mother out. The ulcer on her leg had worsened during the last week so that she had to use a stick to walk with. How she had aged, Ben thought, in such a short space of time. She looked almost at death's door herself.

When Ben had been a boy, his mother had brought him and Duncan here in the summer and let them run wild. Extra-curricular activities had not been on the agenda then. If you were young and lucky enough to get to a place like this you were put down, given a bicycle or a horse if you were really lucky and left to get on with it. His father would come from Edinburgh at weekends and things would be a bit more organised then because sometimes there would be people to stay; there would be other children (like Diana and Hugo Forbes) and tennis parties and organised swimming picnics at Moss Yard or Cardoness or Carrick, the best of the local beaches, but mostly they were left alone to roam about on their own on their bikes, or saddle, if they wished, the rather fierce pony, Boadicea, who lived with a retired hunter that had once belonged to the Old Man when he was going through a riding phase, in a field beyond the walled garden.

The Old Man had never tired of telling them the story when they were boys of how he had rescued their mother from the strange situation in which she had found herself. As the only daughter of a widowed father, she had been living at Ardgay with him and her two identical twin maiden aunts, Edith and Ada, caring for her increasingly eccentric relations with the help of a widowed woman called Jessie Paterson who had been in service at Ardgay since a very young girl.

Jean's family, the Speights, had been lairds of Ardgay since the eighteenth century but death duties had eroded their fortune and by the time young Macarthur came to Ardgay by accident on a bright spring day in the late nineteen fifties, things were in a wretched state in every sense of the word. As the lack of money bit, old Ben had shut up one room after another, boarding up broken window panes, nailing the front door shut, establishing gun emplacements on various window sills from where he could shoot seagulls and any cat that was stupid enough to wander into sight, or the district nurse if she so chose. He hoarded newspapers and Spam and developed an obsession about Fray Bentos tinned stew that he kept in boxes under his bed together with innumerable tins of cashew nuts. The aunts, utterly engrossed in each other, lived in a bedroom on the first floor emerging from time to time, other than for Jessie's meals, wearing tweed coats over their nighties for walks to the walled garden and back, like two ladies out of a Jane Austen novel.

The walled garden, Jean's mother's great project, was running wild with only Jean to weed it and a man to put in the potatoes in the spring. When a particularly severe winter storm smashed every pane of glass in the greenhouse the vine died. Jean told the Old Man that she felt that that was the moment she accepted that the end had come. The vine was very old and had come to symbolise in her mind what her family was: a dead thing in a smashed-up casing. The same winter the aunts contracted pneumonia (if one was ill the other invariably followed suit) and died in their beds, two rigid wooden dollies with bright cheeks, wearing scratchy tweed coats over their nighties. The day after their funeral at Greyfriars Parish church in

Kirkcudbright was the day Jack Macarthur turned up driving a Bugatti and wearing a tweed overcoat with very large caddish checks that Mr Toad would have given his eye teeth for.

Instead of shooting at him, Jean's father had come downstairs wearing an old dressing gown with the stuffing coming out of the lapels that his grandfather had worn in the Crimea, over an embroidered kaftan last worn for a tableaux vivant sometime in the late eighteen nineties. He had given up buying clothes during the Second World War and simply wore the things he found in the dressing-up box. When it was warmer he went nude because it annoyed Jessie and that silly arse of a district nurse. Nevertheless, he had his gun over his arm when young Macarthur appeared, just in case.

Young Jack immediately offered to take him for a drive in the Bugatti which was painted Cambridge blue and shaped like the thorax of some gigantic, metallic insect. It had brass headlights and a leather strap round its bonnet. The hubcaps and wheel arches were painted a soft Lamonty yellow. He offered old Ben a pair of goggles and they set off with Jean and Jessie watching from the area steps.

'Mebbe that's the last we'll see of him,' Jessie had said, wiping her hands on her apron, leaving it unclear whether she meant Sir Ben or that young whippersnapper who had just turned up. Jean rather hoped it wouldn't be the latter. Macarthur was a tall, swarthy fellow with thick hair and shining dark eyes like sloes who looked commanding and great fun, and she so wanted to have some fun particularly after burying the poor little wooden aunts in their pathetic coffins. She didn't want to die immature and untried like Ada and Edith whose white little legs the colour of unripe conkers made her think of old babies being entombed.

Jean's father came back smoking a cigar – his first since VJ Day (anything slit-eyed would be shot on sight) – and invited Jack to stay the night.

Three months later Jack and Jean were married in Greyfriars on a late August day in a heat wave, just one of a number of miracles Jack Macarthur seemed able to perform in a country where it appeared to rain almost without cease whatever the season.

The locals had gawped, gossiped and predicted doom but they had underrated Jack. It was like an eagle arriving in a hen house. He took charge of things in a dashing sort of way. It was useless and cruel to remove the old boy so Jack found him a keeper, a retired forester, who had fought in the war and was trying to manage on an inadequate pension, installing him in the octagonal cottage at the end of the drive. He was charged with instigating minor repairs and keeping a watching brief on the old boy. Jessie, who had fallen in love long since with Sir Ben, continued to produce his meals for him. And thus the old order was allowed to appear to prevail until Sir Ben died at the end of the sixties, sometime during the Woodstock Festival, an event at which he would have passed unnoticed either naked or clothed.

Jessie Paterson married the retired forester, now

dead, and their daughter, Moira, and her husband, now lived in the octagonal cottage at the end of the drive. Moira had taken over Jessie's role as housekeeper and as soon as Patrick vanished up to the nursery, Ben left Charles to see to his mother and went down the back stairs to the kitchen to see what Moira had left them for supper.

He opened one of the doors of the enormous refrigerator Duncan had shipped from America three years ago, a great chrome giant of a thing with juicers and icers and endless compartments for the vast amount of food Americans seemed to need to store merely to survive for a few days, and saw that Moira had left a shepherd's pie, a salad, and what looked like a rhubarb crumble. There was a bowl containing cooked chipolatas (Patrick's favourite) and in one of the endless freezer compartments he found a tub of the chocolate chip ice-cream that Patrick had once informed Moira gravely that he liked to eat in the middle of the night 'if it was available'. Where, Ben wondered, had the boy learned to talk like a retired bank manager? Neither his father nor his mother ever used expressions like that but there were some children, his mother said, who were born old and maybe Patrick was one of them. Or perhaps it was to do with being an only child; Ben wasn't certain, but there was something about the boy's mannerisms and phraseology that made him in his position as honorary uncle both tender and apprehensive for the odd little fellow.

At that moment Lolly barked outside the back

door and scraped at the paintwork with her paw, something she had been forbidden over and over to do, which made no difference whatsoever as she went on doing it anyway.

'Come on,' he said, letting her in, pausing for a moment to admire the way the fur along her back lay in ripples as if a wave had impressed itself on her like a fossil, 'it's your suppertime.'

She had a basket in the corner by the table and there was a sack of all-in-one dog food in the back pantry but first of all he would call Patrick and get him to feed the dog. It was good for the boy to look after an animal and for some reason Luke and Alice didn't have a dog although they had space to spare plus a garden in front and behind, quite a luxury in a city.

He went back up into the hall with Lolly glued to his heels, and called the boy. The hall felt dark and cold and unused, although he could hear the faint sounds of Charles in his mother's room which looked out over the front.

He could also hear the grandfather clock that stood just inside the drawing-room door measuring off the seconds like a brass heartbeat, the faithful background sound of one's life slipping away with nothing to show for it. As a boy that reverberation had been the sound of eternity, the long afternoons of childhood where time seemed to stand still and even in some ways to go into reverse. It would never be teatime, never be suppertime, let alone bedtime and sleep, the great dark ocean across which one had to make one's way into another day of eternity.

'Patrick,' he called again, loud enough so that Lolly barked. In the ensuing silence Ben suddenly had a vision of himself as an old man with a crazy dog at his heels, barking mad like his grandfather before him, passing the days by shooting squirrels and seagulls out of the window, with the long nights huddled over a shotgun waiting for the sound of breaking glass. That prospect lay in wait for him in this house like a threat, but he was beginning to realise that he could choose his own future instead of merely allowing himself to be swept along like driftwood on a wave, a piece of flotsam on a great green wall of water. That was what the passing of the baton meant; his father's death had released him to act.

'Sorry,' said Patrick, coming down the last flight of stairs two at a time, something his mother did not allow him to do at home.

'I got tied up.'

Another bank manager's phrase. 'What were you doing?' asked Ben. 'I shouted and shouted for you.'

'Oh, this and that,' said Patrick airily. 'What about you? Hello, lovely Lolly.'

'You could feed her,' said Ben, 'while I put the supper in the oven.'

'Two scoops or three?' Patrick asked as Lolly skittered behind them down the stairs to the kitchen.

'Three, I think. Poor thing's hungry after all that swimming.'

After supper, which his mother took in bed, Charles and Ben and Patrick played racing demon until Patrick drooped and was sent off to clean his teeth and get into his pyjamas. Ben tidied up, bade goodnight to Charles and then went upstairs with Lolly who had a basket in his room. Patrick was in a room at the end of the upstairs corridor that had belonged to Ben when he was a boy and remained more or less unchanged. The poster of David Bowie had gone but the photographs of prep school and public school remained, the endless dreary line-ups that punctuate childhood and adolescence. Patrick liked the room but Ben found this reminder of the person he had once been painful: all that promise, all that hopefulness, all those scrubbed faces. Now those boys would most likely have boys of their own (except for him of course) and the whole thing would start again. The photograph was like the sediment at the bottom of a glass of wine, dried-out but still faintly pungent, not something to linger over.

The boy got into bed, turned on his side and fell asleep instantly, one of the sudden graces of childhood. Ben kissed him, turned out the light and went into the passage, leaving the door ajar. Once in his bedroom, he lay down on his bed and began to read but got up again swiftly when car headlights swept across the ceiling of his room.

At the window he watched as Luke got out of the car and walked across the carriage sweep to the steps of the house. Lolly barked but stopped when Ben hushed her. The last thing in the world he wanted was Patrick to wake up. He threw up the window and called out to Luke to wait there and he would come down.

'What brings you here?' Ben asked, pulling the door

to behind him to prevent Lolly from escaping. There was a colony of rabbits at the place where the lawn sloped down towards the walled garden and he didn't feel like hunting for her in the dark.

'Alice has thrown me out.'

'Why?'

'It's a long story. Can I come in?'

'Yes, of course you can, but be quiet; I don't want Patrick to wake up. He's just got to sleep.'

He followed Luke into the hall, closing the door behind him. Even to Ben's forgiving eye Luke looked like hell; he was unshaven and his abundant hair looked lank. A boil was forming under his left ear.

'Let's go down to the kitchen. We can talk down there.

'So what's going on?' he asked, when Luke was sitting at the table over a large whisky and water.

'After you'd gone, Duncan came to see us, without warning. You see, he'd found out who was responsible for giving the original newspaper the information about Justine and Elly and so forth.'

'And who was it?' asked Ben, glancing over his shoulder as Charles came quietly into the room.

'It was me,' said Luke.

'I don't understand,' said Ben. 'When I spoke to you some while back you more or less told me that if the journalist did contact you you'd tell him to take a running jump.'

Ben glanced at his cousin and then down again at the backs of his hands. He had scraped his knuckles earlier without noticing and his right hand was throbbing slightly. He had thought of a whisky but decided against it. Drink late at night kept him awake and made him bad-tempered in the morning and he wanted Patrick to have a good day on Saturday. Now, he regretted it – he needed any strength he could get, false or otherwise.

'You remember that I told you there was a girl,' said Luke carefully – one had to be cautious how one framed things to Ben otherwise he got the wrong end of the stick – 'a student of mine, an Arab girl; we had an affair. It ended badly; she's been writing letters, some to Alice, some to me, blackmailing letters. I told you.'

'But I thought you'd sorted it all out, for God's sake. That's why I lent you the money. I mean an affair with a student is hardly a big deal these days, or am I wrong?'

'No, you're not wrong,' said Luke, who was slightly thrown by Ben's attitude but unable to determine quite which way to play what he wanted to say next, 'but she made allegations and appeared determined to follow them up if she didn't get what she wanted.'

'What, then?' asked Ben, looking up, unable to comprehend the full enormity of what Luke was trying to tell him.

'That I beat her up, that sort of thing,' said Luke, taking a mouthful of whisky.

'And did you?'

'What sort of question is that?'

'Well, if she made those allegations, then you would no doubt have had to find answers to them.'

'I paid her off,' said Luke. 'I had no choice. It was her word against mine and in the present climate she would have won hands down. My whole career would have been ruined. Gerry arranged it for me. Alice and I went to see him.'

'You should have thought of that before,' said Ben flatly. 'Go on. You paid her off, then what happened? What made you sell the whole fucking family down the river? Do tell me; I'd love to know.'

But in spite of his surface anger, a voice in his head said, 'Beware! You cannot tear down everything at once; the reins have slid through Duncan's hands, and now it's up to you to take control of the bolting chariot with its terrified occupant, otherwise something even worse will happen. A cornered man will do something violent or stupid, or possibly both. Beware!'

'There were further complications.'

'With the same girl?'

'No, with another. The journalist had pictures of us together. I didn't want Alice to know. She'd already found out about the first thing. She threatened to leave me and take Patrick. I only managed to stop her by promising to try and sort myself out.'

'Another! Weren't you already in enough trouble?'

'The other thing had started before the first girl decided to blackmail me.'

'Christ!' exclaimed Ben with uncharacteristic vehemence. 'You really have fucked up big time. How could you be so incredibly stupid and indiscreet?'

'I know,' said Luke, 'I realise it now.'

'So Alice knows about the next girl on the conveyor belt?' asked Ben.

'Duncan told her everything. I pleaded with him not to, but he wouldn't listen. He showed her the photographs of me with the girl.'

'When he's angry,' said Charles, 'he can't be stopped. What did Alice do?'

'She threw me out. She's going for a divorce. I couldn't get her to change her mind, so I left but I didn't know where to go. I couldn't tell my parents, so I came here.'

'My mother's here,' said Ben, 'you do realise that, don't you? She was exhausted after the events of last week. Dad's dying was bad enough, but to have the press vultures on her heels has made her ill. I want you to know that.'

'I do,' said Luke, looking up at Ben and then back at his empty glass. He waited the requisite beat for his sorrow to register, be accepted and then fade.

Then, seeing his opportunity, he added, 'I want to ask you a favour. Can you give me houseroom until I get things sorted out? It means I could be near them and see Patrick as often as possible; otherwise I don't quite know where I'll go. Money's going to be a problem too.'

'Houseroom?' said Ben, trying to keep the dismay out of his voice.

At the same time he realised he was completely cornered. Luke had made him a request that he couldn't refuse, in spite of what he had done. The family honour code dictated that they came to each other's rescue in times of emergency.

'Did you come all this way to ask me that?'

'Not exactly. I had to get out. Alice insisted.'

'Where are your parents?'

'I told you. I don't want to worry Mum and Dad at the moment. He's busy on some new commission and Mum, well you know Mum; she'll just panic and start bleating about Patrick and it's bad enough as it is.'

'Of course you can have a room,' said Ben quickly, melted by the thought of Patrick quite as much as his disgust at his own momentary lack of charity. 'I've got enough space, for God's sake. Of course you can. Do you want more whisky?'

'No, thanks. Houseroom here would be much appreciated tonight too.'

'You'd better work out what you're going to say to Patrick in the morning,' said Ben. 'He'll be flabbergasted to find you here. I'm not going to tell my mother yet.'

'I'm also going to have to work out what to say to him about me and his mother,' Luke added. He didn't seem to have heard what Ben had to say about his own mother. His problems were so pressing that he could only deal with the immediate horror.

'Does Patrick know how bad things are between you and his mother?' asked Charles quietly.

'I'm not sure. He knows something. Children are quick to sense an atmosphere, particularly an only child like Patrick.'

'Why not just say that his mother needed a break

and you decided to come and join us here. It's the truth, after all, and she might have changed her mind by the end of the weekend. She might be regretting it even as we speak.'

'Possibly,' said Luke as neutrally as he could, thinking that it was highly unlikely but that it would not do to disagree at this particular moment.

In the night, Ben was woken from a deep sleep by Patrick, a small, sodden creature stinking of pee. He realised that he had been dreaming of Marianne; that he had told her about Luke and she had said, 'But he's a snake in the grass,' and they were just discussing this when Patrick woke him.

'I've wet my bed,' he said, when Ben put the light on. 'I'm terribly sorry,' he added politely in one of his little old man phrases, but Ben could see that he was struggling to keep the tears back.

'What happened, old thing? Did you have a nightmare?'

'I think I must have done.'

'Do you want to tell me what it was about, while I get you some clean sheets?'

'I can't really remember,' said Patrick. 'Something about a tank coming up the path and Mum answering the door; then I woke up. I'm really sorry, Ben.'

'Don't give it another thought.' He thought about telling the boy that his father was also in the house but changed his mind. It would have to be a surprise for the morning when they were all feeling stronger. He got Patrick into his clean pyjamas and put him in the other bed, then stripped the wet sheets off and put them in the basket in the nursery bathroom next door. By the time he came back Patrick was asleep again, the traces of tears still visible on his cheeks. He wanted to kiss him but didn't for fear of waking him; instead, he allowed himself to stroke Patrick's cheek; there was still baby down on his jaw line and his own skin felt rough and dry like a little animal's. His vulnerability made Ben want to put his arms round him and hold him close.

Back in his room Ben reflected that he had never known about the trouble in his own parents' marriage. His mother had carried on as if everything was perfectly in order, as if she had the happiest marriage in the world. He had never seen his parents argue or even appear to have the faintest disagreement. The Old Man had a powerful, almost feudal sense of the importance of family which extended outwards to include his brother's tribe and his wife's family, even people who had worked for Jean's father before the Old Man had come on the scene; people like Jessie were members of the clan and subject to its protection as well as its laws. He thought of his father as being a bit like the boy holding his finger in the dyke. Now he was dead the force of the water might very well sweep them all away or at the very least turn all their interlinking worlds upside-down. There would be casualties; there was no doubt about that.

Cressida and Pete lived in the centre of Kirkcudbright in a handsome town house with dove-grey double doors, which were folded back during the day. From these doors you could see the granite war memorial to the dead of two wars in the shape of an obelisk (why always an obelisk?) and a wedge-shaped slice of the harbour where the fishing boats still came into roost as they had done time out of mind. There was a ruined castle (in very good repair) and Greyfriars church (where Jean and the young Macarthur had been married so many years before) and a little raised park with railings and a view of the estuary where at low tide the grey-brown mud lay in dull striations above the deep and treacherous channel where miniature whirlpools boiled and the green, green reeds rustled in the wind.

If you stepped into the small lobby between the outer and the inner door with its clear glass panels you could look right into the house where a wide hallway tiled with black-and-white tiles led to a broad staircase with an elegant balustrade that swept up and then round to a square landing with a dome where the filtered green light fell onto the polished boards. Behind the staircase to the left, a door led to the kitchen and the warren of rooms beyond, where another door opened onto the walled garden at the back of the house. The drawing-room was on the right of this hallway and the dining-room on the left; big square rooms that wouldn't have been out of place in a house in the New Town in Edinburgh, for this house was the same vintage.

Whenever Marianne came to Robert Maclaughlin House (for it was important enough to have a name as well as a number) she felt as if she were entering the kind of broad-shouldered dwelling that wouldn't have been out of place in a nineteenth-century French or even a Russian novel. There was something about the proportions of the place that spoke of solidness and seriousness of purpose, of the family as the centre and the aim of life; the family as an achievement in itself.

As soon as Marianne entered the house on Archie's heels she felt this aim, everything spoke of it from the children's toys in the hall – a tricycle and little container on wheels full of wooden bricks – to the faint scent of a hundred nutritious meals cooked in the kitchen beyond. It would be there upstairs in the settled look of the comfortable bedrooms; the way the last of the day's sunlight fell across the polished boards of the upstairs hall, catching the nap of the old and beautiful carpet in Cressida and Pete's room; the delicate edges of pillowcases; the fat fullness of the chintz roses in the spare-room curtains.

Cressida heard them come in and called out from the kitchen for them to join her. The kitchen, like the rooms at the front of the house, was large and square with wooden cupboards painted dark blue, a large table in the middle, and an old sloping tiled floor that was probably original. There was a dresser where Cressida displayed the lustreware she had started collecting when she was a student and a sofa under the window that looked out onto the garden.

She was stirring something in a saucepan on the inevitable Aga and looked like an advertisement for country living, Marianne thought: plump and prosperous.

'Smells good,' said Archie, going over to where Cressida stood and taking the spoon from her so that he could try for himself whatever it was.

'Not enough salt,' he said, handing it back.

'Here!' said Cressida, smacking him playfully on the backside. 'Leave off!

'He always thinks he can do everything better!' she exclaimed over her shoulder to Marianne, who was standing in the doorway thinking to herself that the pantomime had already started between Archie and Cressida. They each played up to the other as if they were some kind of bloody comic duo. It was impossible sometimes to get a word in when they were together arguing over recipes or politics or paintings, with Pete, who was usually exhausted after a day's work, going along with it on the side pretending to be entertained. Or perhaps he was. Perhaps he didn't feel as she did the perpetual outsider between her elder sister and her father; perhaps one had to be a sibling to know this feeling, this dull ache that lay somewhere between jealousy and boredom.

Once upon a time there had been her mother when she felt the need to retire from the gladiatorial combat that being Archie's child seemed to demand, but now there was only Archie strutting and posing like some sort of fighting cock demanding a contest.

Even going to Janet's grave had turned into a challenge as to who could show the least emotion.

They had walked out from the shore over the rippling sand past the deeper pools amongst the rocks, the water warm in the sunlight, where once Marianne would have spent an entire afternoon staring into the depths; those apparently aimless moments during which she was now convinced the self was somehow formed, as if the hard wiring of the brain needed this imaginative, bird-haunted solitude: the mournful cry of gulls wheeling amongst the thermals. The island was a scramble: stones turning to rough grass like iron filings that tore at one's hands, thistles as tall as a man, the deep, damp scent of the stands of bracken concealing what? Snakes and scuttling things. Marianne looked for flowers, dandelions like butter-yellow Catherine wheels of fire, the odd bit of ragwort, despised and poisonous but beautiful in its way, while Archie stumped along in his lace-up shoes like an elderly schoolboy in a grump.

Marianne watched him as they reached the cairn at the top of the island, a conical heap of stones gathered from all over with one large smooth oval stone to crown the pile, her name, 'JANET MACLEAN' and the dates of her birth and death; nothing else. No beloved this or that or even 'RIP'. Archie's curious eyes that were sometimes green and sometimes almost the colour of citrines gave nothing away as he looked down at the stone. Not a tear, not even a grimace, just a blank, a hard blank. Marianne put her bouquet down and looked away out to sea. There was another island beyond and beyond that probably another. We have to believe in the things we cannot see. 'Holy mother, pray for her,' she said to herself and then turned away, ignoring him.

'Archie will get us some drinks,' said Cressida, putting the lid back on the saucepan. 'There's wine in the fridge, Archie, or gin if you'd prefer,' she added, looking at her sister.

'Gin, I think,' said Archie. 'I'm in a gin mood. What about you?' he asked, also looking at Marianne.

'Whatever,' she said.

'Whatever is not an answer, madam. Wine or gin; just make your mind up.'

'Wine then,' she said abruptly, going over to the window and looking out at Cressida's pretty garden. There were some roses that caught her eye: palest pink with darker pink stripes that suddenly put her in mind of Ben's roses and the bouquet on his father's coffin that had shed their petals like sweets; roses that had seemed to condense a whole summer's sweetness. When she had come in the next day they had dropped most of their petals over her desk and she had liked them for that too, as if they had got bored of waiting to be admired and just given up the ghost.

She thought of Luke with a kind of scorn mingled with despair. She had loved him for a little while in a curious sort of way, but the spell was broken for good; that last time she had seen him as he was: needy, contemptible, intelligent, emotional, but ultimately cruel; all the good in him sacrificed to those moments when one dark facet of his nature ruled him completely. No one is all bad, she thought, or all good for that matter, but in the end one is forced to make a judgement.

'Penny for them,' said Cressida, handing her a glass. 'You're very quiet,' she said, 'and very thin. Do you eat properly?'

'Sometimes,' said Marianne, wondering how Cressida would react if she made comments about her size and asked if she ate properly, which she clearly did. Since the twins' birth four years before, Cressida had remained plump, which she grumbled about but made no apparent effort to correct.

'She needs fattening up, like me,' said Archie, patting his stomach.

'You should go on a diet,' said Cressida disapprovingly. 'You're far too fat. You'll have a heart attack.'

'I am on a diet,' said Archie. 'A grapefruit diet.'

'Yes, and we all know what that means. You eat a grapefruit first and then anything else you feel like. You always were a greedy pig.'

'You take after me,' said Archie, helping himself to a fist-full of nuts and eating one or two out of the corner of his hand like a child. 'You'll have to watch it yourself otherwise your husband will run off with his nurse.'

'No, he won't,' said Cressida. 'He likes me the way I am. He doesn't like his women too thin.'

'Just as well,' said Archie.

'Oh, shut up.'

And so it had gone on until Pete came in, hands and forearms scrubbed, white shirt open at the neck, jeans, deck shoes; very much the prosperous vet at home, the family man; Marianne could never look at his hands without wondering where they had been (she had once seen him delivering a calf up to his shoulder in the birth canal) but she liked Pete who was kind and good-humoured and put up with her bossy sister where another less patient man might have wanted to wring her neck.

'Can I see the kids?' asked Marianne when Pete had taken Archie off somewhere to show him some new piece of machinery he had acquired.

'They're asleep,' said Cressida, 'or should be.'

'I thought you might keep them up for us.'

'If I keep them up they won't sleep and then we get hell through the night. Pete's working terribly hard at the moment.'

'You're something else, aren't you?' said Marianne, fed up. 'I am their aunt and I never see them.'

'Well, you should come down more often and then you can see them in the day,' retorted Cressida. 'Dad says you're having a bad love affair. What's up?'

'Nothing's up. He's making it up as he goes along, as usual.'

'He seemed convinced about it.'

'Nothing's going on,' repeated Marianne stubbornly.

'But who is this man?'

'There isn't one.'

'Is he married? Is that why you're being so cagey?'

'I'm not being cagey. I just don't see what business it is of yours, that's all.'

'I do happen to be your elder sister.'

'And don't I know it,' said Marianne angrily. 'Stop pushing me around.'

'You're a hopeless case,' said Cressida, shaking her head. 'We try to help but you won't let us.'

'I don't need help.'

'Is it Mum? Is that what the matter is?'

'What about her?'

'Dad says you never grieved for her.'

'He won't let me,' said Marianne, getting to her feet. 'He won't bloody let me, that's why. We walked out there to her grave this evening but he just blanks me. He shows no emotion. I don't know why he suggested it in the first place or why I was stupid enough to go along with it.'

'Maybe it's hard for him too. Maybe he doesn't know how to show what he feels. He's always been a bit like that, you have to admit. We've always had to employ a bit of guesswork there. Mum said the same. It drove her mad. It's as if he daren't take the risk of revealing himself in case he gets damaged.'

Marianne noticed that her tone of voice had changed. She was always good when she stopped being bossy and really listened.

'But it's no good telling me I don't show enough emotion over Mum when he's like a stone himself.'

'I agree with you,' said Cressida. 'He's a hypocrite.'

'Did you know he was having an affair with Ben's ex-wife? She's coming to Carrick tomorrow night. I don't want her there. It feels like a violation somehow. Mum's house and all that.'

'He doesn't really tell me much about that side of things,' said Cressida, 'but I knew he was seeing her. She's quite a handful, or so I hear.'

'She ate Ben for breakfast, but I don't think she'll find Archie so chewy.'

'She's not his normal type,' said Cressida frowning. 'He hates all that aristocratic stuff.'

'Pretends to hate,' said Marianne, 'but loves the prestige it conveys, if the truth be known.'

'Don't let him hear you saying that. It'll offend all his cherished notions of meritocracy.'

'He's a hypocrite, as we've already agreed. Says one thing, does another.'

'What are you two squabbling about?' asked Archie, as he came back in with Pete.

'We're not squabbling,' said Marianne. 'We were just talking about the Macarthurs.'

'And your new girlfriend,' added Cressida, just to show her sister that she was with her on this one.

'What new girlfriend?'

'Oh, come on,' said Cressida. 'Your secret is out.'

'I don't know what you're talking about.'

He knew perfectly well of course, but definitely did not wish to discuss it with his highly critical daughters. He feared them together although he would never have admitted it. This evening at Janet's grave he had found that he could not recall his wife's face, a disconcerting thing for an artist, but he had been able to conjure Mrs Mackenzie's without even trying. He had decided that he could love her if she would let him, but he wasn't at all sure she would. Diana he had not given a thought to.

'Do you want a walk up to the house to see what's happening?' Hugo asked Diana on the Saturday morning. They were sitting in the kitchen having breakfast or what passed for it.

Only Hugo could still enjoy the Mother's Pride or its white, flabby equivalent and find the coffee not stale, having not been kept in an airtight jar. It was all very well to be comfortless in grand surroundings – at least one could feast the eye if not the body – but not to have a clue how to live properly in reduced circumstances really was the pits, Diana thought, pushing her cup of pigswill away from her. She was secretly longing for a drink but didn't want Hugo to know this.

'Do I have to?'

'No, of course not. I thought you might be interested in what the Loebs are doing.'

'Why should I want to know that? I think you should have gone somewhere further away,' said Diana, 'and not just hung around on the doorstep. It's not healthy, this obsession with seeing what's happening; it's like picking a scab, for God's sake. Is there any orange juice?'

'There's a carton in the larder,' said Hugo, rising to his feet. 'I'll get it.'

While he was out of the kitchen, Diana took a glass from the draining board and went along the dark tiled passage to the sitting-room where there was a tray of bottles and decanters. She caught Macneil's eye as she took the stopper out of the decanter of gin and laid it with care on the silver tray, which she knew bore the inscription 'Baghdad, 1919', under all the bottles. 'Piss off,' she said aloud in Macneil's direction. 'It was all right for you. Anyway, you look ridiculous in that outfit.'

Her ancestor was dressed in a kilt with a tartan cape over one shoulder and a bonnet with a feather in it. On his feet he wore elaborate cross-laced black leather pumps.

When she left, as she looked in her driving mirror Diana could see Hugo standing in the porch at the front of the house holding Bracken, the lurcher, by the collar. Hugo's sparse hair was standing on end, one of his shirt tails was hanging out of his trousers and he was wearing his red leather slippers whose appearance invariably shocked her. As she watched him recede it occurred to her that he was the only man she had ever truly loved.

Archie had got up early and gone off painting by the time Marianne woke up. From the kitchen window she could see the sea, the same colour as cellophane, lying in glittering sheets on the horizon. The tide was right up because the phalli were just visible, their tips glistening in the sunlight. Sometimes when it was hot, as it promised to be today, the butter-coloured Charolais/Hereford crosses that the local farmer favoured wandered ankle-deep across the shore wading through the in-coming tide, the bull leading a column of heifers oriental-style. It was one of Archie's favourite sights and one he had painted many times (there was one in the Scottish National Gallery) not least, Marianne suspected, because it was his view of what relations between the sexes should be.

She made herself coffee and then, having dressed, took her swimming things and went out of the house towards the sea. She crossed the overgrown lawn at the front of the house, ignoring the unweeded border by the wall where a few brave peonies were blooming defiantly in pink-satin splendour, and walked down the slope to the place where the lawn joined the grassy track that led towards the sea. Once, before she got ill, her mother Janet had made a vegetable garden to one side of the lawn, a large oval of earth surrounded by wire to stop the rabbits and the roe deer from helping themselves to the spoils; very little remained of this endeavour now; just a grassy mound sprouting the odd carrot or leek, although the rocket had seeded and run wild in scarecrow shapes providing a rich harvest for the rabbits. At one end there was a row of lettuces gone so toweringly, grotesquely to seed that even the rabbits and roe deer ignored it. Since her mother died the whole place was overlain with this feeling of desolation as if war or revolution had swept away the loving care that had once been lavished on it, rather than merely the more commonplace theme of illness and death.

Archie loved the house but his anarchic streak meant that the garden was as interesting to him untended as it had been when Janet had been alive. He liked the long grass and the feeling of being overrun by nature. He did not seem to feel, as Marianne did, that the wreck of her mother's garden was a symbol for the wreck of their little family. Her grandparents were dead, and as both her parents had been only children, there were no cousins to offer sanctuary. She loved her sister Cressida but Cressida had inherited their mother's knack of being able to make a house a home; such tired, overused little words, but so essential to being able to function properly and without which one quietly starved to death, emotionally speaking; and she no longer needed Marianne in the same way now that she had Pete and the children.

Archie had set up his easel and was painting, as a warm-up exercise, a view of the jetty and the beach by the ruined summer house which hikers or kids from Kirkcudbright had set fire to a few years before; the graffiti of doped-out lovers adorned the stones. 'Jenny sucks Kevin's dick', etc, and the remains of fires in several places in the ruins of the interior testified to its continued illicit usage.

The upper part of the beach was composed of stones and boulders, but the lower part was smooth, pale sand. As a child, Marianne had swum in the Easter Sea, her limbs mottled with cold; so cold in fact that she remembered the sensation of coming back into the thawing edges of her body as if the whole of the rest of her, the jelly centre of the bones, the blood and water, had frozen solid, rendering her

241

impervious to the element in which she plunged. She had been a passionate swimmer on this treacherous coast. The water had pulled her into its embrace like a lover in a trance.

Then, at fifteen, she had gone to Spain and found a warm, tideless, glittering sea which, unlike her own restless shore, simply rocked to and fro like wine in a glass. The first time she swam in the Solway after that she had felt as if her body was descending painfully into a tub of needles and she realised she had lost her childhood immunity to her own coastline. From being an elemental part of it she became an adult picking and squealing along the edge of the waves, where once she had plunged thoughtless into its sandy, salty depths heedless of the jellyfish that drifted like sightless eyes.

'Hello,' Archie said, reaching down for a tube of colour, and then squinting up at her, seeing her not as face but as an exercise in light and shade, the gleam of cheekbone or the bridge of a nose as a dab of white lead, a cloud of hair a dash of charcoal with an underpinning pinch of red like a trace of flame.

'Hello, Dad. It's me, Marianne, your daughter.'

'I know who it is,' Archie replied unsmilingly, leaning down again to rummage for something else in the ancient canvas knapsack he used for carting his gear around in when he was painting outdoors.

The more she pushed the further he retreated from her.

'I'm going for a swim,' she said, turning away. It was hopeless to try to talk to him when he was in this mood, 'and then I'm going to take the car and go into Kirkcudbright to get a few things. Is there anything you want?'

'We'll need some more drink if Diana's coming. And something for tonight's dinner, a joint maybe?'

'OK. Money?'

She thought that she would talk to him in future using as few words as possible; he probably wouldn't notice.

'There's some in my jacket pocket. I think it's hanging over the back of my chair in the kitchen.'

He glanced at her. 'Are you OK?'

'Fine. I'm off now. See you later.'

If he felt rebuffed he didn't show it. When she glanced over her shoulder as she picked her way down the beach he was engaged in some painterly task or other. She had always envied painters their accoutrements; there were so many displacement activities they could legitimately indulge in: fiddling with colour, washing brushes, mixing things; whereas writers had paper and pen or a screen and that was it. Anything other than staring out of the window was an illegitimate activity, punishable by lacerating feelings of guilt, or so her writers told her.

Ben had avoided seeing Luke on Saturday morning by taking Patrick with him on an early site visit to Barhill. He told the boy that his father had arrived late in the night as a surprise but would need to have a lie-in if he was to be on form for their picnic lunch on the beach, an explanation Patrick accepted without demur.

Barhill was an eighteenth-century house – unusual for the locality – and particularly unusual in its design, which was based on Lord Burlington's breakfast pavilion at Chiswick House in London. One of Andrew Murray's forbears had been on the Grand Tour and had been determined to introduce his own little piece of neo-classical beauty into the familiar landscape of his own estate; a long, winding driveway led from the road and meandered towards the house which suddenly revealed itself around the last corner and invariably made people who saw it for the first time gasp slightly. The simple stucco façade concealed an interior of considerable beauty that had been allowed to decline over the last century into an unloved white elephant.

The Victorian owners had removed the graceful double staircase and put in a solid, carved wood affair encased in brown varnish. The kitchens and pantries had become squalid; the beautiful marble floors were discoloured and, in places, simply boarded over; the bedrooms had ceilings that leaked; and some of the fireplaces had been removed by Murray's father for reasons unknown.

Ben's job had been to restore the house according to the plans drawn up for Percival Murray in 1780 and he was extremely pleased with the results, as was Andrew Murray himself who greeted Ben with relish when he arrived and made a fuss of Patrick.

'Hello, young man,' he said. 'Let me show you my new/old house, restored by your uncle.'

He took Patrick by the hand, with Ben in tow, and explained the glories of the copied double staircase, reproduced faithfully in every detail by an artisans' cooperative started by the Old Man near Biggar some years before; the marble floors cleaned and re-laid, and in certain places such as the dining-room completely renewed. The mouldings had been copied by skilled plasterers, the dry rot cured, the windows copied and replaced; the whole effect being one of restrained elegance with a pleasing and somehow gleaming austerity which made visitors exclaim and Murray beam with pride.

Towards the end, Murray, still holding Patrick by the hand, led him into a back sitting-room which had the blinds drawn down. He went to the window and let one set of blinds up, allowing sunlight to flood the embrasure.

'Do you know who that painting is by?' he asked, pointing to a Monet of water lilies that hung over the fireplace. In the partial light, the painting seemed to float in space as if a little fragment of the lake itself had been captured within the frame.

'No.' Patrick shook his head, glancing round for Ben.

'It's by Monet,' said Murray proudly. 'Beautiful, isn't it?'

'Yes,' said Patrick uncertainly.

'Your uncle said it should hang there,' said Murray, 'and I think he's right. He's been right about everything else. That's why I've recommended him to the Prince of Wales, if he's got the time of course now that he's so busy. How's the Castle Forbes project coming along?' Murray asked, going to the window and drawing the blind down again so that the room was once more in the half-dark and the lilies retreated into their own mystery.

'Slowly,' said Ben. 'I do plans; they like some things and don't like others, but the whole process takes a long time because they're always on the move. It's also a matter of restraining some of their wilder ideas which the planning committee would simply throw out.'

'Such as?'

'One thing I had to squash was their idea of having an indoor swimming pool in the old servants' hall. Even Victorian additions are held to be sacred these days.'

'Unlike in our parents' time,' said Andrew, 'when they appeared to glory in destroying what had been handed down to them. You were fortunate in that your father was always one step ahead of the game in that respect. How's your mother, by the way?'

'Not very well, I'm afraid. The strain of the last weeks has completely exhausted her.'

'Give her my best wishes,' said Murray. 'Now, young man,' he said to Patrick, 'would you like a swim before you go?'

'Thanks so much,' said Ben swiftly, answering for him, 'but we have to get on into Kirkcudbright for various reasons. A kind offer.'

'What did you think of Mr Murray?' he asked Patrick once they were in the car.

'He looks like a hamster,' said Patrick. 'He wouldn't let go of my hand. I'm not a baby, you know.'

'Of course not. Did you like his painting?'

'No. I thought it was boring.'

'Cost a few million,' said Ben, glancing with amusement at Patrick.

As they were talking, Ben's mobile phone rang.

'I'll get it,' said Patrick, snatching it up before Ben could stop him.

'It's Dad,' he said excitedly, 'but he's going to meet us in Kirkcudbright.'

'OK,' said Ben. 'Sit down, Lolly,' he added over his shoulder.

'She thinks it's time for a walk,' he said to Patrick, 'I meant to give her a run along the beach, but I didn't have time.'

Marianne parked Archie's old Volvo by the war memorial and glanced in the direction of Cressida's house across the road, but the double doors were shut, a sure sign that the family was out on some Saturday expedition somewhere. She then turned and walked down the broad pavement in the direction of the harbour with the car park in the centre of the square to her right and the ruined castle directly ahead.

As a boy, Archie had grown up in Forge Cottage opposite the castle and had fished for crabs from his bedroom window when the tide was up. Marianne crossed the car park and walked up the worn steps between the railings, past the old mine that had been turned into a collecting box for beleaguered fishermen. She was heading for the little park with a bench or two in it next to Greyfriars Church that had a very good view of what fishing boats happened to be in harbour at that time. When she had been a pupil at the Academy she had lingered in this place for an illicit fag or to meet some boy or other before they went home on the bus but it felt odd to come back here as an adult, somehow dissociated from the person she had once been; the same but different. She intended to sit there for a moment in order to enjoy the harbour view before going to do her shopping. Then she would meet up with Ben.

As she sat there, she noticed a boy with a dog quite far away from her up at the other end by the church. The boy was throwing sticks for the dog who didn't always return with them when she should. He was calling to her to come back to him.

As she was watching, the dog did something very strange: it took the stick that it had dropped back into its mouth and began to run in demented, ever-widening circles; after a few laps it suddenly took it into its head to rush off the length of the small green, past Marianne, down the steps and out into the car park.

'Lolly, come here!' yelled the boy, but the dog paid no attention whatsoever.

The boy, whom Marianne now realised was Patrick Macarthur, ran after it, shouting with excitement.

A car, a four-wheel drive, with massive bull bars, was coming out of the car park at a fair clip. Marianne watched as the boy ran straight in front of it. The dog was out in the road by this time, which ironically was empty of traffic. There was a noise, a kind of thud; the child was picked up, as if by a giant hand, and thrown to one side where he fell and lay motionless.

Then several things happened at once. The car stopped abruptly, so abruptly that another vehicle behind ran slap into it. Someone somewhere screamed. Later, Marianne realised it had been she who screamed. At the time, the sound seemed to come from somewhere below her. Everything seemed to go into slow motion. The driver of the car leapt out and ran to where the child lay. She had a mobile telephone in her hand and was gabbling into it. The driver of the car behind, another woman, also ran to the child, leaving the driver's door open. Marianne by this time was also moving herself in the direction of the child. To her right, she saw that someone had grabbed the dog and was holding it very tightly by its collar.

Then she saw Luke, his face contorted. She couldn't understand what he was doing there. It was like a dream where the people one is connected with all appear at once in surroundings both familiar and yet strangely alien. Luke didn't belong here; she couldn't understand it. There was the sound of a siren; by the mercy of God the local ambulance station was round the corner. The vehicle tore into the car park and came to an abrupt tyre-squealing halt, like something out of a TV drama. Marianne remembered noticing the light revolving like a synthetic egg yolk in the continuing brilliance of the sunlight.

A man and a woman in green overalls on their

knees and Luke again, his face tender with grief (she had never seen him so broken down, so softened before) staring down at the child who lay as still as a stonefish resting on the bottom of the ocean, his head to one side, the angle unnatural as if some internal stalk had been snapped. The ambulance people gabbled into their fronts and then conferred. A third one appeared with a stretcher onto which Patrick's motionless body was deftly manoeuvred as if he weighed no more than an ice-cream wafer. Luke followed the stretcher through the open doors of the ambulance.

The dog, poor beast, was still being held by an onlooker and was twisting inside its collar, desperate to get to its owner. The ambulance doors closed and it swerved away towards the war memorial, turning right in the direction, Marianne assumed, of the cottage hospital.

At that moment a police car appeared, siren going, revolving egg-yolk whirling, and two heavily built policemen got out. The driver of the Range Rover that had been going too fast out of the car park, Marianne now recognised as Diana Forbes. She was standing next to where Patrick had been deposited by the impact and was talking loudly to Ben Macarthur. The two policemen and the driver of the other car joined them at the same time as Marianne.

'He ran right out in front of me, silly little bugger,' Diana was saying or, rather, shouting, clearly distraught. 'He was chasing your fucking dog. What was I supposed to do, tell me that? It's typical of you that you weren't watching him carefully enough. You never had any bloody sense.'

'Now calm down, madam,' said one of the policemen sternly. 'We need to establish exactly what happened.'

'I've just told you what happened,' said Diana. 'If he,' she pointed at Ben, 'had been paying attention, this would never have happened, but he's always in a bloody dream; always off somewhere else in his head.'

'Look; can we go somewhere else?' said Ben quietly to the other policeman who was thinner and fairer than the first one. 'She could do with a cup of tea. I think she's in shock.'

'The first thing we have to do is to breathalyse the driver of the car that hit the boy,' the fair policeman answered, sensibly sticking to basics. 'If you'll come this way, please, madam.'

'No, I fucking won't,' said Diana furiously. 'Why don't you listen to what I'm telling you? He ran out in front of me. It was an accident. I didn't bloody mean to run him down. You carry on as if it was something I . . .'

'Have you been drinking, madam?' interrupted the first policeman, whose meaty face and fat pink forearms gave him the slightly swollen look of a cartoon policeman.

'What sort of question is that?' demanded Diana. 'I tell you, it was an accident. There was nothing I could have done to prevent it.'

'If you'll come this way, madam,' said the cartoon policeman, taking Diana's arm.

'Do as he says, Diana,' said Ben urgently, 'otherwise you'll make everything worse.'

'She was driving too quick,' said a different male voice. 'Those big cars give the driver an illusion they're not travelling as fast as they are. I watched her. She was doing about forty which is hellish speedy in a confined space like this.'

'That's not fucking true!' shouted Diana. 'You're all out . . .'

'Diana,' said Ben, 'do as you're told. There is nothing to be gained from behaving like this.'

As the cartoon policeman was taking Diana away, the second policeman began to interview the driver of the car behind. Marianne went over to where Ben stood and touched his shoulder.

'I saw everything,' she said. 'There was nothing you could have done.

'You couldn't have done anything,' she repeated. 'I was there. I saw it all. Everything. It was one of those things. You mustn't blame yourself. But why was he by himself with Lolly? I didn't realise whose dog it was until too late.'

'I didn't leave him alone with her. I left him with Luke,' said Ben. 'I'm not that stupid; I know what she's like. She hadn't had a walk this morning.'

'Well, where was Luke then?' Marianne was aghast. She couldn't believe Luke had just left Patrick on his own – it wouldn't have mattered too much if there hadn't been the dog, but everyone who knew Lolly knew she was the canine equivalent of an hysteric, and one hell of a handful.

Ben wiped the back of his knuckles across his eyes like a schoolboy. 'I don't know where he was,' he said. 'I left them together while I went to the electrician round the corner.'

Marianne stared at him, not knowing what to say, then she put her arms round him and held him close, as a mother might do. He was trembling.

'Do you want me to come with you to the hospital?'

'No, I'll be all right. Thanks anyway.'

'Diana is supposed to be coming to our house at Carrick.'

He stared at Marianne and then looked away. 'I'll have to deal with her first. If the breath test is positive she could be charged with manslaughter.'

'You don't know what's happened yet,' said Marianne. 'I'd better go and call Archie and tell him what's happened. Will you ring me and let me know about Patrick?'

'Of course.'

He stuffed the piece of paper into the back pocket of his jeans. Looking at his feet, she noticed he was wearing the same make of boots that Archie liked to buy from the harbour shop and wondered why she hadn't noticed before.

She watched him go across to where the policemen stood. He obviously mentioned her name because the policemen glanced in her direction and the younger, blond one indicated that he would be with her shortly.

Diana was sitting in the police car looking straight

ahead. It was not clear what the outcome of the breath test had been. When Marianne glanced at her watch, she realised it was only eleven thirty. A whole lifetime seemed to have passed since she parked the Volvo by the war memorial. She found that she wanted to cry. Cressida would still be out and her mother who she yearned for was dead. There was Archie, but he would probably be unavailable, as usual; never there when he was needed. She looked in her bag for her mobile phone and dialled the number at Carrick but there was no reply.

She could visualise the phone ringing and ringing in the kitchen. The tide would be on the ebb by now, the cattle would have returned to the higher pastures and the little boy, held forever in her memory as a silent shape on the ungiving tarmac, might have moved beyond to the unknown regions, his childhood ended as randomly as one might decide to blow out a candle. Even when her own mother died she had not been quite so aware of the difference between life and death; it was not a border post or a river, as the ancients had thought but a thread, finer than a hair, which could break at any point without warning.

The thinner of the policemen, a youngish blond man with a crew cut, approached Marianne in order to question her about what she had seen. He looked ridiculously vulnerable and young without his hat, a baby in charge of law and order and Diana. Marianne did not envy him his task there. Corralling Diana was like trying to capture a wild animal; only a stun gun and a big stick would do. How could such a woman have been married to Ben? How could her father be interested in a woman like that? Maybe he was just 'sick in the heed', as her fellow Scots would say.

When she had told the policeman what she had seen – the boy with the dog and then the car, simple but deadly, she decided to go to the cottage hospital and see if she could find out what was happening. It was then that it occurred to her that Luke would be there. In the shock of it all she had forgotten the physical presence of Luke; in her mind he was compartmentalised as a man she saw in Edinburgh but never in her own place in Marchmont and never in his; there was nothing to anchor him to her domestic life (what on earth had he been doing here for instance?) or to any other part of it she shared with people she knew; they had no common environment, no mutual friends – other than Ben of course – only a sexual connection: an act performed in a certain place at a certain level of intensity that she had firmly dissociated herself from upon that last occasion.

The cottage hospital was a small place, cosy in comparison to the huge hospitals in big cities that Marianne had occasionally encountered. She had come here as a child with Saturday-night tonsillitis that her mother thought might have been meningitis, and dimly remembered her grandfather Maclean dying in here when she was about three or maybe less; Archie holding her up so that the dying man could see the future like Simeon and the infant Christ. Lord let now thy servant depart in peace, but only if it's time, Lord; not a child, please God, not that. All right some

255

dribbling old man. But where the hell are you when you're needed? Lord God of Saboath by cool Siloam's shady rill on a green hill without a city wall, where are you?

When she got there, however, she found that Luke and Patrick had been taken by ambulance on to Dumfries Infirmary where there were the facilities to deal with serious medical emergencies. Luke must have informed Ben by mobile phone of what was happening because there was no sign of him when she went back to the car park. It might never have happened. Under all the horror she found herself thinking tenderly of Ben. She could remember the shape of his body in her arms, the deep cleft in his back where his spine ran into his buttocks. His obvious anguish had torn at her like a claw; she wanted to comfort him. What did it say in the 'Song of Solomon'? 'Stay me with flagons, comfort me with apples.'

Cressida was still out so Marianne went to the supermarket just up the hill. Inside, she tried to remember what she was doing there amongst the gross banality of the special offers, the cheeky chappies behind the cold meat counter in their white overalls and paper hats, the world of oven bags and greaseproof paper. Accidents happen. The world goes on wiping its arse and descaling its taps or thinking about gadgets to stop the fizz going out of plastic bottles. In the drinks section she selected a bottle of wine and then dropped it with a huge smash onto the linoleum floor. The manager came, a boy she had known at the Academy, Iain Cruickshank. He instantly recognised her, told her not to worry; accidents happen, and then, when Marianne burst into a storm of tears, took her into his office and found his secretary who stayed her with flagons in the shape of a cup of extremely hot, sweet tea in a Styrofoam cup.

Marianne sat on Iain's hideous office chair, a revolving object covered in a particular brand of grey-flecked tweed apparently only available to car manufacturers and the makers of office furniture. She called Archie again on her mobile and got hold of him this time. When she told him what had happened, he said that she had better come and fetch him as Diana would probably need help with the fuzz, who always got everything wrong, and if he knew anything about Diana she'd probably rub them up the wrong way. She had a knack for it, he said; it was *noblesse oblige* gone rancid; one more reason for bringing on the guillotine.

Why do you care if you feel like that, Marianne wanted to ask, but knew better than to ask. It was abundantly clear to her, yet again, that Archie was enjoying himself hugely. Like a gleeful schoolboy he loved other people's trouble. And, as for Diana, it was clear to Marianne watching her performance with the police that she was a woman in deep, deep trouble, not just because of what had happened with Patrick – as if that wasn't bad enough – but also because it was clear that her whole attitude to the world was built on a platform of aggression, and the only reason for that, Marianne reckoned, was pain. Aggressive people were people in pain; it was a *sine qua non.*

She drank up her tea, found Iain and thanked him.

'I'm married now,' he said, 'to Kirsty Johnson. You could come and have tea with us.' He was living up in some of the new housing by the cemetery, he said. 'Come round.' She thanked him and said yes, knowing she wouldn't.

Back at Carrick, Archie was ready to take charge. He had put on a suit, a Harris tweed three-piece that would repel bullets and hail stones should they attempt a *putsch*, the kind of suit Mallory and his friends would have worn in the nineteen twenties to scale Everest in, the kind of suit that would have scaled Everest on its own given half a chance.

'Why are you wearing that?' asked Marianne, drawing up outside the back door.

'Authority, my dear,' said Archie, getting into the car. 'The fuzz up here still respects a man in a decent suit.'

'A suit of armour, do you mean? Where's your lance?'

'Don't mock me,' said Archie, lighting a large cigar although it was still early for such indulgences. 'Seriously, hen,' he said, 'something pretty awful occurred, huh?'

'Terrible,' said Marianne. 'It all just happened in a flash: man, dog, boy, stick; then suddenly out of all the joy something terrible: a car going too fast, a child not looking, a dog not obeying. It was terrible.'

And terrible because afterwards it had seemed inevitable, as if someone had choreographed it.

'And how is he, the wee man?'

'Nobody knows,' said Marianne. 'I went to the cottage hospital but he'd been taken to the Infirmary. I suppose I should have known.'

'Go straight to the hospital,' said Archie. 'I know the matron. She can ring through and find out what's going on. Let's set your mind at rest.'

'Are you sure?'

'Aye.' Archie put his hand on her arm. 'I can see you need to know. So that's what we'll do. We'll find out the important stuff first and then take it from there, OK, hen?'

At the cottage hospital Archie continued to smoke his cigar with lordly indifference to the 'NO SMOK-ING' signs that were displayed everywhere.

'That's just to keep the masses down,' he said when Marianne pointed it out to him. 'You can't expect a man to put out a good Havana cigar until he's ready to.'

When Matron came, a lardy blonde run to fat with a bosom like a landslide, she also ignored the cigar to Marianne's astonishment.

'I haven't seen this young lady for a while,' she said to Archie, as if Marianne was still a child (an autistic one at that). 'It's great to see you, Archie; how's life treating you these days? Pretty good by the looks of it,' she added admiringly, taking in the suit and the cigar, and the brogues he now bought from Edinburgh's most exclusive men's shoe shop.

'We need to know about a wee boy,' said Archie. 'Patrick Macarthur. Got run down this morning in the car park. He was chasing a dog and ran in front of a car, a big one, you know, with bull bars.'

Matron tut-tutted and shook her head. 'If I had my way, those cars would be banned. We've had several sets of injuries this year alone due to those things and there's no need for them. Give me a moment and I'll see what I can find out. He's gone to the Infirmary, I dare say; if it's very serious they'll have taken him to Glasgow, poor wee thing.'

She came back after five minutes. 'He's badly concussed and they're running checks on him for internal damage at Dumfries, but it looks as if he might have been lucky, God be thanked.' She crossed herself.

'A child's death is always a hard one. Thank the Lord it didn't happen.'

'I saw him,' said Marianne, wiping her eyes, 'and he looked terrible. I was convinced he was dead.'

'Well, Mother Nature has a way sometimes,' burbled Matron, looking as if she would rather like to employ one of Mother Nature's other ways with Archie.

'She fancies you rotten,' said Marianne crossly when they were back in the car.

'Who?'

'Matron, Nancy or whatever she's called.'

'I have that effect on women,' said Archie modestly.

Diana was sitting in an interview room in the police station in a state of helpless despair. The breath test had been positive, as she knew it would be. She had made another visit to her father, the second in a short period of time, which had necessitated a visit to the Craigie Arms, a pub at the end of the road where the home was. The Craigie Arms boasted what was grandly termed a 'cocktail lounge', which merely described a dark brown room where women could drink out of sight of the public bar and the leering males who hung about in such places during the day.

Diana had been in there alone apart from a tiny shrivelled old woman in a heavy tweed coat who was hunched over a glass of Guinness; an escapee by the looks of things from the home up the road. The sort of person, Diana feared, that she might become herself. She'd had several whiskies – even 'large' pub whiskies seemed pathetic by her standards and hardly seemed to dent the functioning of the conning tower – and then set off for the centre of Kirkcudbright where she wanted to get some drink for Archie before making her way to Carrick. She had intended to go slowly along the beautiful road via Borgue that followed the shore, and had even considered stopping to lose herself in the view: the grey-blue bars of sea running into the pale hyacinth of the horizon, the eerie sound of gulls to comfort her. She had thought of herself walking across the rutted fields towards the sea and finding some kind of peace by communing with nature as Hugo did.

The sound of the child's body as it connected with her car would haunt her forever. She remembered a time in France some years before when she had been on honeymoon with Ben; she had been driving down a tiny lane very fast and had run over a cat; the sound had been much the same: a heart-stopping thud and then a bump as the wheel went over the body. The cat had screamed and then stopped abruptly. Ben had been terribly concerned about the cat; she remembered that and she had felt so guilty that she had lost her temper with him and said something horrible like 'It's only a fucking cat so stop fussing.'

When Archie came in she got up and then sat down again. The girl, the young, sulky one, Marianne, was with him. For some reason he was dressed like Edward VII at Sandringham; all he lacked was a Homburg hat and a cane.

'God, you look extraordinary!' she said, starting to laugh. When Archie came over and put his arms round her, the laughter turned to tears.

'It's all right,' said Archie. 'He's OK. You didn'y kill him, somehow; he'll live; he's OK. But you shouldn't drive so fast; I'm always telling you.'

'How do you know that?' she asked sharply, ignoring the second part of what he said.

'I went to the cottage hospital and got them to ring Dumfries. He'll live, it's official.'

'Oh, thank God!' she said. 'Thank God, thank God!' Then she started to cry again. Archie winked at Marianne over Diana's head and raised his eyebrows. See what women are, he seemed to say; see how they need us. Marianne scowled at him and made as if to leave.

'Where're you off to, may I ask?'

'I'm going home,' she said. 'You two can stay here. I've had enough for one day.'

'OK,' said Archie. 'You take the Volvo and I'll bring Diana back when they've finished with her. I happen to know she's insured for anyone to drive.'

Patrick was in a special room on his own surrounded by machinery. He was on a drip. His father sat by his side and looked up when Ben's face appeared at the glass, motioning with his head for Ben to come in.

'How is he?' he mouthed across the hump under the blanket that was Patrick. His head on the pillow looked too large for the thin outline beneath the blanket. Hospital did that to you, Ben reflected, gazing down at the child; illness drew attention to certain parts of the anatomy like a magnifying glass; he thought of the other invalid now dead who had been so close to him and of how death had drained him out so that he had lain beached in his bed like a rotting hulk that had once been human. In Patrick's stillness he thought he could see a similar process at work.

'He's concussed,' said Luke quietly, 'but they don't think it's any worse than that. They'll keep him here for a day or so to be sure, however. Thank God we're in Scotland where you can still get what passes for decent emergency medical care.'

Ben frowned. 'Has he come to? Has he spoken to you?'

'He did a bit earlier. He said, "Hello, Dad," and something about Lolly. Did you get her all right?'

'Yes, thanks,' said Ben. He waited for a moment,

wondering if he could ask the vital question now or whether he should leave it. It occurred to him that perhaps Luke hadn't given an account of his whereabouts out of respect for the sickroom. Instead, he asked about Alice.

'She's on her way,' said Luke, avoiding Ben's gaze.

'Did you tell her what had happened?'

'Of course I did.'

'Where were you?' asked Ben. 'He was on his own with Lolly.'

'I just nipped off to get a packet of fags from the newsagents on the corner. I could see him from where I was the whole time. If Diana hadn't been driving so fucking fast it would never have happened. I hope the police are going to prosecute her.'

'You shouldn't have left him with Lolly on his own,' Ben said. 'You knew that.'

'Well, look,' said Luke, getting up and motioning to Ben to go out of the room, 'all's well that ends well.'

'That's all very well for you to say now,' said Ben angrily, 'but he was very nearly killed.'

'Your ex-wife is responsible for that, not I,' said Luke.

'You left him,' said Ben. 'You were the primary failure, not Diana. Why don't you admit it?'

'Because there's no point in dwelling on it,' said Luke. 'If it gets your ex-wife off the road, then all is indeed well.'

'I don't believe this,' said Ben. 'Look at him! If you'd been there, this would never have happened.'

There seemed to be something missing in Luke, as

if a vital piece of moral machinery were simply not functioning. Ben could tell his cousin didn't understand what he was getting at, or possibly couldn't understand because he did not have the means. It was this lack that had enabled him to sell the story to the press without compunction, to weigh things only according to how they affected him, not anyone else. The remorse came from being found out but did not spring from the original act of treachery.

'I think you're making a mountain out of a molehill,' said Luke, fumbling in his pocket for a cigarette. 'My main hope is that they'll do Diana. That's what I told Alice and she agreed with me. She's a danger to others, she said.'

'They will without the shadow of a doubt,' said Ben wearily, reminded of his earlier feelings about Luke the previous night, and that it was up to him somehow to hold all this together. 'She failed the breath test. The desk sergeant called me to tell me.'

'So what happens now?'

'They'll charge her with dangerous driving, bail her and release her.'

'I'm going to press for a custodial sentence,' said Luke, getting up to go back into the room where Patrick was. 'She's lucky not to be on a manslaughter charge.'

'I know,' said Ben, following him. 'I realise that.'

He wanted Luke to calm down a little. It couldn't be good for Patrick, semi-conscious, to hear the venom in his father's voice.

'What time is Alice coming?'

'She should be here in about two hours.'

'Do you want me to meet her?'

'Thanks,' said Luke, bending over his son, every inch the solicitous parent, 'I'd be very grateful.'

'You'd better tell me what happened before we go in,' said Alice as she sat with Ben in Luke's car in the hospital car park. 'If I know Luke, he'll alter everything subtly. I want the unedited version first.'

'What did he tell you?'

'Just enough so that I knew Patrick was OK. That was all I cared about.'

She looked at Ben. 'I suppose he told you about Duncan's visit last night?'

'Yes, he did.'

'I'm going to leave him,' said Alice. 'I've had enough, Ben. It was the last straw. I wanted to be angry with Duncan, I wanted to be able to say I didn't believe him, but I knew he was telling the truth and Luke wasn't.'

'I'm sorry, Alice,' said Ben, putting his arms round her. Her shoulders were dreadfully thin and sad. She felt unloved and lonely. She sobbed in a dry, terrifying way as if emotion were an infection to be spewed out as quickly as possible.

'I'm sorry too,' she said, opening her handbag to look for a tissue, 'but Patrick on top of everything is more than I can deal with at the moment.

'What exactly did happen this morning? I know Patrick's a handful sometimes. Luke said he ran away after the dog and wouldn't stop.

'He's like that. He takes it into his head to do something and doesn't stop to think of the consequences, but that's boys for you. It's your ex-wife that caused the problem. I hope they prosecute her. I actually hope they might send her to jail.'

'Luke left him on his own with Lolly,' said Ben. 'Did he tell you that bit?'

Alice looked at him in disbelief. 'No, he didn't,' she said. 'He just said that Patrick ran off and then Diana ran him down. He must have been too ashamed of himself to admit the truth. Why did he leave him?'

'He told me he went to buy some cigarettes in the corner shop opposite the park where Patrick and Lolly were. I couldn't get him to understand that if he hadn't done that, then what followed would probably not have come to pass. Diana deserves what's coming to her, but Luke is also responsible.'

'That's Luke all over,' said Alice wearily. 'I used to think he was confused and complicated – he is both – but I've since come to believe that he is also amoral. I can't take any more. I want a marriage that I'm a loving part of, not this sham; I want better for Patrick. I want somebody who protects me, not the other way round. Your father paid me to stay – did you know that?'

'What?'

'He paid me – or rather he put money in an account for Patrick – and I stayed.'

'I knew he was paternalistic,' said Ben, 'but I'd no idea it went that far. Family always meant everything to him. It's his Italian blood. But I am shocked, I have to say, horrified even, that he should interfere to such an extent. What did Sandy and Hannah think about it, for God's sake?'

'Sandy's got his head in the clouds and Hannah is quite an aloof person, quite cold. Luke doesn't confide in them.'

'What did he do to the girl who was blackmailing him?'

'Moderate to severe S&M, I should think; that's his bag. He probably beat her or tied her up. That's what he enjoys most.'

Ben shuddered. 'Why is he like that?'

Alice shrugged. 'Why is anyone like anything? Who knows what forms a person? Busy father, aloof mother, rather bossy superior kind of sister – Sukey tormented him as a child, he once told me, and loved scoring points off him – he's got a lot of anger in him, unresolved stuff. But that's his problem. I'm still young. I want out now.'

'Did you know about it when you married him?'

'He revealed that side of himself to me once or twice; I was inexperienced and I didn't know then that if someone shows you something about themselves and then you don't hear any more about it, it doesn't mean it's gone away; it's there, you just don't see it. We were young, we were in love, and he was very good-looking. It was enough. And he was a member of a powerful family. I admit I liked marrying Sandy Macarthur's son. I grew up worshipping Sandy. When I was a schoolgirl, I thought he was Scotland's greatest writer. By the by, did you know the girl, the latest girl, was Marianne, your Marianne?'

'Marianne! Surely not! She'd never go in for that sort of thing.'

It was like a blow in the solar plexus. 'His' Marianne would never countenance such things.

'According to Duncan, there are photographs of them together. That's what Luke was desperate to suppress. I'd already found out about the other girl, and he promised there would be no more. How naïve can you be? He was already seeing Marianne when he made the promise.'

Ben looked at her and then shook his head. He felt as if something that belonged to him had been torn from his grasp. He realised that he had begun to allow himself to believe in the possibility that he and Marianne were made for one another; and now that was gone. How could he not have known about that sordid and perverted side to her nature?

When Alice came into the room, Luke stood up. He made as if to hug his wife, putting his arms round her, but Alice stood woodenly, not leaning into the embrace. 'I'll leave you on your own with him,' he said. 'He did wake up for a little while.'

'How did he seem?'

'Fine. A little disoriented, but the doctor said that was only to be expected. He'll be along in a second to talk to you.'

'I've already put in a request at the nurses' station,' said Alice. 'They know I'm here now.' She looked at Luke. 'Ben says you were at the newsagents. Is that right?

Luke hesitated, and then said, 'I think we should have this conversation outside. I don't want him upset.'

Alice glanced at Patrick and then at Luke. There were tears in her eyes. In the silent battle that was raging between them, she recognised that Luke had made a masterstroke by claiming the moral highground. Patrick must come first, he was saying; you are a selfish mother if you do not agree. The near-death of his child and the terrible torrent of emotions it must have unleashed inside him couldn't alter his basic nature, which was to lie.

'I'll go now,' said Luke, 'and I'll be back in half an hour or so. Is that OK?'

'Whatever,' Alice replied stonily.

'It would be better for him if we could present an appearance of unity,' Luke said in French. 'It won't help him recover if he thinks his whole world is going to fall to bits.'

'It has fallen to bits,' Alice answered, also in French, 'as you well know.'

'He doesn't know that,' said Luke, stroking Patrick's forehead – he was still nearer the child than Alice in the cramped space – 'and that's all that matters.'

'Why are you talking French?' asked Patrick sleepily, opening his eyes. 'Hello, Mum; what are you doing here?'

'What are you doing here, more to the point?' said Alice, moving closer so that she could kiss his cheek. 'I'd hug you but you're on a drip.'

'I chased Lolly and then someone ran over me,' said Patrick. 'Hello, Dad.' He held up his arms to his father.

'Hello, darling,' said Luke, still stroking Patrick's forehead. 'I'm going to go out for a while and let Mum have you to herself.'

'Don't go,' said Patrick, 'please don't go. I don't want you to go. I've got a terrible headache,' he added.

'Where?' asked Alice, looking into his face. 'Show me where it hurts.'

'Everywhere,' said Patrick, exploring his hair with his fingers. 'I think I'm going to be sick.'

'Call the doctor,' said Alice urgently to Luke. 'Get him here at once. Press the emergency button.'

Archie took charge of Diana when the police had finished with her and drove her back to Carrick, leaving Marianne to follow in the Volvo.

Half-way back to the house on the shore, Marianne stopped in a lay-by and called Ben on his mobile phone.

'It's Marianne,' she said when he picked up. 'How is he? I went to the cottage hospital but they said he'd been taken to the Infirmary. The Matron said he would be OK. You said you'd call. Why didn't you? I've been so worried.'

'You can't use mobiles in hospitals,' said Ben. 'They

upset the machines or something. The news is bad, I'm afraid.'

'What's happened?'

'He seemed all right – Luke spoke to him for a moment or two – then he slept for a little while. When Alice arrived, he woke up, and said he had a headache. All hell broke loose, doctors everywhere and machines and God only knows what, but they couldn't prevent him from slipping into a coma.'

'So he's in a coma, then?'

'I'm afraid so.'

'How bad is it?'

'I'm not sure. They're measuring him on some scale they have. It'll take a while to run all the tests.'

'So what are you going to do now?'

'I'm going back to Ardgay to wait – Charles is coming to pick me up – there's nothing I can do here. Mother is very upset according to Charles. I should be with her.'

'I'm so sorry,' she said, 'so very, very sorry. I thought he was going to be OK. I was so happy when the Matron told me that he was all right.'

She paused, aware that beyond the sorrow and the horror there was some other constraint. She knew Ben well – he was voluble in trouble – so why was he so silent now?

'Yes, well . . .' he said bleakly.

'Ben?'

'What?'

'There's something else; I can tell. What is it?'

'I don't know what you're talking about.'

'Yes, you do. You're keeping something from me.'

'Look,' he said, 'Patrick might not make it, isn't that enough?'

The cruelty of this remark made her gasp.

'That wasn't what I meant.'

'I have to go,' he said.

She didn't know what to say to this. 'Will you keep me informed?'

'Yes, if you want me to.'

'Why are you being like this?' she exclaimed, as the line went dead.

At the house, Archie had taken Diana upstairs and made her undress and get into bed.

'You have to sleep,' he said. 'It'll do you good. You can't think straight until you've had some rest.'

'I don't want to sleep. I want a drink.'

'No more drink now,' came Nurse Archie's reply. 'If you hadn't been drinking this would never have happened.'

'That's why I want a drink. I need one. I don't want to sleep. They'll get me if I sleep.'

'Sssh,' murmured Archie, pulling up the shiny old eiderdown. 'Hush now. Just sleep and you'll feel better.'

Marianne put her head round the bedroom door whilst this pantomime was taking place, listened for a moment, and then withdrew disgusted. Diana was being treated as if she were the victim, not the per-petrator, although of course Luke had been equally to blame, but there was something about the way

273

Archie was soothing her that made Marianne feel slightly queasy.

In her own room at the end of the passage, her girlhood bedroom, she lay down and wept hot tears for Patrick that ran down her neck into the pillow. And as she wept, she continued to go over the conversation with Ben in her mind. There was something else behind his distracted coolness, of that she was certain, but what? When they had arranged to meet this weekend, it had been his idea. He had been warm and eager towards her then, so what had changed?

It occurred to her that Luke might have told Ben what had transpired between them, but Luke had already confessed to her that he had sold the Justine/Elly story to the press in order to prevent the truth being known about their affair or those pictures being published, so why would he tell Ben such a thing? It made no sense at all.

Archie was in the first-floor kitchen looking out of the window, glass in hand, when Marianne came along the passage from her bedroom.

'How long is she staying here?' Marianne asked, getting a glass from the cupboard and opening the fridge in order to pour herself a glass of wine.

'Until this evening. I've called Hugo and told him what's happened. He's going to come over and fetch her.'

'What about her car?'

'I'll drive it back to town on Monday morning. She can't be driving around in it at the moment.'

'Have they banned her?'

'If they haven't, they should have done,' Archie replied. 'I'm banning her for the time being. She's in a very bad state of mind and that car's a killing-machine. She shouldn't be let loose in it.'

'What do you mean, "bad state of mind"?'

'She's suicidal. The child has crashed through her defences where nothing else could, if you'll pardon the expression.'

'He's in a coma,' said Marianne, recalling Diana's spectacular performance in the car park. 'I just spoke to Ben in Dumfries.'

To her shame, she felt a rush of power as she made this remark. Superior knowledge always bestowed the power to hurt, and she felt a desire to cause pain to someone.

'But I thought Nancy said he was OK?' came Archie's gratifyingly bewildered reply.

'She did. But there've been further developments since then.'

'Oh my God!' said Archie. 'That's terrible. What are his chances?'

'No one knows.'

'Don't mention this to her at the moment, whatever you do,' said Archie. 'It might send her right over the top.'

'She should have thought of that before,' said Marianne cruelly. 'Why are you protecting her any-way? I thought you said the affair was over.'

'What's eating you?' demanded Archie, settling down in an armchair. 'You're not normally this waspish.'

*   *   *

275

Jean Macarthur, nervously awaiting Ben and Charles's return from Dumfries, hobbled down the front steps using her stick and across the gravel to the grass on the other side. She stopped briefly to poke at an impertinent weed with her stick before moving slowly on.

She longed for movement of some kind, but since Jack had died she felt as if she had seized up both mentally and physically. The sense of exhaustion and despair was overwhelming, particularly the feeling she had that things were now running out of control, as if they'd all been used to Jack being in charge for too long and had atrophied; it was also odd how the chaos inflicted by the press intrusion had changed her sons. Duncan, understandably perhaps, had fallen apart, in as much as Duncan was capable of doing such a thing; once during the last week he had turned up drunk at her house and she had heard Charles trying to calm him, another time she saw him in the street looking terribly bleak, dragging a recalcitrant Theo behind him. The two men, absurdly but rather sweetly, had divided Theo's week up between them so that Charles had him Monday to Thursday and Duncan Friday to Monday.

Ben, on the other hand, seemed not so much happier as somehow more in charge of himself than before; having to take over where Duncan left off suited him and lent him stature. His indecisiveness, the stammer that occasionally afflicted him, the general falling away that he was known for in the family (and that had worried Jack so much) seemed to be vanishing. If life was indeed a long race as whoever it was had observed, then Ben was galloping up from behind.

As for the events of the morning, she had been more than relieved when Ben told her on the phone that it was Luke who had left Patrick unattended. She would not have wanted that hanging over her son.

Now, waiting for Ben, she was taking herself on a slow walk towards the walled garden in order to inspect what was going on. Gardening always soothed her soul; there was something immediate in it that prevented the mind from wandering aimlessly and somehow centred it so that the quantity of blossom on a tree or the amount of fruit it was about to yield both absorbed and calmed one, and prevented one from thinking about such things as a dying child run down by her former daughter-in-law.

Moira Paterson, the housekeeper, watching her from an upstairs window with Agnes who helped out when the family were in residence, shook her head.

'She's slowed up to nothing since the Old Man died. I've never seen anyone deteriorate so fast. Last time she was here, she was skipping around.'

'She's had an awful lot to deal with, losing the Old Man like that and then all the scandal,' said Agnes, with relish.

'And now the wee boy,' added Moira, nodding her head, as if they were a committee putting some crucial statement to the vote.

'How is he?'

'Very bad,' said Moira. 'He's in a coma. Charles has gone to fetch Ben from Dumfries. She'll be waiting for them to come back.'

'The lad wet his bed,' said Agnes. 'Did you see the sheets? He's a wee bit old for that, wouldn't you think?'

'There are troubles at home,' said Moira darkly. 'Luke's a fine man in some ways, but he's right pleased with himself. Mother says he was like that as a boy: charming and good-looking and all that, but he knows how to play you.'

'Well, he must be feeling terrible now,' said Agnes.

'Oh, yes,' said Moira, who wasn't going to have Agnes claiming the moral high-ground. 'I wouldn't be in his shoes for all the tea in China.'

Half-way back to Ardgay when they were just coming through Castle Douglas, Ben took a call on his mobile. It was Marianne again.

'I want to see you,' she said, without preamble. 'We have to talk.'

'I can't, not right now. I'm with Charles and we're on our way home. I'll call you later.'

'You said that before.'

He was less distant with her this time, but she felt it had to do more with the proximity of Charles than with any change in his own feelings. His voice still contained a chill note that angered her by its injustice, as if the tragedy belonged to him alone and was not a universal sorrow: she had after all been present when it happened.

'I will, I promise.'

This did not reassure her either. He was panicking, no doubt hoping to God that she wouldn't say anything too embarrassing.

'How is he?'

'No change. I'll call you when I hear anything.'

'Do you promise?'

He could hear the tears in her voice.

'Of course I do,' he said quickly, 'I'll get back to you as soon as I can.'

'That was Marianne,' he said to Charles, to whom he felt he owed an explanation.

'Ah,' said Charles cautiously. 'How is she? It must have been tough for her to be involved in all that.'

Jean had confided in him that she hoped Ben would have the sense to move ahead with Marianne after their false start, but Ben's tone of voice with her was not reassuring to Charles, expert decoder of relationships. It sounded to him as if Ben was fending her off for some reason at a moment when it would have been more logical for him to lean into her embrace.

'Involved?' said Ben. 'What do you mean?'

'Well, she was there, wasn't she? She saw it happen. People can have heart attacks from shock, you know.'

'Heart attacks,' Ben repeated stupidly. He knew he was being dense but it was as if he couldn't grasp what Charles was saying about it being hurtful for Marianne. He was so angry with her for another reason that in his mind he had disallowed her any feeling whatsoever over the accident.

'It's hard to be involved and then excluded,' said Charles carefully. 'She must feel completely power-less.'

'I suppose she must,' said Ben, mortified. The cruelty of his own action struck him like a blow.

His mind swung between his own bad behaviour and Marianne's – or at least what he had learned of it from Alice – but then it occurred to him that he had not even told Marianne why he was being so cold with her, allowing Patrick's accident to take up the slack and be excuse enough for anything, and that was extraordinarily unjust. He had acted as judge and jury, condemning Marianne before she had even had a chance to defend herself. He decided to ring her later when he had some privacy, not wanting Charles to overhear what would be a difficult conversation.

His mother was in her cosy little sitting-room at the back of the house with Duncan when Charles and Ben returned. They were both drinking what looked like large gins and Duncan was smoking a cigar, a habit he had recently acquired. The rich, dark, leather smoke hung in the air, reminding Ben forcefully of his father and the world of earthly pleasures the Old Man had so effortlessly inhabited.

'I felt I had to come,' said Duncan, glancing at Charles. 'What a thing to happen – for God's sake help yourselves to drinks. Mother tells me Luke was off buying fags or some such. What the hell was he thinking of leaving Patrick in charge of Lolly? Everyone knows the bloody dog is psychotic. You'll have to think about having her put down,' he said to Ben. 'She's a public menace. Where is she, by the way?'

'Locked in the pantry,' said Ben, determined to keep control of himself, although the suggestion about Lolly (a typical Duncan-like piece of steam-rollering) had made his blood boil. 'And you can't blame the dog. Luke shouldn't have left them together.'

'Luke would never listen as a boy,' Jean put in. 'If you told him not to do something because there were consequences attached, he would never pay the slightest heed. Today's behaviour is an extension of that, I'm afraid. He doesn't understand or doesn't want to understand cause and effect; it's a form of moral selfishness.'

'You know why he came here in the first place, I suppose?' enquired Duncan theatrically, looking at each person in turn.

Ben nodded, wondering whether it was his imagination or had his elder brother become more *grande dame*-like than ever since his father died.

'Why?' asked Jean, reaching for the silver cigarette box.

She hardly ever smoked any more but there were times, and she could tell that this was one of them, when it was called for. She allowed Duncan to light her cigarette with the big silver table lighter that Jack had won at a local clay pigeon competition years ago.

'Alice threw him out last night after I'd been round there.'

'Why did she do that?' asked Jean, drawing deeply

on her cigarette and feeling her head swim deliciously.

'Because I've discovered that it was Luke who sold us as a family to the press. And do you know why he did that?'

In the ensuing silence, Ben could hear the faint sounds of Lolly barking in the pantry. He found himself hating the note of smugness in his brother's voice. Duncan was wallowing in scarcely suppressed self-righteousness.

'Why?' asked Jean, putting out the cigarette with shaking hand.

When Duncan told her the whole story she was silent for a moment.

'And you thought that telling Alice what her husband had done would help? Is that what you're saying?'

'I thought it was my duty to tell her, yes.'

'Why? What good would it do? What good has it done? All it meant was that Luke left home, came here, was inattentive to his child because he was too anxious to go on without a cigarette and then look what happened?'

'So, it's my fault; is that what you're saying?'

'You should have thought it through. And Alice should learn to be more tolerant. What was the point of throwing him out?'

'And Luke gets off scot-free?'

'I would hardly describe what has happened to Luke as getting off scot-free,' said Jean. 'Your father believed in containment. Surely there was a better way to deal with this than tearing everything down out of a desire for revenge.'

'Luke has to pay for what he has done,' said Duncan in a cold voice, getting up and going to the drinks tray. 'I'm rather baffled as to why you find that so hard to understand.'

'Because it's cruel,' said Jean, 'and I was brought up to detest cruelty. He's done wrong, yes, but you should have thought out more carefully how you would deal with him. As it is, you rushed in unthinking and then all hell broke loose.'

'And what would father have done?'

'He would have bided his time, that's all I'm saying.'

Jean turned her head away so that she did not have to look at Duncan. Her jaw was trembling. She was not used to having a position of authority and it unnerved her. Damn Jack for making her so useless.

'I don't think this is a very productive conversation,' said Ben, who was worried about his mother whom he had rarely seen so impassioned. 'I think we should all cool down a bit before we go into the detail of what happened, or at least until we know what's happened to Patrick.'

He wanted to stop Duncan and his mother saying things in the heat of the moment that couldn't be reversed; his father had believed in total control, keeping everything in compartments; now that he was dead all the barriers had fallen and one area of family life was leaking toxically into another.

'Ring the hospital now,' said Duncan, dropping the glass stopper in his hand so that it rolled and clattered on the silver tray.

'I need to lie down for a little,' said Jean. 'Help me upstairs, Charles, will you?'

'I'll take you, Mother,' said Ben. 'Then I'll call the hospital.'

'You can do it from my room,' said Jean.

She walked upstairs very slowly and in silence. In her room, she sat down on the bed with a sigh and looked up at Ben.

'I wish I knew what to do,' she said. 'I feel so powerless. It's not just Patrick; it's everything. Since your father died, things have got out of control. Patrick's accident is just another part of it.'

'I know, Mother,' said Ben, taking her shoes off for her and helping her get her legs up onto the bed.

'I always thought family was everything,' said Jean. 'I went along with your father on that one, but now I'm beginning to wonder. How could Luke have done such a terrible thing? And how could Duncan have been so blind to the consequences of his actions? It beggars belief. That poor little boy. Call the hospital now, darling, please.'

Ben did as his mother asked, but there was no change in Patrick's condition.

'Do you want anything to eat?' he asked his mother, but she shook her head. 'I'm going to have a little sleep,' she said. 'Then I'll feel better.'

'Is your leg very painful?'

'In a nutshell, yes. But I don't care about that. It'll get better; Patrick might not.'

'Don't blame Duncan too much for what he did,' said Ben. 'He wanted revenge on your behalf. He's seen what the events of the last few weeks have done to you.'

'You know what they say about revenge. Luke must be unhinged. It's the only explanation I can think of.'

'Or just desperate and confused and out of his mind with worry,' said Ben.

'You're kinder than your brother,' said Jean. 'Duncan has no heart.'

'Go to sleep now, Mother. I'll come and wake you if there's anything you need to know.'

Marianne looked round Diana's bedroom door at about six o'clock the same evening to see if she was awake.

Diana was sitting bolt upright in bed smoking a cigarette. She gave Marianne a hard stare and then looked away.

'There isn't an ashtray,' she said, as if Marianne was some kind of servant for whom she had rung.

'Would you get me one please?'

'You shouldn't be smoking up here,' said Marianne. 'It's a fire risk. Archie won't have it.'

'Where is Archie?' asked Diana, tapping ash into her hand.

'Downstairs with Hugo. He's come to fetch you home.'

'Joke,' said Diana.

'What?'

'Never mind.' Diana shook her head. 'How is the child?'

'There's no change,' said Marianne more gently, watching Diana for signs of remorse.

'I see.' There was a pause whilst Diana got out of bed and looked round for somewhere to put her cigarette end. She was wearing a white shirt over her knickers. Her trousers and the boots she had been wearing lay in a heap on the floor.

'Well,' she said savagely to Marianne, 'what are you waiting for?'

'Nothing,' said Marianne, feeling like a child found out doing something illicit.

'Tell them I'll be down in a minute.'

'There's someone on the phone for you,' said Archie when Marianne came back into the kitchen where he was sitting with Hugo, both men nursing whiskies. Hugo looked unshaven and slightly trembly. His shirt looked as if it had been worn once too often and his socks didn't match.

'Who is it?'

'Some man. Didn't ask his name.'

'Plenty of those around, I should think,' said Hugo, in a horrible attempt at being arch. When he opened his mouth it was apparent that he needed to go to the dentist urgently.

Marianne took the call in the sitting-room at the end of the passage. Like the kitchen, this room had a sea view; she remembered her mother sitting here just before she died looking out to sea in a way that had scared Marianne, as if she could see beyond the horizon.

'It's Ben,' said the voice at the other end of the line. 'I began to wonder if Archie had forgotten I was on the line.'

'He had to find me first,' said Marianne. 'I was seeing to Diana. Hugo's here to get her. How's Patrick?'

'No change. Luke and Alice are there with him. I'm going to go in later and take over. I think they need some sleep. I'd like to see you on my way in.'

'OK.'

Whatever it was earlier that had made him so cold and distant had vanished entirely from his voice.

'Are you all right? It must have been terrible to see it all unfolding in front of your eyes this morning.'

'I'm OK,' said Marianne. 'I just can't get it out of my mind, that's all; thanks for asking though.'

'I should have asked you this morning; it's just that . . .'

'Don't,' she said, 'just don't. We were all half out of our minds.'

'I'll come and collect you,' he said, 'and we can go somewhere for a drink about eight or so.'

She had a generosity about her that was incredibly touching; the way she would allow bygones to be bygones; maybe that was one of the greatest qualities one could hope to find in a woman or in anyone come to that. But why all that stuff with Luke, all that perverted crap? What did she see in that? And why hadn't he known she had that side to her?

*　　*　　*

'Hello, sis,' said Hugo with as much *faux* jollity as he could muster, getting up when Diana came into the room. 'I've come to take you back home. Best place for you right now.'

'I want a drink,' said Diana, ignoring her brother.

'OK, OK,' said Archie, who could see this was not a moment to mess with Diana.

She accepted a large whisky, and drank it in silence. Hugo, made nervous by her behaviour, attempted to engage Archie in conversation about his work, but the whole thing had the air of a painful travesty.

'When you've finished that,' Hugo said to Diana, after a few minutes had passed, 'we'll go. I don't want the supper to burn.'

'Tastes the same whatever you do to it,' said Diana, getting up.

She looked in her handbag and took out a small mirror, proceeding to apply some lipstick, as if she were alone. Her hair was scraped back and whatever make-up she had been wearing in the morning had long gone, but her handsomeness could endure such treatment, Marianne thought, coming back into the room, slightly elated after her conversation with Ben.

'Well, then,' said Hugo, 'shall we be on our way, sis?'

'If you want,' said Diana, putting her compact away and glancing at her brother with what looked like contempt.

'Thanks for doing the honours this morning,' Hugo said to Archie as they went down the stairs to the courtyard where his ancient Land Rover was parked.

'Glad to be of assistance,' said Archie.

To Diana he said, 'Behave yourself,' as if she was a schoolgirl returning to the penitentiary, but Diana appeared to not to hear him.

'She's in shock,' Marianne said, as Hugo drove off, a couple of his dogs glaring balefully out of the back window at Archie and Marianne.

'I wouldn't be surprised if she's suicidal. I've seen that look before,' she added, with sudden conviction.

'Best thing that could happen to her,' said Archie, 'she's made such a mess of things.'

'I don't believe you just said that,' Marianne replied, walking off round the front of the house. At the entrance to the water garden, she sat on the wall and watched the tide come in.

Families were such complex things, she reflected: both a force for the good and a source of astonishing disappointment and heartbreak. Archie still had the ability to shock her with his callousness: what he himself would call honesty, but which in fact was a negative view of the world.

In Archie's universe there was no turning back, no forgiveness, no making amends; just a predetermined journey towards oblivion, a kind of post-Calvinism for the shabby new world of modern Scotland, with its self-delusions and posturings.

And yet there was a kind side to him too; he had rescued Diana this morning and given her shelter for the day until poor, absurd Hugo had come along to fetch her this evening. Maybe it was useless to try to categorise people, Marianne thought.

Human beings were so complex they could always surprise you.

Ben came to fetch her a little later than he said. He rang her from the courtyard with the van's engine still running, not wishing, he said, to run the gauntlet of Archie of whom he was wary.

They drove out onto the main road and then proceeded for a few miles in silence until they were the other side of Kirkcudbright, when Ben pulled over into a lay-by without warning and turned the engine off.

'Why are you doing that?' Marianne asked, startled out of her reverie.

Ben grabbed her by the shoulders and pressed his thumbs into her collarbone with as much force as he could muster.

'Stop it!' she cried out.

'You don't like it, do you?' he said, pulling away from her.

'Of course I don't like it; I hate it. Why did you do that?'

'You liked it when he did it?'

'What are you talking about?'

'You know what I'm talking about; come on. Don't pretend.'

Marianne put her hands over her face.

'Who told you?'

'Alice.'

'How did she find out?' She was still talking through her hands.

'Duncan found out. He got our solicitor, Gerry

Lamont, to help him. Gerry knows everyone and everything. Duncan wanted to know who the mole was.'

Marianne took her hands away and gazed at Ben without speaking.

'You knew,' he said.

She nodded, caught his eye and looked away as if she couldn't stand to see his reaction.

'He told me the last time we met.'

'Why?' asked Ben. 'Just tell me why. Why didn't I know about that part of you?'

'Because it didn't exist,' she said.

'What do you mean?'

'It was something Luke led me into, little by little. I think he does it to everyone; and by the time you realise you're in too deep, or at least that was my experience.'

'Are you still seeing him?'

'No.'

'Why not?

'Because it went too far. He got scary and I didn't want to see him any more.'

'Scary?'

'Yes, scary. He's too needy. I couldn't deal with it; I doubt any one woman can. He'll just have to keep moving from girl to girl.'

She glanced at him sideways and saw that he was thinking about what she said, and wondering whether he could believe it.

'You were angry with me,' she continued. 'I thought

that was unfair. It was none of your business what I did with Luke.'

'Yes, it is,' he said quickly. 'I couldn't stand the thought of you being some kind of S&M pervert.'

'I still can't see why it was any of your business.'

He was so quick to judge and label, she thought, so slow to try to understand anything; nothing had changed.

'Because Luke sold our family out in order to protect his relationship with you.'

'That's not my fault,' said Marianne indignantly, 'and it still doesn't make it any of your business. I didn't ask him to do that. He didn't consult me. What do you want me to say?'

'I don't understand why you took up with him in the first place.'

'Because he listened to me,' she said angrily, 'which is more than you ever did.'

'What?'

'He listened to me. I could talk to him. He wasn't so self-obsessed that he couldn't help another human being.'

'And I was; that's what you're saying, isn't it?'

'Yes.'

She was too angry to stop now. 'You were self-obsessed and you played the victim. "Oh, look what's happened to me; oh, it wasn't my fault; oh, my family don't think much of me," – you were pathetic. You acted as if no one else in the world had any problems but you. I ended up feeling quite sorry

for Diana. No wonder she went off the rails trying to decipher you. It would have driven anyone
to drink.'

He made no reply to what she had said for a
moment; then he said, 'I think I'd better drive you
home.'

'I think you had,' Marianne agreed furiously.

He drove her back to Carrick still in silence and
dropped her off by the entrance to the courtyard.
Marianne got out of the van, slammed the door and
walked away without looking back.

After a short pause, she heard Ben accelerating
away down the drive towards Dumfries.

Well, she thought, that's that. Another wonderful
screw-up. Self-righteous bastard! But under it all lay
a deep regret that the last chance she had had with
him had gone.

When Ben got to the hospital, there was no visible
change in Patrick's condition. Luke and Alice, sitting
on either side of his bed, looked tense and exhausted.
Patrick himself, wired up to various machines which
monitored his progress, was still and white and
broken-looking. Alice had brought a favourite old
teddy from home (the one he had brought with him
on the night of the Old Man's death), which lay in
the crook of his arm.

When Ben appeared, Luke said something to Alice,
laying his hand on her shoulder, and then went out
to greet his cousin.

'Any news?' asked Ben.

Luke shook his head. 'We're just waiting and watching. Alice is being amazing. I'm not sure I'll be able to get her to leave though. You might have a go. She can't do anything here and she's shattered; look at her.'

In the room, Ben kissed Alice and then sat down in Luke's chair and took Patrick's hand in his. He wanted to stroke his foal-like cheek but didn't dare for fear of disturbing the machinery.

'Luke thinks you should get some sleep,' he whispered.

'I can't leave him,' said Alice. 'The hospital will give me a bed if I want one. What kind of mother would leave her child at a time like this? Luke can't seem to understand that,' she said, adding, 'but he is being fantastic in every way he knows how. We've been able to talk while we've been here. An odd time to do it, I know.'

'Good talk?' said Ben gently, who was thinking that breaking and mending happened in the oddest ways between people. Forty-eight hours ago, Alice had been angry enough with her husband to throw him out into the street with nowhere to go. And now, restitution in the face of death. One had to hand it to Luke, he thought; he was nothing if not a smart operator. And what had happened to Patrick provided Luke with the perfect shield against criticism. It was not possible to feel anything else for him but compassion. The rage and bewilderment his treachery had provoked seemed something that had happened years ago in the distant past.

'Yes,' she said. 'We need to make a fresh start. If he recovers,' she nodded at Patrick, 'then we're going to go somewhere else. We need to get out of the claustrophobic cocoon of Edinburgh life. There's too much history there for all of us. He swears it'll be a completely new beginning. We just have to hope that the little one makes it. His vital signs haven't deteriorated any further since this morning. I have a gut feeling he's going to be OK. That's why I can't leave, but I don't want to tell Luke. He'll get over-excited. You know what he's like,' she added, her tone of voice a mixture of fondness and exasperation, which was, as Ben suddenly realised, the glue that kept them together. Luke as much as Patrick was Alice's naughty little boy, always promising to reform, never quite coming up with the goods.

'That's good,' said Ben, 'very good. Better than I'd hoped.' He didn't want to say that it was a complete turn-around from his last conversation with her, because he had realised almost too late that human beings were hugely contradictory and perfectly capable of a *volte face* every five minutes.

'Why don't you go and lie down for a couple of hours and I'll sit with him. Luke can stay or go to Ardgay as he wishes. The house isn't locked.'

Luke said he would stay if Alice agreed to lie down for a while. Though she did, half an hour after he'd arrived, Ben found himself alone with Patrick.

He had dozed off a little and was deep in a dream in

which, with Lolly, he was swimming in an unfathomable, waveless sea when he was aware that someone was talking to him.

'Wakey, wakey,' said the voice, Patrick's voice; one of his old-fashioned phrases picked up from God only knows where.

Ben tried to surface and failed. He was back with Lolly in the bottomless deep when the voice spoke again.

'Where's Mum?'

This time he surfaced to find Patrick looking at him. He had taken the oxygen mask off his face and laid it on the pillow beside him, as if it belonged to some party trick he had grown tired of. Somewhere a machine was bleeping urgently.

'You're awake!' said Ben, taking Patrick's rough, dry little hand in his. It was warm, as if life was flooding like the sea into every extremity.

'You're the one who was asleep,' said Patrick calmly. 'Where's Mum?' he repeated.

'Having a bit of a sleep,' said Ben, 'but she'll want to know you've woken up. Shall I get her?'

At that moment, several people entered the room at once: a doctor, a nurse, an intern, plus Luke and Alice.

'He's awake,' said Ben proudly. 'He took the mask off himself.'

'Out of the way, please,' said the nurse, as if Ben hadn't spoken.

Ben got up and left the room. The waiting area was littered with plastic cups and out-of-date, dog-eared magazines, but he had never felt so glad to see anything in all his life. Patrick would live! That was all that mattered.

After some time had passed, Luke came out.

'He's going to be all right!' he said, wiping the tears from his eyes. Both men were weeping as they embraced.

'I'm going to go now,' said Ben, blowing his nose. 'I'd better get some sleep. Call me later on and let me know what the score is. I've got to make a site visit to Castle Forbes at some point, but obviously that can be fitted around your plans. How long will they keep him in for?'

'We don't know yet,' said Luke, 'but it may be a few days.'

'You can stay at Ardgay as long as you like,' said Ben. 'You know that.'

'Thanks,' said Luke, putting his hand on his cousin's shoulder. 'I'll never forget what a support you've been over all this.'

'It was nothing,' Ben shrugged. 'See you later.'

He drove through the ugly, shuttered town and out onto the A75, heading for home. He turned off by the ICI factory that had been belching chemicals into the unpolluted Galloway air since he was a child and drove slowly along the back road that would eventually bring him to Dalbeattie.

The dawn was breaking as he stopped the car at a high point and got out to admire the low, clean line of the hills and the pearly smoothness of the dawn sky as it filled with light. It would be a fine, hot day, that rarest of commodities in this part of the world and it seemed to him then that the sky and the light spoke of Patrick's miraculous recovery and celebrated it.

When he got in and drove on, however, he found that he had begun to go over in his mind what Marianne had said to him, as if he had not been able to come back to this until now.

She had said Luke listened to her and indeed it was true that there was something cosy about Luke. Ben was aware that he had a gossipy, warm, cuddly side to him that drew women to him; the other side of the coin was that the women he had drawn to him then left him or shopped him; in short, his cousin was a confused and needy fool, but he was also highly likeable and forgivable, whereas he, Ben, withdrew emotionally, tended to blame others, as Marianne had pointed out, and was generally less alive in certain respects than Luke. He was living cautiously as if he were immortal when he was anything but. If he had learned anything from Patrick's accident, it should be that time was alarmingly short.

When Archie came to pick Diana up on the following Monday, he found her sitting at the kitchen table in Hugo's house smoking. She nodded in his direction but made no other effort to greet him.

Hugo, who had come out when he heard the sound of the car coming into the yard, was worried.

'I got her home on Saturday night,' he said, 'but she hardly spoke, although she drank plenty. When she went to bed, I checked on her and found her sitting fully clothed on her bed staring into space. I said, "Don't you want to get undressed, sis?" but she carried on as if she hadn't heard. I was worried she might burn the house down or something. Yesterday I told her the news about the child, but it didn't appear to register.'

'Have you called the doctor?'

'He came out last night, old Doc McCluskey it was. Said he couldn't find anything the matter with her; she's probably mildly shocked was all he could come up with. Said to keep her warm, all that stuff, don't let her drink too much, but that's easier said than done. You know what she's like. Ben came by yesterday – he's overseeing the work at the Castle for the Loebs – but she wouldn't speak to him; wouldn't even see him. I don't know what to do with her.'

'Wouldn't she be better here than in Edinburgh on her own?' asked Archie.

'She won't stay. Says she wants to go home. I can't stop her; she's so bloody stubborn. Good news about the boy, though. His parents must be very relieved. I know how I'd feel if it were Alec.'

'It is indeed,' said Archie, who was more concerned about Diana. 'Has she any private health insurance?' he asked.

'Probably. She seems to have most things. The Macarthurs provided for her very generously. She was a favourite of the Old Man's, you know.'

'Well, find out and call her Edinburgh doctor. I think she needs to lay off the booze and sort out her head.'

'The same thought had occurred to me,' said Hugo, touching his moustache nervously, 'but she won't contemplate the idea.'

'Well, I'd better be on my way,' said Archie. 'I'll give you a call when we get there.'

'Very kind of you to do this,' said Hugo. 'What about your own car?'

'My daughter took it back to Edinburgh last night,' said Archie. 'Children do have their uses from time to time.'

Marianne had driven herself up to Edinburgh alone on Sunday, leaving Archie, who was going to collect Diana the following morning. Duncan had rung through on Sunday morning to tell them the news about Patrick and had spoken to Marianne, but she had heard nothing from Ben. His lack of response confirmed her feeling that whatever there had been between them was dead. And it was her own stupid fault. How could she blame Ben for his reaction to her own aberrant and morally culpable behaviour? When the smoking clouds of her own anger and pride had cleared she was forced to realise that he had developed and grown since they had parted and she had not. Her admiration for him was unbounded; her sense of regret equally so. She had lost the thing she most cherished. This conviction made her feel sad and flat as if all the fizz had gone out of her life and nothing would ever take its place.

She left the Volvo at Archie's studio, where the

great tit of the State provided a free parking space, and took a cab back to her flat in Marchmont. Neither Nadia nor Jim were at home and the place was a tip. There had obviously been some kind of a party the night before and the kitchen was full of dirty glasses and putrid ashtrays; the smell of stale smoke hung in the air. Someone had slept in her bed. Marianne cursed flat life before lying down on her bed to have a good cry. She couldn't even be bothered to change the sheets.

On Monday morning, the office was buzzing; not only had Justine returned from holiday, but the news of Patrick's recovery was a hot topic. Justine summoned Marianne into her office to hear the full story before they began on the book committee meeting that had been put back to midday in order to allow Justine to get a grip of her correspondence.

Marianne was describing the drama to Justine in graphic detail when Justine's telephone rang.

'For you,' she said to Marianne, putting the phone down. 'There's someone to see you downstairs.'

'I'm not expecting anyone,' said Marianne.

'Probably someone delivering a manuscript. You know what they're like, but I don't know why Doug couldn't take it. He gets worse and worse. Now Jack's dead we may have to retire him.'

'It would save being groped on a regular basis,' said Marianne, getting up. 'I'll go and see whoever it is, then I'll be back as quickly as possible.'

'Take your time,' said Justine.

Marianne went downstairs slowly, dragging her

feet. Recounting the detail of Saturday's events to Justine merely increased her feeling of depression. She was plagued by a feeling of emptiness, of having come to the end of something without meaning to, of being without any purpose. Nadia said there were three categories in life that mattered: job, flat, man. In her case, all three stank. The flat was a pit, the job a painful reminder of the Macarthur family, the man situation bleak beyond description.

Ben was standing by the open door of the Press holding a bunch of flowers as big as an umbrella in his arms. Doug was in his glass sentry box in the hallway pretending to sort the post, but in reality he was watching for Marianne on the stairs.

'Visitor for you,' he said, grinning so widely she could see all his fillings. 'Told me not to say who it was. It's that romantic, so it is.'

Marianne stopped in her tracks. She was aware that she had forgotten to clean her teeth or put on any make-up. She was wearing an old pair of black trousers and a tight black shirt with a stain on it that she had found on her bedroom floor that morning; not exactly what she would have chosen for a romantic tryst.

'What are you doing here?' she asked, when she had got her voice back. She was aware that she didn't sound particularly welcoming. She didn't want to be 'friends', if that was what the flowers meant. She didn't want to make 'amends' in honour of what they had once meant to one another; she just wanted never to see him again. It was easier that way. Cleaner and safer and much less painful in the long run.

'Don't look so dismayed,' he said, coming towards her, holding the flowers like some sort of battering ram. Marianne had a mental picture of herself smothered by lilies and roses.

'I've come to apologise,' he added, tucking the flowers under one arm and taking her hand in his.

'Where are we going?'

'Outside, so that Doug stops leering at you.'

'I don't want to go outside. I'm busy. It's the book committee meeting.'

She was already getting angry with him for being so bloody breezy. How dare he come in and destroy her Monday morning like this?

'Not too busy for what I have to say,' he insisted, and dragged her down the tiled hallway and out of the door. Once on the steps, he took her arm and walked her very fast a little way down the street.

'Look here,' he said, 'I've been a bloody fool. I love you and I don't want to lose you. I think we should get married.'

'You what?'

'I think we should get married.'

'Are you OK?'

'I'm sane, I'm not unhinged. I love you. Life is short. Let's do something with it. Will you marry me?'

She stared at him. 'Do you mean it?'

'Yes.' He put his arms round her and kissed her on the mouth.

Somewhere, over on the other side of the street by

the railings, someone wolf-whistled. This was, after all, Edinburgh: cosy, provincial, beautiful, claustrophobic Edinburgh, where such acts in public still cause a stir.

'All right then,' she said, 'go down on one knee.'

He did so without protest. 'Now ask me,' she said, ignoring the cluster of people that was beginning to gather.

'Will you marry me?' he said, having laid the flowers on the pavement.

At that point, Archie drove past at the wheel of Diana's Range Rover. He slowed at the sight of two young people making a spectacle of themselves – it was before the Festival when such behaviour was commonplace – until he realised who the protagonists were. Then he accelerated before Diana noticed, although glancing at her profile he saw that she had seen them and noted what was going on.

Marianne saw none of this.

'Will you marry me?' he said, taking her hand in his and kissing it.

'Of course I will, you idiot,' she replied. 'Now get up and stop making a spectacle of yourself.'

Then she began to laugh and as she laughed so did Ben and then he cried and she cried too; and they walked away and left the flowers until someone came running after them.

'These are for you,' he said, handing them to Marianne.

'I've never seen such a huge bunch in my life. What am I to do with them?'

'Put them in water,' he said, 'and admire them. What else?'

Back at the Press, she said, 'I'm supposed to be in a meeting with Justine and the others. They'll wonder where the hell I've got to.'

'Let them wonder,' he said, taking her arm. 'We're going home to bed.'

On an evening several days later, Diana lay on the sofa in the sitting-room of her flat in Howe Street, the apartment she had bought with the money the Old Man had shovelled her way after the divorce. The Old Man wanted to keep her in Macarthurtown because he believed in applying the same principle to relationships as to any other aspect of life: waste not want not. She had been a Wife and even if she was now a former Wife, she should be kept inside the clan. He often remarked that the Queen could have learned something from the way their family worked. Once in, keep them in and keep their loyalty.

The sight of Ben and Marianne, however long ago it was, (two, three days ago?) haunted her and triggered a whole set of images of her own happy days with Ben she rarely allowed herself to recall; to bring them to mind was too painful and the agony of the breakdown of her relationship with Ben had been a large part of the reason she began to drink and take drugs to excess. Ben had disliked the drinking but the cocaine had induced in him a real sense of fear and loathing, which had led to terrible rows between them. But drink and cocaine numbed and dulled the sledgehammer sense of failure she had felt so powerfully when it became obvious to her that she couldn't reach him, that he lay somehow behind a glass screen of, not exactly indifference, but of his own fear of feeling and what those feelings might bring down on his head if he allowed them free rein. Cocaine had become her friend; as necessary to her ability to get through the day as breathing. And now she had seen someone else reaping the reward she had yearned for. The thought of Ben doing such a thing in her time would have been unthinkable.

The dealer from whom she used to get her stuff, only a little cocaine here and there, had just rung; or at least she had thought he had just rung to say he was on his way. She had left the front door on the latch for him downstairs and her own front door slightly ajar to save the effort, the intolerable effort, of having to get up once more. He sounded aggressive on the phone; something about her owing him money. She was sure she didn't but the cash machine had rejected her card on several occasions lately for reasons she wasn't certain of and didn't really want to investigate, although she knew she would have to at some point. She had tried to borrow from Archie but he never lent money, or so he said.

After a pause of some minutes, he buzzed and let himself in; it was like being burgled by consent. But she had asked him to come here and she couldn't tell him to bugger off. He was called Juan, or at least she thought that was his name.

Diana, from long force of habit, got up and looked

in the mirror. Since she had returned from the week-end she hadn't really brushed her hair, only sort of patted at it; as a consequence it was looking pretty wild. Her face was unmade up and she was wearing a black tee shirt and a pair of denim jeans. Her thin, prehensile toes were dirty. Archie had always complimented her on her beautiful hands and feet.

Archie, she thought; what a joke. She had taken up with him to embarrass Ben when he had started to see that little Marianne person, and then she had ended up rather falling for him. How useless was that! Archie always kept a distance; he was an old hand at not getting too involved.

Gazing at her face in the mirror, Diana thought she looked like an old hippy; her face hadn't collapsed yet but it was showing signs. The marble quality of youth was vanishing to be replaced by something more leathery and reptilian. The lines from nose to mouth were getting deeper by the day. She also had a lop-sided look that puzzled her as if someone had remoulded her face in the night and then she remembered she had tripped and fallen before she went to bed last night or, rather, sofa; she didn't always bother with going to bed any longer, choosing instead to fall like a soldier in whatever part of the battlefield of her flat she happened to find herself in at the time.

That flat with its high-ceilinged, handsome rooms was dishevelled and dirty, rather like its owner. It looked a bit like a student flat after a party: overflowing ashtrays, empty bottles, dirty cups and bits of newspaper lay about, their glossy innards spilled across the floor advertising cheap loans and weird household appliances. She must have bought the newspapers at some point but she couldn't remember when.

Her cleaning lady, Mrs Drabble, had stopped coming. Said it was too dirty, but what was the point of these people if they didn't clean up what's dirty? It was baffling. Absolutely baffling; like so much else that had happened recently, she just couldn't get her head round it.

Juan let himself in. Diana was standing by the mirror in the sitting-room; she saw Juan enter in the looking glass (as her mother would have had her say); it was suddenly like a play, one of Sandy's perhaps, a drawing-room comedy with a vicious undertow of suppressed violence fused with anguish. She wanted a man so much; and she had slept with Juan before, or so she seemed to recall.

He looked terribly handsome in a rather dago-ish sort of way. His dark, curling hair stood on his head in glistening spirals giving him a Medusa-like quality; he was thin and angular and had an excessively pronounced jaw that made him look absurdly like the tough guy in a cartoon strip. His dark eyes were as hard as stones. She wondered whether he had a knife in the pocket of his leather jacket or concealed against his bum in those tight-fitting jeans he thought he looked so cool in, poor little piece of flotsam that he was.

Juan drew a bottle of vodka out from behind his

back, Stolichnaya; Diana recognised the red and silver label. Perhaps this was the dagger, she thought, giving way to her fantasy; Juan had come to bring her some stuff and then they would go to bed together; she could almost feel the tip of the knife as it cut into the soft skin under her chin, leaving a fine line of bloody dew drops in its wake.

'I've brought you what you asked for,' Juan said, holding up a little bag containing some white powder. 'I thought we could have a bevvy first. Have you glasses?'

She watched him looking round with distaste at the squalor, wrinkling his nose at the smell, which was pretty repulsive. After days of smoking and drinking without opening the windows, the room stank.

'You'll have to wash up,' she said, knowing he wouldn't, but allowing herself the fantasy of Juan with a little frilly apron over his jeans and a maid's cap, like in one of those books of cheap bondage fantasies their grandparents kept in locked drawers in their libraries. Her grandparents anyway, not Juan's, who came from some swarming tenement block in Glasgow or Naples or wherever it was dagoes came from.

When Diana entered her own kitchen she was briefly shocked before indifference set in once more. The place was unbelievable. A black bag of stinking rubbish sat in the middle of the floor; there were open packets of food on every surface; a great, glistening, hummus-fed bluebottle banged against the window over the sink. She found a couple of

tumblers, washed them up and went back to the
sitting-room.

He looked at her with contempt when she came in,
but waited while she poured the drink, watching as
she took one gulp and then another. Its oily coldness
coiled down her gut like a glass rope.

'I need the money,' he said. 'You're not getting the
shit until I get the cash.'

'What are you talking about?'

She could hear herself sounding more and more like
her mother addressing some tiresome minion.

Clarity returned to her when he hit her. She was
suddenly as sharp as an icicle.

'You're always wasted,' he said, looking at her
coldly. 'You can't remember anything half the bloody
time.'

The ring on the fourth finger of her right hand was
worth several grand; the diamond held the light with
a kind of white glitter he couldn't take his eyes off.

'Pay me now,' he said, suddenly at her side like
a viper.

'Get out,' she said, trying to sit up and finding she
couldn't, 'or I'll call the police.'

'Pay me now, or I want your ring,' he said, grabbing
the wrist of her right arm and holding it up high to
further disable her.

'Fuck off!' she screamed, thrashing like a reptile on
the sofa. 'Let go of my arm!'

'Give me the money and I will.'

'Let me go then,' she said, suddenly quiet. He could
feel the tremor in her body.

Juan let go of her arm and she was suddenly off the sofa and at the telephone, quicker than she would have believed possible. She tried to dial 999 but he was on her before she had the chance. He ripped the phone out of her hand and flung it at the wall and then he was at her, tearing and ripping. She felt a piece of her hair go like a slice of turf. Looking round, she grabbed a candlestick but he had her from behind and quite suddenly she lost her footing and fell against the fireplace, cracking her head on the marble surround with a noise like a pistol shot.

Diana lay with her head by one of the columns of the fireplace. Some minutes after Juan had gone she regained consciousness and tried to crawl in the direction of what she thought was the telephone, but gave up after she had moved no more than twelve inches.

She lay like this for a day. On the second day at around midday, she died.

In the meantime, several things had happened.

Patrick had made a spectacular recovery from his injuries and had become a celebrity in the children's ward. Ben and Marianne drove down to visit him and found him chasing a football round the ward with a couple of other boys.

'They're discharging him tomorrow,' said Alice, giving Marianne a hard look. She was trying not to judge and, after all, she knew what Luke was like, but it was difficult. This little piece had gone from one man to the other knowing damn well Luke was married. Would they have done it, she wondered, watching Patrick, if they knew what it meant in terms of heartbreak? Patrick needed a mother and a father or he would end up as damaged internally as he had briefly been on the outside, and needing life support of a different kind. Wait until she had a child, Alice thought, eying Marianne, and then she would tell her what it felt like.

Luke had greeted the news of Marianne's return to Ben as if he had not only been expecting it but had been somehow responsible for it. He embraced Ben and kissed Marianne genteelly on the cheek as if she was someone he had met a few times at family parties but nothing more than that. Marianne was the same with him: distant, a little cool, and remarkably composed.

In the end it was Alice, the feminist, who had compromised, adopting the Old Man's blinkered view. If you wanted family life to work out, you had to turn a blind eye to certain things. It was disgusting in a way, but it worked. There had never been a point in human history, as their marriage counsellor had pointed out, when married couples expected more from each other than nowadays. And she wanted her son to grow up in a warm, congenial environment; that was the pact she had made with God whilst waiting to know whether Patrick would live or die that terrible night. If he lived, she would put up with Luke; that was the deal.

'Hello there,' said Ben, capturing Patrick by the cord of his dressing gown. 'You don't look as if you should be in here at all. All the nurses look petrified.'

'They're letting me out tomorrow,' said Patrick, 'and then Dad's taking us to the sea for a few days.'

'Where's that?'

'Somewhere in Galloway?' asked Marianne, leaning on Ben's shoulder.

'No, we're going to the Côte d'Azur,' said Patrick. 'I want to do windsurfing and Dad says he'll teach me.'

'How grand you are,' said Ben, catching Marianne's eye. 'You'll be in a yacht next. Just look what you're doing when you cross the road, OK?'

'I promise,' said Patrick solemnly. 'You won't have Lolly put down, will you?'

'No, but she's got to go to school. I can't have her running wild like that. There's a place near Forbes Castle where they train delinquent dogs. You'll have to come with me and see her when she's there.'

He ruffled Patrick's hair. 'When are you off?' he asked Luke, who was standing by the door of the children's ward.

'After the reading of the will,' said Luke. 'I asked him where he wanted to go, expecting him to say Disneyland or something and he said, "The Côte d'Azur," as if he always went there. When Alice asked him how he knew about it he said he'd read a travel brochure and liked the look of it.'

'Old before his time,' said Ben. 'The Côte d'Azur is where money launderers and tax evaders go.'

'I can think of a worse fate,' said Luke, putting his arm round Ben. 'Have you forgiven me, Benno?'

'For shopping us, you mean?'

'You know that's what I mean.'

'I'll forgive you,' said Ben, 'but I won't forget. And I can't feel the same about you; I don't trust you any more. I'm sorry, but it's true; you've forfeited all that. I hope you're going to get help of some kind before you start destroying the family afresh.'

'I am; yes,' said Luke meekly, bowing his head as if accepting his fate. 'Alice has arranged for me to see someone; a man. She didn't want me seeing a woman in case I tried anything on.'

'Very sensible of her,' said Ben drily. It was clear to him that Luke was only capable of drawing a moral conclusion from his actions when someone else did it for him and presented him with the results. The therapist, poor bastard, would have a hard time with a man who kept a part of himself outside any form of control; particularly such an intelligent man as Luke who'd run rings around him. He'd do it again; that much was for sure.

On the second day after her fall, Diana was found dead in her flat by Archie Maclean. He had telephoned her countless times since he dropped her off on the Monday after the child's accident, and had eventually managed to persuade the police to help him break in.

She was lying on the floor on her back with a blackened gash across her temple.

Archie looked at Diana and then round the sitting-room. The police officers glanced at one another and then one of them spoke into his chest as if the reel, temporarily suspended, had suddenly speeded up again.

'Looks as if a small war has taken place,' said Archie, as the tears came into his eyes. 'What was she playing at?'

'A burglary, would you say, sir?' asked the policewoman.

'I don't think so,' said Archie. 'She was depressed and an alcoholic. She'd been involved in an incident at the weekend to do with the running-down of a small boy. He was badly hurt but he's going to be OK. It made her a bit loopy.'

'It would make me loopy,' said the policewoman, raising her eyebrows.

'Can I make a phone call?' Archie asked. 'I think I'd better call her brother Hugo Forbes. He's her next of kin.'

'By all means,' said the policewoman. 'We'll just take a look around the apartment while you're doing that.'

Hugo answered the phone after many rings. It was nine o'clock in the evening and he'd fallen asleep fully clothed, despised red leather slippers and all, on his bed with his dogs, at the factor's house. Rowena never allowed them in the bedroom during their marriage and it was one of the few things that gave Hugo any pleasure anymore. He'd rather have Bracken, the lurcher, in bed with him any day; at least she didn't give him the cold shoulder like Rowena had latterly.

When Archie told him what had happened there

was a silence and then a gasp. A rumbling clatter announced that Hugo had dropped the receiver, and then the line went dead.

Archie waited a moment and then called again, but got the engaged tone. He wondered what he should do – drive out to find Hugo or just wait. It seemed to him extraordinary that he should have become almost the guardian of this disjointed and unhappy pair of siblings.

When the phone rang again, Hugo's voice, choked with tears, said, 'Look, I'm sorry, Archie . . .'

There was a pause during which Hugo tried to get control of his voice, then he said, 'She was the only woman I've ever really loved, you see. I loved her much more than my wife. We spoke the same language, you see; even when she was so unhappy she knew what I was talking about. We were like the only survivors from a great cataclysm and now she's gone. I can't really believe it.'

'It'll take a while,' said Archie gently, who was very moved by what Hugo had said.

'I was afraid of this,' Hugo was saying. 'She's been drinking like a fish. Patrick's accident upset her terribly.'

Now that he had started to talk he seemed unable to stop.

'Had you spoken to her recently?' asked Archie.

'We talked a day or two ago. You could never tell if she'd answer the phone or not. I suppose I should have known. I tried to get her to come here to live with me for a bit, at least until the court case, but she wouldn't. She said she was damned if she was going to live like some pensioner on the Loebs' doorstep.'

'So she was in her usual form, then?'

'Not really. She was in despair, but you'd have to know her to realise it. You know what she's like. She's so damn argumentative.'

'I do know,' said Archie. 'I think you'd better come, Hugo. I think they want to take her body for a post-mortem to determine the cause of death, but I'm not sure. Have you a mobile?'

'A what?'

'A mobile phone.'

'Can't stand the things. And you have to go up to the attic here to get any reception although Loeb has said they can erect an aerial on the back hill. I always told them to go to hell, but he believes in progress, of course. He probably owns the company. I'll leave as soon as I can, but I'll have to sort the dogs out first. Shall I come to Diana's flat?'

'Come to my studio,' said Archie. 'I can put you up on the sofa.'

'Very kind of you, but I think I'll stay at Diana's.'

'I wouldn't recommend it,' said Archie. 'The place is a hell-hole. I don't think it's been cleaned for a while.'

Hugo took Bracken and the old black Labrador, Bob, down to the kitchen. They'd been fed earlier and Mrs Mac, the cleaning woman, would put them out in the morning. He filled their water bowls with fresh water and kissed the top of Bob's shining, seal-like head and made Bracken get into her basket with many kind gestures.

The phone call and the ensuing activity on Hugo's part had thrown Bracken's clock out and she made it quite clear that in her view it was time for the morning constitutional up one drive at the castle and down the other, through the mossy, mushroom woods with a swim in the burn thrown in for good measure. As he did these ordinary, domestic things Hugo found he was crying without realising it. He couldn't remember when he'd last cried – not even when he left the castle for the final time; that had been so traumatic that it had not occurred to him to cry – perhaps it hadn't been since childhood. Stupid girl, stupid, stupid, adorable girl, he muttered to himself, swallowing the tears back.

He adored her; they'd always been close, but she was such a blasted handful, always had been, even as a girl. Their father had been the only person who could manage Diana but it had been a love/hate relationship and now their father was senile and in a nursing home thinking about the plot of *Neighbours* or what was for lunch if his one-hundred-and-five-year-old brain was capable of thought, which Hugo doubted. Why was it always the wrong person who died? He wiped his nose with the back of his hand as he locked the back door.

Outside, the dawn was a line of milky dark on the horizon. On impulse, he drove up the back drive towards the castle – the Loebs were away somewhere (they were invariably away somewhere in the restless manner of the very rich) and stopped outside the steps that led up to the front door. He got out of the car and walked across to where the lawn fell away in a great sweep of dark velvet. As children they had rolled down this slope and climbed the lower branches of the enormous oak at the bottom.

If one listened hard one might almost be able to hear their childish voices calling to each other. 'Hugo, Hugo, bet you can't find me . . . I'm here . . . you don't know where I am, do you . . .', her face peering out of the branches like a little goblin's.

Hugo set off into the gloom and then turned round knowing suddenly and uncannily what he would see.

The fox paused at the top of the lawn and looked at him for what seemed like a long time, man and animal in silent communion, and then it walked away into the dark. It was a last sighting of her. He knew it then in that ghost moment.

A week later, the family gathered at the offices of Lamont & Lamont in Charlotte Square: blonde stones, rustication, polished ashlar, swags of laurel and Grecian urns; the New Town cocktail of severe architectural perfection. A black male receptionist sat at a desk in the front hall, adding a touch of exoticism.

The New Town had suited the Old Man because of just this exclusivity; he had loved the secret gardens, those woods beyond the world not available to the hoi polloi, and the homogenous but individual splendours of its squares and crescents; the same but still individually different.

He'd once said, Duncan recalled, that he hoped God had taken a leaf out of the Adams' book and laid out Paradise as a kind of celestial New Town. The New Jerusalem with fanlights and the grey, velvet call of wood pigeons.

Duncan himself had arrived first and stood with Gerry by one of the bookcases, greeting the family as they assembled. He was more splendid than ever in a pristine suit with an amethyst lining – a modern equivalent of a toga in his view – as befitted the new head of the family and a slightly paler tie that came from Hermès. All that was missing was the laurel wreath.

Gerry Lamont's office was a tall room with long shutters and rows of books running from floor to ceiling. Gerry himself was waiting for the family in this room, slightly flushed in the jowls from the close shave he had to perform twice a day. He was wearing a chalk-stripe suit with the chalk stripe in palest shell-pink, Duncan noticed; a variation on a theme, rather like the exceedingly comely black receptionist. He could almost hear Gerry saying, 'Don't want our clients to think we're too predictable, eh?'

Jean entered the room wearing a dark grey flannel suit with a severe but chic black velvet collar, the sunburst diamond brooch, and pearls at her throat. She was accompanied by Charles and walked with a stick, although the ulcer on her leg was beginning to show signs of healing. She missed the presence of her husband more than she had thought possible. Without him, she felt vulnerable and defenceless. If it hadn't been for Charles, she didn't know what she would have done.

She was also worried about Duncan who had taken to coming round to supper with them and then sloping off home on his own with poor Theo. It was both comical and painful but Charles was determined to hold out a little longer on the basis that it was good for Duncan to suffer and he'd really done remarkably little of it during the course of his life. In adversity, Duncan had not been as impressive as one might have supposed.

Ben, on the other hand, was flourishing now that his father was dead; he had really come into his own, thank God, and not before time.

Jean was pleased about Marianne but also curious about how in the story Duncan had told her, the girl had moved from Ben to Luke and back again. Modern girls seemed so somehow ingenious; perhaps, Jean wondered, if she had taken a lover then Jack might have taken more notice of her instead of taking her completely for granted as he had done and which she had allowed him to. Presumably, the point of the exercise had been to attract Ben's attention and, if so, it had been remarkably successful.

But she liked the fact that Marianne had returned to the fold and was now going to marry Ben. Marianne was a warm-hearted girl with spirit who appeared to be able to manage Ben with aplomb; and Ben was besotted. His mother had never seen him so in love, certainly not with Diana. Of course Marianne was not here today. This occasion was for family only and as Marianne was not yet family she could not attend.

Luke and Alice arrived with Sandy and Hannah for protection. Luke had got away with a great deal as far as his family was concerned – only what had happened to Patrick prevented Duncan from banishing him into outer darkness for a spell. Jean watched the way he guided Alice to a chair and whispered something in her ear that made her smile. Jean wondered how long he would be faithful to his wife for: not long, she would wager. He was incorrigible. He had been like that as a boy and nothing had really changed. The true hallmark of a sterling character was the ability not to reinvent oneself as modern people were so fond of saying but truly to change; Luke would never be able to do that, unlike her Ben, she thought, indulging her mother's pride for a moment.

Once everyone was assembled, Gerry cleared his throat and plunged into the long list of instructions the Old Man had left him.

Lady Macarthur was left the life interest in the estate and the house in Ainslie Place; Ardgay was of course in her name and would eventually be left to Ben.

The Old Man had left instructions that Mrs Mackenzie's name was not to be mentioned at the reading of the will, in order to spare the feelings of his wife.

The two sons, Duncan and Ben, had already had the bulk of their inheritance passed to them by the Old Man long ago; there were holdings in trust and cash squirrelled away in Swiss bank accounts; Jack Macarthur had been a generous man and a tremendous philanthropist but he had not been stupid when it came to money.

All his pet projects received cash boosts – the unmarried mothers, the half-way house in Craigmillar for recovering addicts, the money for a community centre in another disadvantaged part of town – and there was money for the old socialist Sandy Macarthur and his wife, not to mention the Macarthur Foundation and various other philanthropic projects close to the Old Man's heart.

Gerry glanced at Luke Macarthur and noted his downcast expression. He had kept news of the Macarthur legacies until last, out of sense of theatre, and because the Old Man had had a wicked sense of humour when it came to members of his own family.

'Lastly,' Gerry said, 'there is the sum of three hundred thousand pounds to be left to my niece by marriage, Mrs Alice Macarthur, and a further three hundred thousand pounds for her son Patrick Macarthur.'

'But that's preposterous,' expostulated Luke, before he could stop himself. He half rose from his chair, looking round the room as he did so, and then subsided.

Ben glanced at his mother and then looked away.

Duncan raised his eyebrows and glanced up at the ceiling. Alice, always alabaster, actually blushed with pleasure. Then she gazed at her husband and smiled the smile of the victor.

'In addition,' Gerry added, 'the money already left to Patrick Macarthur is to remain under his mother's control until Patrick attains the age of twenty-five.'

'Charles has made lunch for all of us,' said Jean, standing between her two sons, on the steps of the offices of Lamont & Lamont. 'Marianne is waiting there for us, with her father. It's a formal occasion and I insist that everyone attends, whatever else they may have had in mind.'

Charles glanced at Duncan who met his eye yearningly. He wanted his wife back and longed for the return of the ordered calm of his domestic life. He wanted to spend weekends with Charles again, beginning with breakfast in bed with Theo hovering alongside like a crocodile waiting for titbits; he wanted to come home to the smell of dinner cooking and a house full of flowers.

'You'll come?' Charles murmured in Duncan's ear. 'It's an engagement lunch. I've really pushed the boat out. I've got someone in to help.'

'Of course I'll come,' said Duncan, 'but only if you'll have dinner with me tonight. What do you think? It's been a long time, or it seems like a long time.'

'It feels like an eternity to me,' said Charles.

They fell back together behind Ben who was helping Jean into the car.

'I'll go home now with Mother,' Ben said to his
brother. 'We'll see you there.'

'Are the Luke Macarthurs not coming?' Duncan
asked Charles after Ben had driven off.

'It was not felt appropriate for the moment,' Charles
replied, 'if you know what I mean.'

'Sure do,' said Duncan, making a face. 'Our family
needs a bit of time to reform, if you ask me.'

'The star of the show being Ben, of course,' said
Charles, half-teasing.

'I agree,' said Duncan slowly. 'He's really the new
head of the family.'

'Joint head perhaps,' said Charles. 'There's no need
to throw the baby out with the bathwater.'

There was champagne in the drawing-room before
lunch and then an official picture taken by the photographer who had covered all the family events for the
Old Man since anyone could remember.

'May I say a few words?' asked Jean, once they were
all lined up, Marianne in a linen suit she'd bought at
the weekend with Nadia in tow, standing between
Ben and Archie in one of his bullet-proof tweeds.

'Go ahead, Mother,' said Ben, taking Marianne's
hand and pressing her fingers gently one by one.

'Our family has been through some terrible times
lately,' Jean began. 'The loss of my beloved husband
being the most obvious one, but there have been
other events that could have set us all at odds but

somehow have not. We are here, we are together, we are family and family we shall stay. All our happiness lies in each other,' she continued, 'and I would like to welcome Marianne into this family with all our love. I know she will be the most wonderful and charismatic addition.'

As she spoke, she reached round her son for Marianne and at that moment the photographer took his first picture of the reconfigured family.

'Father will be smiling down upon us,' said Ben, putting one arm round Marianne and one round his mother.

'Indeed he will,' replied Jean, raising her glass, 'indeed he will.'